ARRIVAL: EXODUS
BOOK FOUR

Praise for Gun Brooke's Fiction

Fierce Overture

"Gun Brooke creates memorable characters, and Noelle and Helena are no exception. Each woman is "more than meets the eye" as each exhibits depth, fears, and longings. And the sexual tension between them is real, hot, and raw."—*Just About Write*

Coffee Sonata

"In *Coffee Sonata*, the lives of these four women become intertwined. In forming friendships and love, closets and disabilities are discussed, along with differences in age and backgrounds. Love and friendship are areas filled with complexity and nuances. Brooke takes her time to savor the complexities while her main characters savor their excellent cups of coffee. If you enjoy a good love story, a great setting, and wonderful characters, look for Coffee Sonata at your favorite gay and lesbian bookstore."
—*Family & Friends Magazine*

Sheridan's Fate

"Sheridan's fire and Lark's warm embers are enough to make this book sizzle. Brooke, however, has gone beyond the wonderful emotional explorations of these characters to tell the story of those who, for various reasons, become differently-abled. Whether it is a bullet, an illness, or a problem at birth, many women and men find themselves in Sheridan's situation. Her courage and Lark's gentleness and determination send this romance into a 'must read.'"—*Just About Write*

Course of Action

"Brooke's words capture the intensity of their growing relationship. Her prose throughout the book is breathtaking and heart-stopping.

Where have you been hiding, Gun Brooke? I, for one, would like to see more romances from this author."—*Independent Gay Writer*

September Canvas

"In this character-driven story, trust is earned and secrets are uncovered. Deanna and Faythe are fully fleshed out and prove to the reader each has much depth, talent, wit and problem-solving abilities. *September Canvas* is a good read with a thoroughly satisfying conclusion."—*Just About Write*

Soul Unique

"This is the first book that Gun Brooke has written in a first person perspective, and that was 100% the correct choice. She avoids the pitfalls of trying to tell a story about living with an autism spectrum disorder that she's never experienced, instead making it the story of someone who falls in love with a person living with Asperger's. ...*Soul Unique* is her best. It was an ambitious project that turned out beautifully. I highly recommend it."—*The Lesbian Review*

The Supreme Constellations Series

"*Protector of the Realm* has it all; sabotage, corruption, erotic love and exhilarating space fights. Gun Brooke's second novel is forceful with a winning combination of solid characters and a brilliant plot. The book exemplifies her growth as inventive storyteller and is sure to garner multiple awards in the coming year."—*Just About Write*

"Brooke is an amazing author, and has written in other genres. Never have I read a book where I started at the top of the page and don't know what will happen two paragraphs later. She keeps the excitement going, and the pages turning."—*MegaScene*

Visit us at www.boldstrokesbooks.com

By the Author

Romances:
Course of Action
Coffee Sonata
Sheridan's Fate
September Canvas
Fierce Overture
Speed Demons
The Blush Factor
Soul Unique
A Reluctant Enterprise
Piece of Cake
Thorns of the Past

Supreme Constellations Series:
Protector of the Realm
Rebel's Quest
Warrior's Valor
Pirate's Fortune

Exodus Series:
Advance
Pathfinder
Escape
Arrival

Novella Anthology:
Change Horizons

ARRIVAL: EXODUS BOOK FOUR

by

Gun Brooke

2017

ARRIVAL: EXODUS BOOK FOUR

ISBN 13: 978-1-62639-859-7

This Trade Paperback Original Is Published By
Bold Strokes Books, Inc.
P.O. Box 249
Valley Falls, NY 12185

First Edition: December 2017

Credits
Editor: Shelley Thrasher
Production Design: Susan Ramundo
Cover Design By Sheri (graphicartist2020@hotmail.com)
Cover Art By Gun Brooke

Acknowledgments

I love writing. I adore hearing from readers. I still pinch myself when I think of the fact that I'm a published author. All this is not due to me alone, and I want to thank the people who have a hand in all this.

Len Barot (aka Radclyffe), my publisher, you create the best of homes for writers and I'm glad I'm one of the first you signed. I couldn't be happier being among the "inventories." :-)

Dr. Shelley Thrasher, my editor, who is i-n-v-a-l-u-a-b-l-e to me in her professional capacity and as my very good friend. (And she is an author too—go check out her books at BSB!)

The rest of the BSB gang, Sandy, Connie, Cindy, Stacia, Lori, Carsen, Sheri, and all the ones I'm not sure about their names—you do an amazing job. Thank you so much for your help, ideas, assistance, and encouragement.

My first readers, thank you for keeping me from making too much of a fool of myself from silly mistakes and logical gaps.

My dear readers—without you, my words fall empty to the ground. You are so loyal and show me so much appreciation, it makes me blush! Thank you for sticking with me through all my different adventures, whether romance or science fiction.

Thank you also to Elon, for discussing spaceship blueprints with me and for reminding me to eat. Malin, Henrik, Pentti, grandkids, Ove, Monica, Laura, Joanne, Maggie, Birgitta, Soli, Shafieqa, my family and friends, you are the absolute best and I love you.

Lastly, and no less important, my dogs. Hoshi and Esti, you do help me write, unless you are trying to persuade me to come out and play by placing your heads on my keyboard and writing six pages with the letter p before I can pry you away. :-)

Writing used to be a lonely profession, until there was the Internet with first readers (beta readers) who enjoy the writing process. Also, being able to do research without leaving your seat, is darn cool. That in itself doesn't complete a novel, though. So much work goes into it and that is why it is essential for me to have a great publisher, amazing editor, attentive publishing company staff, enthusiastic first readers, and wonderful family and friends.

Dedication

For Elon

You share everything with me and always put me first.

Everything I value most, comes from you.

PROLOGUE

The scars had faded into white, jagged lines, and that alone was a testament to the time span between when Pamas was captured and when she escaped from the changer called Nestrocalder. That was not the changer's real name, of course, but an ancient Oconodian word meaning "poisonous soul." Always dressed in flowing, black garments, Nestrocalder kept the mystery alive by never revealing its identity. Some said Nestrocalder was male; some claimed the enigmatic leader of the illegally organized changers was a woman. Others insisted Nestrocalder did not even exist—or was a blend of several different malevolent changers high up in the hierarchy.

Lieutenant Commander Pamas Seclan didn't care. All she knew was how one day stretched into the next while she was held in bunkers deep in the jungle in the Kirano sector on Oconodos. They moved her intermittently, which made her realize the changers had an entire web of bunkers. They somehow managed to make the compounds invisible to Oconodian sensors. The hope of being rescued seeped from her soul as the days turned into months and the months into years.

During her capture, Pamas feared for the welfare of her children. About to leave her abusive husband when she was taken, she now stressed over the fact he had sole custody of Aniwyn and Pherry.

She couldn't remember how she was taken. One moment she was driving her hovercar to Fleet Admiral Caydoc's office for a pre-mission briefing. She'd blinked, and the next time she opened her eyes, Pamas was in a room so dark she was certain she'd lost her sight. It turned out she was half right. During her capture, she had lost her right eye. For years, she bandaged and protected her empty eye socket with strips of fabric ripped from whatever clothes they provided her with. She refused to give them any information, military or otherwise, not even when she suspected Nestrocalder was interrogating her. This steadfast refusal infuriated her captors, and they never treated her with kindness or compassion.

When she escaped after almost twenty years, she learned how close the pending Exodus mission was and about her daughter's part in it. While her son Pherry led a family life on Oconodos, working as an agronomist, her daughter, Aniwyn "Spinner" Seclan, had walked in her mother's footsteps and carved out a military career. A skilled pilot, she was part of the Advance Team, sent to scout for a planet able to sustain life for the Oconodians desperate to leave the volatile situation on Oconodos. The malevolent changers were on the verge of taking over, and the government had decided long ago that this was the only solution.

When Pamas found Pherry's name on *Pathfinder's* passenger roster, Pamas used her stolen identity, which had kept her safe from the changers she had escaped from, and secured travel documents for the Exodus ship when it launched.

CHAPTER ONE

Standing among the cheering crowd, Pamas knew she attracted attention for having an eyepatch. Anyone suffering the loss of an eyeball would replace it with either a cybernetic one or a much more expensive transplanted real eye. Pamas had yet to prioritize either of those solutions. Having an eyepatch didn't bother her as much as it did other people.

Another announcement echoed throughout the entire ship. "Please brace for impact. Restrain small children, the elderly, and others who may need assistance. Cube eleven will touch down in one hundred secs."

Now as she stood by the large screen at the main square aboard cube eleven, she marveled at the technology that made it possible for the cube to travel across the vastness of space while attached to the other twenty vessels. Having arrived at this planet, the Oconodians' and the Gemosians' new home, called Gemocon to commemorate the merging of the two people, the twenty-one cubes separated and were in the process of landing. This was the tricky part, as no one had actually performed a landing sequence before cube one set down only half an hour ago in the very center of what was to be named the capital of Gemocon.

Holding on to one of the trees growing around the square where they all watched the exterior cameras filming their descent, Pamas breathed slowly as her stomach clenched. She had managed to remain incognito for the entire duration of the journey, and now she had to finally decide whether to assume her true identity or stay hidden.

❖

One day later, Pamas stood in line to one of the south exits. Twice already she'd had to prove her identity. The name she had used during the long journey, Pamas Dagellion, was connected to her retinal scan and genetic makeup records. She had found it easier to use her real first name, as it was common enough.

The buzz around her nearly split her eardrums. Young people couldn't stand still from pure excitement, and right next to Pamas, a small child, perhaps three years old, asked the man whose hand she held on to if the ground hummed on Gemocon, like it did on *Pathfinder*. No doubt the child had been very young when they boarded the massive spaceship to find a new home.

"No, Miela," the man answered her, chuckling. "The ground is very still, but what you can feel is the wind."

"What is the wind?" The little girl's mouth became a perfect little *o*.

"It's when the air moves really fast and caresses your face." Miela's father smiled wistfully. "I have missed that during our journey, but now we're here, and it will be wonderful." His voice was cheerful, but his eyes had something sad in them as he smiled at the child.

Miela nodded and turned to look at the young people cheering loudly now when crewmen prepared to open the hatches. Her gaze passed Pamas, and her green eyes grew wide at the sight of Pamas's eyepatch. "Oh...what happened to your eye?" Miela looked stunned but not afraid.

The man she was with turned to see who she was talking to and seemed taken aback and embarrassed as he pulled the child closer to him. "Miela. It's not polite to ask," he said hurriedly.

"It's all right," Pamas found herself saying, her tone mild. "I had an accident and my eye got injured."

"Does it hurt?" Miela tilted her head, peering up at the eye patch.

"No. Not anymore." But it had. When the torture had reached that level, Pamas had for the first time asked for death to claim her. After they took her back to her cell in the jungle bunker, she knew her eye had been destroyed. She received some rudimentary treatment, perhaps because she would have been even more of a problem if it had become infected. Once the worst of the pain was over—and it took several weeks—Pamas swore never to wish for death again. If she could endure the agony of what they had done to her eye, she could take anything. They never fully broke her, and she didn't give up any information.

"I apologize for my daughter. Miela is only three and a half, and she hasn't learned yet what is polite to ask and what's not." The man cleared his throat. "I'm Toggion, by the way."

"It's fine," Pamas said and winked at Miela. "I prefer questions to stares or murmurs behind my back." Truthfully, she cared about neither, but she didn't want the little girl and her father to feel bad. This sentiment surprised her. Only a year or so ago, she wouldn't have minded either way.

"Thank you. May I ask why you haven't had it replaced? Just tell me if I'm being too forward," Toggion said.

"For a long time, I wasn't motivated, and then, when I was, I figured it could wait until we reached Gemocon. During the journey, I thought our health-care system should focus on real emergencies."

Toggion looked impressed. "That's very selfless. Not a lot of people would think like that."

"I'm not selfless," Pamas said, cringing. "Just practical."

A muted metallic sound was followed by a squeaky tone as the crewmen began to lower the hatches outward. A gush of new, fresh air made the old air that had been perfectly fine just before seem stale and recycled—which it was, of course.

Miela gasped and clung to her father's hand. "It's the wind, Daddy! It's the wind!" Her entire face lit up. "I can feel the caress."

"I know, I know," Toggion said, wiping at his eyes. "Creator of all things…I can't believe we made it."

"But we did, Daddy." Miela kissed Toggion's hand.

"I just wish your mother could have been with us." Toggion lifted the girl up onto his shoulders and grabbed his suitcase with the hand that wasn't holding her legs securely.

Pamas shifted the shoulder straps of her backpack, which held all her belongings. She knew of people who had brought much more with them, filled every storage space in their quarters with belongings they clearly couldn't live without, despite the clear instructions from the authorities.

"Do you think we'll spot the Red Angel, Daddy?" Miela asked. "She works at the hospital in our cube. I've only seen her on the screen."

Pamas had seen the woman who went by the moniker Red Angel, an empath changer who could not only sense emotions from others, but also read thoughts. Rumor had it that she and her sister, who possessed the ability to see the future, had stowed away aboard *Pathfinder* despite every precaution the engineers and authorities responsible for the Exodus mission had taken. Strangely enough, President Tylio trusted both changers and credited them for saving the ship and a multitude of lives on several occasions.

Toggion answered his daughter. "I don't know, sweetie. She might be working, or assisting the president. You know she does that."

"I just want to see her. Just once." The little girl looked around them, obviously hoping against odds to see the famous and revered changer.

A loud humming noise permeated the large hall inside the hatches. An automated, metallic-sounding voice came over the speakers. "People of cube eleven. Form lines and keep together with family members. Move in an orderly fashion. Anyone cutting in line will be pulled aside and made to wait until last. You will be greeted and scanned as you reach the gates. Keep moving, and do not stall the lines by asking redundant questions. Everything each of you needs to know will be given to you when required. Welcome to Gemocon, your new home. Go in heavenly splendor." Pamas swallowed against the sudden dryness in her throat. She wanted to push herself to the front of the line, get off this ship, and make her way out into the fresh air. Suddenly the vast cube felt constricting and as if it were about to pull her back in. A lot of people would keep residing in here to keep the hospitals going. If she had been one of them, she would have escaped and gone into the wilderness despite potential dangers.

The line moved fast enough to keep people who felt like Pamas in check, but not so fast the greeters at the gate didn't have time to do their job. Men and women from the advance team stood there smiling broadly as they scanned them and gave initial information. Pamas ended up in the far-right line and found herself looking down at a stunningly beautiful woman. Large, black curls framed a triangular face, and her blue-violet irises told of her Gemosian descent. Her lips were full and curvy, her nose narrow and slightly upturned, giving her an impish expression. A nametag on her uniform gave her name: Darmiya Do Voy.

CHAPTER TWO

Darmiya Do Voy stood at gate eleven, ready to greet the passengers as they disembarked cube eleven. It had been a majestic view when the enormous cube broke through the light clouds, still emanating heat and scorching the ground as it touched down. As soon as it was cool enough for the crews to approach, a steady stream of men and women rushed forward to attach hoses and vents required to sustain life support within the cube now that it was no longer traveling through space at an unimaginable speed.

Now, twenty hours later, it was time to greet the ones leaving the cube and guide them toward their habitats or tents. Habitats were mainly for families with young children, the elderly, or others with special circumstances. The rest would stay in tents until they had chosen whether to reside in any of the denser populated areas or the countryside.

Darmiya hadn't slept many hours during the last three nights, going over checklists and trying to anticipate any potential mishaps. Now she was standing here at the opening to the long corridor that would take the new inhabitants farther into the part of Gemocon's future capital that held provisional housing. Darmiya had meant to greet the newcomers with her usual exuberant self, but now all she wanted was to return to her own habitat and go to bed. She didn't used to succumb to exhaustion like this, but the last year had been insanely busy. A lot of the medical issues and planning had weighed heavily on her. Her best friend Spinner, the commander of the air group for the advance team, claimed Darmiya would be back to her old self as soon as *Pathfinder* had arrived and the responsibility didn't solely lie on the advance team. Not only that, Darmiya and Calagan would have some 100,000 of their fellow Gemosians and not feel like they were so outnumbered.

Darmiya didn't feel outnumbered. That wasn't it. And besides, these two people had agreed to merge and refer to themselves as Gemoconians. She didn't want to seem overly dramatic, but she doubted the arrival of *Pathfinder* would solve everything for her in an instant. Yet she also didn't think it was right to bother Spinner and her wife with her fears. They had so much on their plate, currently standing in for President Tylio until she arrived. Darmiya wasn't sure it was the hard work, not entirely anyway, which was good, since she did realize if they had worked hard before the Exodus ship arrived, their duties would only increase once the cubes landed. Her mood swings and bouts of depression were something…something else. She couldn't pinpoint the problem herself.

The hissing sound of the metal walkway extending from the open hatch to cube eleven drew her attention from her inner musings. People began milling out in single file through the walkway. Some of the engineers had suggested they should construct totally closed arms from the cubes to the gates, but Darmiya had fought, and won, for building them without a roof. "Don't you think they've longed to see the sky? They've just spent more than two years in space without the types of shore leaves we had. Even if our pit stops were dangerous, some of us stepped on solid ground and breathed air. We will have much less stress and discontent if the walkways don't have roofs." She had glared around the conference table, seeing Spinner and her wife, Admiral Dael Caydoc, nodding to themselves. Some idiot had objected by saying, "But what if it rains?" Only Dael's intervention had stopped Darmiya from igniting on all fuses. Dael put a hand on Darmiya's shoulder and turned to the engineer in question. "If it rains, Lieutenant, they'll get wet."

Now, Darmiya readied herself, holding the tablet steadily. She didn't have to fake any smiles yet today, which was a blessing.

Nodding encouragingly toward a family of five as they walked down the corridor from the gate toward the small hover vehicles that would take them to their provisional habitat, Darmiya then turned her attention to the next on the list.

"Pamas Dagellion?" Darmiya glanced up at the slender, tall woman before her. It was hard to miss the stark appearance of an eyepatch, but she disregarded it and merely repeated the name and smiled questioningly.

Pamas Dagellion didn't reciprocate but nodded briskly, and Darmiya could have sworn that the woman went from a military "attention" to an "at ease" stance, hands behind her back.

"Yes." The woman extended her right hand for Darmiya to initiate the identification procedure. Pamas Dagellion kept her one good eye on her, which made Darmiya's cheeks grow warmer. When she had performed the retinal scan of Pamas Dagellion's right eye, she read the results and nodded affirmatively. "Excellent. Now, according to my list here, you are to take the left corridor and exit toward the settlement area down by the lake. You will find it consists of tents and habitats. Yours is tent 14-DG. The orientation board at the entrance is quite self-explanatory. You will find guards and personnel to assist you if you require help. Do you have any questions?" Still following the script, Darmiya didn't really expect the woman before her to have any special queries.

"Yes. Where can I find the military headquarters?" Pamas asked. "It's important."

"I see." Darmiya really didn't see, but the advance team's counselor had trained her how to address eager new arrivals. "You will find everything you need to know on the orientation boards by the entrance to your quarters. Everything is easily downloadable into your tablet for convenience—"

"No, Ms. Do Voy. You don't understand. This is quite urgent." Pamas glared at Darmiya and clearly tried to keep a civil tone. This was something she was supposed to note on her passenger roster, but Darmiya decided to give the woman some slack. The eyepatch combined with the paled scars on her face awoke sympathy in her. The juxtaposition between that and Pamas's pale-blue eye was mesmerizing.

"It's Doctor Do Voy." Darmiya sensed that she would lose the other woman's interest if she didn't remain firm. Pamas Dagellion didn't appear to suffer fools or weak personalities easily. "No new arrivals are allowed to wander outside the provisional camps until everyone is ashore and accounted for. Once everyone is assigned accommodations, passes will be handed out—your new identity documents."

"That is just it," Pamas said, and now Darmiya could tell others were starting to object about having to wait behind the stubborn woman. "I need to go to the military headquarters for that reason. It is very important. *Very.*"

Darmiya was uncertain what to do. She could insist on Pamas following the rules, but she had a hunch this woman would do as she pleased and find her way to headquarters no matter what—and surely that would make everything Darmiya's fault for not being clear enough.

"Hey. How long is this going to take? I have three kids back here getting restless," a woman called out from the line behind Pamas, who merely looked at Darmiya below raised eyebrows. She was obviously not going to back down.

"All right. Let's do it this way, even if it's not by the book. You go ahead and settle into your new lodgings. Then, once my shift is over, I'll come and get you and walk you over to the military headquarters. It's a bit of a hike, but we have very few hovercars operational at this point, and we can't spare any."

"Thank you. I have no problems going on foot. I'll get out of your way unless I need to know something else."

"No. That's it. Once again, welcome to Gemocon. I hope your tent will be to your satisfaction for now, Ms. Dagellion."

Pamas nodded and began walking down the corridor behind Darmiya, who shook her head. What was it about this woman that got under her skin? She had hoped something or someone would come along that could pierce the armor of indifference and dullness that engulfed her every day, but she hadn't counted on it being a prickly, persistent woman who looked like she'd endured torture at one point.

Going through the motions with the remaining people, one after another, Darmiya smiled and gave the correct information while on autopilot. She really was happy that the Exodus ship, with all its twenty individual cubes, had made it to Gemocon. This was the entire reason for the dangerous journey they had all undertaken, first the advance team and then the 2,100, 000 people aboard *Pathfinder*.

Darmiya's communicator buzzed, and then she recognized retired Fleet Admiral Helden Caydoc's voice. "Admiral Helden Caydoc to Darmiya Do Voy."

Darmiya tapped her lapel to answer. She had never used to wear an Oconodian uniform, consisting of a gray coverall with a thin flak vest over it, but now it had become a necessity when working toward receiving their people. When someone wore a uniform, it was easy to identify the other person's branch and profession. Darmiya was on the medical and scientific side together with her brother Calagan. The woman paging her was Dael's esteemed grandmother, and even if she was officially retired, she was the highest-ranking active military officer among the advance team. "Darmiya here, Admiral. What can I do for you?"

"We have a bit of a situation, and you are among the ones that needs to be briefed. Dael has put me in charge of getting the right group together, Advance team and *Pathfinder* crew alike. Report to headquarters at 20:00 hours."

Checking her timepiece, Darmiya calculated quickly that she might just about make it after walking Pamas Dagellion to headquarters. She would have to order some military police to escort the other woman back, but it wasn't undoable.

"Count me in, Admiral. Will Calagan be there too?"

"Of course. Caydoc out."

Darmiya frowned as she scanned the next person in line. Helden was rarely anything but direct, but even so, she was never this abrupt. What could be so amiss that it required her to slip back into her role as fleet admiral?

❖

Pamas followed the winding corridor, now under a roof again for a few hundred meters. Guided by the signs, she made two turns and then stepped outside. She moved out of the way of the people walking behind her and took in the view. In the far distance, tall mountains rose through the layer of clouds hovering above them. It looked like there might be snow or ice toward the top, and the scene was achingly familiar compared to Oconodos's northern hemisphere. Closer, a vast forest stretched along the horizon, and in front of it lay something resembling the grassy prairie she had hiked across as a young cadet. The area just before her looked like the perfect area to receive the Gemoconian population. Flat, but with beautiful hills to the…gazing up to the two suns above them, Pamas estimated she was looking due north. Slowly she inhaled the crisp air, feeling quite dizzy from its sweet scent. Were flowers nearby emanating this scent, or was it like this everywhere on the planet?

She headed toward the area of habitats and tents where she would reside until the next step of colonization. The area was indeed located by an idyllic lake and was the one closest to cube eleven. Looking back over her shoulder, she was stunned at how enormous the cube was, seen from her current perspective. In the vastness of intergalactic space, each cube hadn't seemed as big, but now it towered 580 meters over what would become the capital, together with cubes one and three. Cube one held the Caydoc Park and all the governmental buildings, universities, and, so far, the residential area for their political leaders. Cube three mainly consisted of the engineering area. It would be entirely dismantled and converted into providing the capital and surrounding towns with much-needed power and computer systems.

On her walk along the gravel path toward the village of tents and habitats, which seemed to wrap around the entire lake, Pamas let her thoughts stray to how the military would receive her once she had revealed her identity. Would they welcome her back into the fold? Would she truly *want* to go back on active duty? A lot had to have changed while she was held in a bunker in one jungle more mosquito-infested than the other. Her knowledge was outdated, to say the least. Apart from the two changers that had snuck aboard *Pathfinder*, the sisters, nobody could use her extensive knowledge about malevolent changers. They were all back on Oconodos.

The orientation board consisted of a six-meter-wide rectangular panel with people standing in line for any of the eight palm sensors available for registration. Pamas hoped they weren't expected to use one each time they came and went. That was a bit more surveillance than she was prepared to allow. After all, getting away from the changers that had held her captive and finding her kids were the only reasons Pamas was here. If Pherry and Aniwyn rejected her, she would purchase what she required and go off into the wilderness. Having made do on practically nothing in the jungle had prepared her in ways she never would have guessed before she was taken.

Pamas placed her hand into the indentation when it was her turn at the orientation board. She also placed one of her large tablets into a connection slot. A purple light ran along her palm, and she hoped it would be forgiving enough and recalculate her palm and fingerprints despite the scars interrupting the sweeping lines. The scanner gave a muted beep, and a dotted line appeared on the map of the paths among the tents and habitats. Her tent was at the far end of a small peninsula that extended to the center of the lake. Not bad for tent real estate. Back on Oconodos, such a lot, no matter how small, would be worth a fortune. She had lived in a regular neighborhood as a child and only moved into a posh district when she married the man she thought she would love forever. When the much-older Gexter Seclan made general, she concluded that the price of trying to stay in the marriage was hurting her, but worse than that, it was damaging her children. She had come so close to leaving him together with Aniwyn and Pherry. Just one more day and—

"Finding it hard to read the map, dear?" a kind voice said behind her, making Pamas wince and step aside.

"No, thank you. I'm fine. Excuse me." Grabbing her tablet, she nodded at the elderly man, hoisted her backpack, and hurried along the well-marked paths among the dwellings to her tent. The tents came in two different sizes, as did the habitats made from nylon-infused aluminum. Pamas wondered if the advance team had stored all of them or had brought some manufacturing equipment with them.

Reaching her tent, she once again pressed her palm against a sensor near the fastening of the tent flap. It buzzed and released its locking mechanism. Pushing the flap aside, Pamas stepped inside.

The tent boasted a real floor, which was a relief. She had had her fill of sleeping on the ground in the jungle or on raw concrete in the bunkers. Seeing the single bed, the blankets, pillow, and sheets folded at the foot of it made her smile. She spotted a simple faucet by a shelf holding a small sink, but nothing resembling a bathroom. A quick glance at the information on her tablet showed that those in single and double tents were supposed to use the common areas that provided bathrooms, aqua showers, cooking possibilities, and recreational areas. Pamas doubted she would spend much time in the latter. The closest facility was only two paths away, which was a relief.

As for her tent, a small seating area with a table and two stools sat next to a rack holding enough space for clothes and personal items. Those who had accumulated a multitude of things aboard the cubes would have to store their belongings outdoors. Pamas traveled very lightly, for obvious reasons, having constantly been on the move after her escape. The habit was hard to shake. She glanced around her new, albeit temporary, home. The whole briefness of this arrangement was perfect at this point. The wilderness was still on the table, should her attempts at redemption where her children were concerned fail miserably. She tried to shake the gloom from her mind, but it was difficult. She had remained aloof and endured the loneliness that had been her existence all through her captivity and afterward. Would life on Gemocon be different?

Pamas placed her backpack on the floor where she could reach it, locked the fastening device on the tent flap, and then set her timepiece to alert her so she would have time to freshen up before she handed herself over at the military headquarters. And who was she kidding? Next to the stunningly beautiful woman of Gemosian descent, she could hope to look clean at the most.

Oddly enough, it was Doctor Do Voy's intense, golden-brown eyes that followed her into a fitful sleep.

CHAPTER THREE

Darmiya pulled the lever back on her hoverskid. She was grateful to be among the few who had access to their own means of transportation, since the only larger vehicles were emergency hovercars. One hovercar served as transportation for Admiral Dael Caydoc when she had to travel quickly between the three major settlements. She usually took her entire senior staff with her, as the vehicle could accommodate eight passengers, not counting the driver. Dael most often didn't use the private vehicle, insisting it was needed elsewhere as an addition to the other emergency vehicles.

One of the junior engineers had invented the tiny method of transportation that Darmiya now skillfully maneuvered among the rows of Gemoconians walking to their new dwellings. The footrest barely had room for her feet, and a rod led up from the rectangular plate to a handle from where she controlled direction and speed. By leaning to either side, backward or forward, Darmiya could make the tiny hover vehicle move or turn faster.

Now she turned into the area where Pamas Dagellion's tent was located. A quick glance at the orientation map showed her to the location, and she had to concede that Pamas had lucked out. As the woman was living alone and hadn't submitted any information about family or other loved ones, she would reside in a one-person tent until a permanent apartment was constructed—or Pamas had built a house with her own hands, which a lot of people would do once they traveled beyond the limits of the three cities.

Darmiya lived in a habitat that she shared with her brother, though they had managed to create separate entrances even if they shared a kitchenette and living area. Because Darmiya treasured her privacy, her bedroom was her private sanctuary. Spinner often looked at her with concern if Darmiya spent too much of her precious free time in there alone.

Reaching Pamas's tent, Darmiya pulled the hoverskid to a stop and folded it up, as always impressed with how small it became and how easily she could stow it in her backpack. She pressed the small sensor next to the fastening on the tent flap and heard a muted signal from inside.

"Just a minute." Pamas's voice filtered through the tent's insulated material. A minute later, the flap shifted to the side and Pamas stepped outside.

Darmiya blinked, trying to fathom that this impressive-looking woman was the same as the worn and torn person she had guided through the arrival gates only a few hours ago. Pamas was now wearing sleek black trousers, a long black coat, and metallic-looking, knee-high boots. The clothes looked brand-new, and Darmiya had never seen anyone carry off an outfit quite like Pamas Dagellion. Pamas still wore her eyepatch, which was part of her intimidating aura, she surmised. The dark-brown hair ran down her back in a thick ponytail.

"Something wrong?" Pamas frowned as she gazed from Darmiya and down at herself.

"What? Oh, no. Not at all. I—I just didn't recognize you at first." Darmiya felt her cheeks color as warmth spread from her cheekbones to her ears.

"So, I take it I made the right decision to change clothes and clean up some." Pamas shook her head lightly. "I figured I couldn't be seen walking around headquarters looking like a vagabond." She pulled up her shoulders and let them down in a fluid, casual gesture. "So, we're walking?"

"It's how we normally get around, if possible. Once you get your hands on a hoverskid, it'll be even faster." Darmiya pointed at one of the engineers she knew who came skidding toward them as they began walking. "They're quite easy to make if you're able to read blueprints and know your way around a laser spanner and some other tools."

Pamas followed the disappearing engineer with her eye. "Interesting. Do you have one?"

"Yes. I didn't have to build my own though. I'm more of a theorist and not very good with tools." Darmiya lengthened her stride to keep up with Pamas. "However, I often walk. Good exercise. Once the workday is over, I'm not much for stepping into a crowded gym."

"Sounds like a good idea." Pamas nodded. She looked toward the mountains in the distance. "So beautiful. I can't quite fathom that we've landed and disembarked."

"You had a much longer journey than we did." Darmiya rounded the gate leading into the area and motioned for Pamas to keep to the right. "Ours felt long enough. If my brother and I hadn't made lifelong friends aboard the *Espies Major*, I don't think we would have been able to keep working such hours." Suddenly worried how her words might sound to Pamas, Darmiya continued quickly. "Not that I'm complaining. Not at all." Feeling stupid, and skinless, for having spoken too candidly, she pressed her lips together to stop making things worse by adding apologies. She spoke too much. It was one of her biggest flaws, and it didn't matter, not lately, that her friends and her brother insisted this was part of her charm. She had been criticized enough for it to know better.

"Your journey must have seemed longer, even if it wasn't. You charted our course. You had no idea what waited behind the next nebula, and you had to be prepared for just about anything. The advance team risked their lives, and you lost an entire ship, to keep the rest of us as safe as possible. There is more to a journey than minutes and hours."

Glad now she was pressing her lips together, as she was close to losing control of her jaw, Darmiya whipped her head around to stare at Pamas. The way the woman spoke was so matter-of-fact and drama free, her words sounding so well thought out and true. And they hit home. It had been a dangerous journey and they had lost so many. That, too, had meant longer hours and more shifts for the rest of them, especially after they touched down on Gemocon.

"I never thought of it that way. It makes sense." Darmiya turned left, and they entered a road that was turning into a street before their eyes. Broad—three lanes in each direction—it would ensure traffic to and from the main military base, and its headquarters would not become congested once hovercars and other vehicles became more common. This would happen soon, as *Pathfinder* had all sorts of transportation in its storage units.

"Impressive," Pamas muttered. "You found material with which to pave the streets."

"Yes. It's not as harmful to the environment as the oil-based cover we used on Gemosis, but we won't have many vehicles running directly on it. The government agrees with the environmental department that hovercraft create a much smaller footprint, so it won't be subjected to the same wear and tear."

"Good that someone is paying attention to old mistakes—at least sometimes." Pamas gazed around her as they passed the buildings constructed along the street.

"Right now, these are shops, but as the commercial areas develop further, they will become military offices instead." Darmiya pointed at the two-story buildings. "The wood they're made from grows fast, and after we treat it to not be combustible, it suits our needs very well. I think settlers who want to build their own houses will find the material quite easy to handle." Blushing now, Darmiya reminded herself about her chatterbox nature. "There I go, lecturing again." She hoped her demeanor showed professionalism rather than the awkwardness she seemed to battle lately.

"You're being most informative, Doctor Do Voy." Pamas still sounded matter-of-fact but not unkind. Tall and wiry, she walked next to Darmiya, who tried to remember the personal information she had been privy to while scanning her at the gate. Forty-nine years old, the woman looked like she had been a stunning beauty when she was younger. Pamas was still good-looking, but her scars and weathered complexion made her seem slightly older and worn. Her one good eye possessed a sharp gleam that belied her years, and Darmiya guessed this woman wasn't easy to intimidate. Something about her made Darmiya's stomach clench, and she wasn't sure what.

The military headquarters was the only structure along the street that stood more than four stories tall. The first floor held the reception areas for the different branches; the second provided conference rooms and a large banquet hall. The third floor, now mostly empty, would become the main offices for junior officers, and the top one boasted large office areas for Admiral Caydoc and her aides. It would initially provide an office for President Tylio and her cabinet members until the governmental building was finished. Now that *Pathfinder* had arrived with material and labor, the plans suggested it would take only about six months for that to happen.

"We're here." Darmiya motioned for the headquarters. "I can walk you to the reception, and then I'm due at a meeting with the brass. I hope everything will work out for your errand."

Pamas stopped and stood motionless in the sunset. "I—I hope so. Thank you for bringing me here. You've been most kind, Doctor Do—"

"Please. Call me Darmiya." Smiling nervously, Darmiya kicked at an innocent pebble on the sidewalk. "Shall we?" She tilted her head.

"Of course, Darmiya. You must call me Pamas, then."

Pamas seemed taken aback but then began to climb the five steps to the headquarters' entrance.

Inside, they both went through the identification scan, and as usual the young ensign on duty smiled in a flirty way toward Darmiya. And, as always, Darmiya sighed inwardly and smiled politely. "Hello, Ensign. I'm escorting Ms. Dagellion to the reception area."

"Always working, Doctor. You need to get out there and have some fun." The ensign winked at Darmiya.

"So you keep saying," Darmiya muttered. "Carry on, Ensign."

They kept walking down the wide corridor. Beautiful stones cut from bedrock not far away from the mountains in the distance by skilled masons made the floor look a beautiful grayish pink. The white walls reflected the sunlight coming through the skylights.

Darmiya sighed in relief. "Oh, good. Ensign Lomoda is manning the desk. That saves us a lot of administrative nonsense."

Pamas turned her head and raised an eyebrow. "What do you mean by 'us'?"

"Oh. Right. Sorry. I mean, I thought I'd just help you…you know, smooth the waves and so on. Silly, I know. You're perfectly capable of doing your own smoothing—Oh, Creator, that came out wrong." Darmiya wanted to sew her lips closed, but to her astonishment, Pamas merely nodded thoughtfully.

"Good idea. You seem to truly know your way around here. I still have no idea what the outcome will be regarding my errand. If I'm not making you late?"

Checking her timepiece, Darmiya shook her head, feeling elated in a curious way. "I have forty minutes before the meeting. I'm all yours." Moaning inwardly at her loose tongue, Darmiya decided to actually bring some strong adhesive for her mouth in the future.

"All right." Pamas walked the last few meters to the reception desk.

"Yes. How can I assist you?" Ensign Lomoda asked politely, clearly trying not to stare at Pamas's eyepatch.

"I'm trying to locate Commander Aniwyn Seclan, commander of the air group." Pamas gripped the edge of the counter before them. "I also need to have my name and status altered back from my alias to my real identity."

Ensign Lomoda gaped. "The CAG...um, isn't here today. At least not yet. She is due in half an hour, approximately. As for the second part of your errand—I'm not sure who to approach for that. Or if it can be done at this office since this is a military installation." She looked helplessly at Darmiya, who returned her attention to Pamas.

"Are you saying Pamas Dagellion isn't your real name?" She took a step back. "Are your scans accurate?" Darmiya didn't think she was being overly cautious. She knew of the stowaway changers aboard *Pathfinder* and had read all the intel, as she possessed a level-two security clearance. Only the president, the cabinet, generals, and admirals had level-one clearance. Could Pamas— what else could she call her—be an undiscovered changer? "Ensign Lomoda. Deploy your sidearm." Darmiya spoke quietly, her voice grave. "Pamas, or whatever your name is, stand back from the counter. I intend to alert security." Sure, the quick scan by the entrance had not detected any changer markers, but that was clearly not enough, judging from what had happened aboard *Pathfinder*. Yes, the first two changers they had discovered while en route to Gemocon had been benevolent, but the situation was more complicated than that. Darmiya was furious at herself. How could she have been so naive as to let a stranger get close to her this way without knowing anything about the other woman?

Ensign Lomoda had just taken aim at the center of Pamas's chest when a familiar voice made them all flinch.

"Darmiya, dear child, who is this—and why does Ensign Lomoda have her sidearm drawn?" Fleet Admiral Helden Caydoc sat straight and perfectly poised in her hoverchair, which one of her caregivers operated. Having suffered a series of strokes, the elderly woman could use only half of her body, but her intellect, not to mention her wit, was fully intact.

"Colonel—I mean, Admiral Caydoc..." Pamas whispered as she turned around. "It's truly you."

"Excuse me?" Helden looked back and forth between Darmiya and Pamas. "Do I know you?" She squinted, and her light-blue eyes seemed to sharpen. "You do seem familiar, thought I doubt I'd forget such an impactful eyepatch, madam."

"It has been twenty years, sir." Pamas had stood straight and rigid, but now she raised her hand to her chin in an unmistakable Oconodian military salute. "Lieutenant Pamas Seclan reporting, sir."

CHAPTER FOUR

W hat?" The aged admiral stared at Pamas, her eyes now huge and one hand pressed to her chest. "It's impossible."

"Sir, I'll have this individual removed," Ensign Lomoda said harshly, rounding the semicircular desk. "She's already told us she's traveled under a false identity."

Pamas didn't care about the ensign but kept her eye trained on Helden. The old woman was frail, she could tell, but her eyes were as sharp as ever, and she was certain her former commanding officer was sizing her up. "Yes, sir. It's me. I will submit to any scans, and you can verify my DNA and retinal scan against the ones in my military files."

"Oh, I will. Nobody stands before me telling me such blatant lies and gets away with it. Not only will I make sure we find out who you really are, but I'm going to make damn sure that you don't hurt Pamas Seclan's children." Helden's voice trembled when she began speaking but ended very strongly. She clenched her one good hand into a fist. "Ensign Lomoda, place this woman in the brig until we have dealt with her accordingly—"

"Fleet Admiral Caydoc? What's going on?" a firm voice asked from behind. A woman stood before a large entourage. She wore a long, light blue caftan over a white shirt and trousers, and kept her golden blond hair in a low chignon. Pamas recognized her immediately. Next to her, a younger, ethereal-looking young woman met Pamas's glance, frowning slightly. Her white-blond hair cascaded down to the small of her back, and the fact she wore a long green dress with gold embroidery made her seem as if she had stepped right out from a children's storybook. Pamas knew them instantly.

"Madam President, Ms. Lindemay." Pamas bowed.

"Now this situation appears more action packed than we anticipated when we called this meeting," President Gassinthea Mila Tylio said sardonically. "Mind pointing that sidearm to the floor, Ensign?"

Ensign Lomoda colored faintly. "Yes, Madam President. Naturally. It's just that we have a situation developing."

"Admiral Caydoc?" The president turned to Helden. "Is either of these two women a security risk?" She motioned toward Darmiya and Pamas.

"This one," Helden replied curtly. She pointed to Pamas. "She claims to be a person who died a long time ago."

Pamas closed her eye. Regretting now that she hadn't found something to eat before Darmiya showed up at the tent, she began to feel light-headed. She had been so eager to reclaim her life now that she was in relative safety on Gemocon.

"She doesn't look too good," another voice said.

"Oh, my. She's going down." Strong arms wrapped around Pamas's waist, holding her close. "Helden. This woman has been adamant about getting here. I'm not saying I trust her implicitly, but perhaps we should hear her out before we toss her in the brig?" She felt Darmiya's arms and heard her voice that spoke gently to the others. "Madam President, I'm Darmiya Do Voy. Welcome to Gemocon. Seems like we're due for the same meeting. I might be a little late. I need to take care of this situation since I was the one who let this woman into headquarters. We have to make sure she isn't an imposter."

Pamas was now struggling against what she recognized as low blood glucose. Ever since her long incarceration, her body was incredibly sensitive to any fluctuations in her system.

"Let's do this the fastest way." The president spoke quickly. "Caya, would you please join Doctor Do Voy and this woman? You can join us at the meeting later."

"Of course, Thea. Sis? I think we need you as well. Whoever she is, she looks like she's about to pass out."

"I'll be fine," Pamas managed to say while opening her eye. Praying this new planet would stop spinning around her, she regarded the woman she recognized as one of the changers aboard *Pathfinder*, Caya Lindemay. Next to her stood a slightly taller woman, her copper-red hair giving her identity away: Caya's sister, Briar, who was also known and revered as the Red Angel.

"Just low on sugar."

"That makes sense," Briar Lindemay said. "I'm a nurse, and I always carry stuff that might come in handy." She extended her mind to determine if any changer threatened to surface, and Pamas took the emergency ration bar and bit into it. "Thank you."

"Why don't we find a place where I can do my reading?" Caya looked around. "Any office area will do, as long as it's private."

"Ensign Lomoda. Follow them into one of the offices," Helden said darkly. "I'll be waiting outside to hear the results."

"So will I." President Tylio rested a hand on Helden's hoverchair. "I suggest everyone else go to the conference room. We have important business to take care of once this matter is resolved, one way or the other."

Pamas was starting to feel better and followed the Lindemay sisters and Ensign Lomoda into a small office.

"I'm going in," Darmiya said from behind. "I brought this woman here, and if it turns out I made an error in judgment, I want to be the first to know."

"Very well," Briar Lindemay said and motioned for Pamas to sit in one of the visitors' chairs. "This won't take long. My sister and I won't invade your mind more than we must. We have no interest in anything but determining who you truly are."

"It's all I ask," Pamas said, still fatigued but not about to let it show. "What should I do?"

"Take my hands," Caya said and sat in the chair next to Pamas. "Then close your eyes and don't think of anything in particular. You won't notice more than an increase in warmth, perhaps. The process is quite harmless."

"All right." Pamas allowed Caya to hold her hands. Closing her eye, she waited for something to feel different despite Caya's statement.

"Oh, dear Creator of all things…" Caya began to tremble. Pamas could feel the slender hands holding hers shake. "This woman is the former Lieutenant Pamas Seclan, mother of Commander Aniwyn Seclan, CAG, and Pherry Seclan, agronomist. She was married to General Gexter Seclan, and he had her declared deceased once she had been missing for seven years. Pamas Seclan found this fact out after escaping from captivity, after years of—no, I can't. I can't." Caya tore her hands from Pamas's, both women opening their eyes. Caya's were filled with tears. Pamas's reflected her shock.

"How can you find that out by a mere touch?" Pamas asked, her voice barely carrying. "I don't understand."

"Caya. Let me get Thea." Briar patted her sister's shoulder. "I can tell your entire mind is in uproar. You can't function at the meeting if this goes on."

"All—all right." Caya tilted her head and looked at Pamas with such empathy, Pamas's stomach clenched. "So many years. How did you survive?" she whispered.

"I had to. I had to get back to my children."

"To get them away from him. The general." Caya nodded slowly. "To save them."

"I was too late. They had to save themselves." Pamas shrugged. She gazed up at Darmiya, who looked at her with wide eyes.

"You really are her. Spinner's mother. She—she migh…oh no. I can't even guess how she will react."

Briar stepped back into the room, the president hurrying along behind her.

"Darling." Thea Tylio knelt next to Caya's chair. "Are you all right?"

"I'm fine. Just taken aback by this woman's past. What she went through while being in the claws of malevolent changers. I can't break a confidence from a reading, but I can assure everyone that she is telling the truth about her identity. She is who she claims to be."

Tylio cupped Caya's pale cheek. "Very well. That's that, then. Why don't we continue up to the conference room after you've had some time to recuperate?"

"All I need is a few minutes of meditation with Briar. I'll be good to go after that. There's so much to do and so little time." Caya stood, wobbling slightly, but held onto her sister and Tylio. "Lieutenant Seclan, or...I don't know quite how to address you. May I suggest you utilize my sister's and my abilities before and during the reunion with your children?"

"How do you mean?" Pamas stood at attention again, hands behind her back.

"It won't be an easy process, but having us present might smooth the waves, so to speak." Caya tilted her head. "I can't really speak for the military here, but from what I know of them, they owe you."

"Caya." Tylio wrapped her arm around the narrow waist of the woman she clearly cared very deeply for. "You will have time to assist Lieutenant Seclan. Right now, go meditate. I'll inform the fleet admiral outside. She needs to know that her former aide de camp is indeed alive and among us."

Caya nodded and said good-bye to Pamas. She left the room with her sister and the president, and Pamas found herself alone with Darmiya and Ensign Lomoda. "This was one scenario I hadn't imagined." Pamas unclenched her fists and straightened her aching fingers. "A mind-reading changer that everyone relies on."

"She has saved *Pathfinder* on several occasions, as you must have heard—through the gossip mill if nothing else." Darmiya sighed and sat down on the desk. "We have received extensive reports about the Lindemay sisters. They're amazing."

"And yet, they're changers. I thought the goal of this exodus was to live in a changer-free world." Pamas had hoped for this, as her experience with changers was less than amicable. In fact, the mere thought of changers existing on Gemocon made her tremble all over.

The door opened, and Helden Caydoc's assistant pushed her hoverchair inside. Pamas stared at the old woman, stunned at how birdlike and frail she looked. But as before, her stern gaze showed no weakness whatsoever.

"The oracle says you are Pamas Seclan without a shadow of a doubt. We will, of course, carry out the other tests available, but she is adamant, and she has no reason to lie. She doesn't know you, or Spinner, after all."

"It's good to see you again, sir." At attention, again, Pamas wanted suddenly to leave, to not be scrutinized in this manner by the woman she had idolized and whose career path she had mimicked to the best of her ability as a young woman. Now, at the age of forty-nine, Pamas had lost most of her best years to surviving the rigors of being a captive among volatile changers. Maybe trying to reclaim some part of her life was a mistake? It might be truly a selfish thing on her part—causing such scenes, such uproars. "Once you have conducted these tests and have a written record of my identity and not the mere words of a changer, where do I stand? Do you know?" And, of course, it might also be truly unfair to ask this old woman, but who else was there?

"I must take this up with my granddaughter, Admiral Dael Caydoc, before we even approach Spinner. I'm not sure you know, but they're married. Have been for almost a year. Darmiya here is Spinner's best friend and part of the family." Helden's voice softened marginally. "And if everything about you checks out, Pamas, then of course you must be debriefed and evaluated. You know that."

"Yes." Pamas was aware of protocol. She had been in enemy hands for twenty years. Nobody here knew if they had turned her. Bent and broken her. She couldn't even be sure herself. Malevolent changers had all kinds of gifts and abilities. What if they had programmed her to go berserk around the president? No wonder Ensign Lomoda was still focused on her with her weapon raised.

"I'm going to the meeting now," Helden said, motioning for her assistant to turn the hoverchair around. "I suggest you start the paperwork. Ensign Lomoda will supply you with a tablet containing the correct forms for you to fill in."

Forms. Of course. The military was, despite its greatness, an administrative nightmare. "Yes, sir."

"Fine. Darmiya. You're expected at the meeting too, right?" Helden asked.

"Yes. I'll be along in a minute. I just want to make sure Pamas has everything she needs." Darmiya motioned for Pamas to follow her. They strode back to the reception desk, where people now were milling about while chatting, tapping on tablets, and carrying equipment. "Oh, my. You can tell that *Pathfinder* has landed," Darmiya said, sounding surprised. "I haven't seen so many people at once in this building before. Amazing."

Having grown used to crowds aboard *Pathfinder* during their long journey, Pamas could still understand where Darmiya was coming from. The advance team had originally consisted of five ships led by the *Espies Major* but had suffered a devastating loss when the Alachcleves had destroyed one of the ships, the *Mugdon*, and all its crew of a thousand souls. Four thousand people working day and night to ready this continent on the beautiful world they'd discovered, for the arrival of more than two million individuals. It had to have been daunting, to say the least. Perhaps that explained some of the dark shadows beneath Darmiya's unforgettable eyes.

When Darmiya had made sure Ensign Lomoda knew which documents Pamas required, and that Pamas would need an escort back to her tent later, she stood quietly for a moment. Looking up at Pamas, Darmiya seemed to hesitate, but then she spoke quickly. "I know Spinner very well. She's straightforward but not always easy to read—or to get along with. She carries some scars, inside and out, and if you push…I mean, if you force the issue, I can promise you it'll backfire."

Pamas swallowed, clinging to the two large tablets in her hands. "I see. What are you suggesting? That I don't even attempt to contact Aniwyn?"

"Of course not. But take your time, and…if you like…I can perhaps be of service? I'd like to help Spinner reconnect with the mother she thought was dead. I'd hate for her to get hurt, or you for that matter. I know she's been very excited about reuniting with Pherry and his family. Your being here is…perhaps that's more than she can take right now. Will you allow me to assist?" Darmiya looked almost pleadingly at Pamas.

"You must be a very good friend to her." Pamas's frayed nerves were beginning to stir again, and she forced the calm she'd had to rely on so many times in the past to wrap around her.

"As she is to me and my brother."

"Very well. I can't afford to mess things up. My journey here…it has been all for my children. I—I accept your kind offer. Perhaps between you and the Lindemay sisters, I can have some sort of relationship with my children."

Darmiya smiled and nodded. "I hope so too. I'll contact you tomorrow, if that is all right with you? I think all your communicators will begin to go active tomorrow or the day after, once our engineers bring them online."

"Thank you." Pamas watched Darmiya raise her hand in a little salute of her own making.

"See you, Lieutenant." Darmiya turned and walked up the stairs next to the desk area.

Pamas looked at the tablets, sighed, and moved to a sitting area farther away. She might as well tackle the administrative part of her coming back alive. She had a feeling that, despite the chore being tedious, it would end up being the easier part of all this.

CHAPTER FIVE

It turned out that the conference room, even if it was the largest in the military headquarters, would not accommodate all the participants. Instead, Darmiya and Admiral Dael Caydoc's aide de camp opened the doors to the large banquet hall by the main stairs to the cabinet members and the military leaders from *Pathfinder*. Representatives from law enforcement followed them, as well as medical professionals.

Darmiya watched as people filled the seats, making sure nobody took any of the ones she had reserved for the president and her entourage. As important as this first meeting was, and a milestone in their new life as a joined people on a new homeworld, Darmiya found it hard to let go of the drama she had just witnessed. Observing the Lindemay sisters do a reading of Spinner's mother had unsettled her deeply on several levels. First, the fact that she now knew that Spinner's mother was alive, and Spinner didn't, not yet, made her feel guilty in a strange way. Second, seeing someone probe into someone else's mind, even if Pamas had allowed it, seemed like a violation. Pamas seemed adamant to prove who she was, but it was disconcerting to listen to the calm, sweet voice of the young woman who read Pamas's mind as if it were little more than a tablet. Caya Lindemay had been kind and reassuring, but that didn't make it right.

A quiet gasp from the people sitting closest to the double doors made everyone look up and brought Darmiya out of her reverie. Four presidential guardsmen entered, shortly followed by President Tylio. Behind her, two other guardsmen escorted Caya and Briar Lindemay, and just behind them walked two women Darmiya would have recognized anywhere: Admiral Korrian Heigel and Chief Social Anthropologist Meija Solimar, the two legendary women who had created the blueprints for the cubes that made up the exodus ship *Pathfinder* about forty years ago. They had to be in their late-sixties to mid-seventies, but they moved with a strength and assuredness that belied their age. Behind them, a tall woman with yet another familiar face glided with lethal grace. She was *Pathfinder*'s chief engineer, Commander Adina Vantressa. Darmiya's high security clearance gave her insight into *Pathfinder*'s command structure and crew manifest. Darmiya's brother Calagan, who was the cynical one of them, always said they needed to quickly make themselves indispensable among the advance-team crew. Now when they were, Darmiya struggled with how to cope and to combat general fatigue. Being irreplaceable could backfire that way.

As the dignitaries took their seats, Dael stepped up to the podium on the dais. She looked at the assembled people from the advance crew and *Pathfinder*, her eyes expressing very little even as she smiled faintly.

"Madam President. Ministers. Distinguished civilian and military leaders. I know you have heard this said many times since you came into high orbit and then successfully landed your twenty cubes, but welcome to Gemocon. No. Welcome home!"

Applause erupted from everyone in the banquet hall. Dael smiled more broadly and then motioned for President Tylio to join her on the dais. The president stood gracefully and climbed the few steps. If she was exhausted from the intense work during her journey aboard *Pathfinder*, Darmiya couldn't tell. In fact, the president seemed to possess the ability to hide her fatigue as well as Dael did. The only one who might persuade Dael to take a break was Spinner.

Dael motioned for the president to step closer to the microphone on the podium. President Tylio did so and stood there for a few moments, taking in the participants in this first meeting. Darmiya followed her gaze and saw how serious Tylio's closest associates, including the two changer sisters, had become.

"I wish this meeting could be just about the sheer joy of having reached our new home," Tylio said, her voice carrying steadily throughout the sound system. "However, you have received some of the intel we brought and the hardships *Pathfinder* has experienced these two and a half years. I regret to inform you that we have not been able to track all the changers that managed to get aboard our cubes. Not only that, but we have it on good authority that these changers are well organized, cunning, and ruthless."

"What about your own changer, Madam President?" a tall woman asked, standing up in row five. "She and her sister were the first stowaways aboard the ship, after all."

Darmiya sighed and wanted to scream. She knew this woman. Her name was Lemdia Baslo, and on several occasions, she had brought work to a complete halt by questioning the tiniest, most minute details for no apparent reason whatsoever. One time, when Darmiya had spent two weeks coming up with a solution to an irrigation problem when her brother Calagan had required help, Lemdia had set them back yet another two weeks by just being difficult and a true pain. Of course, she would be the one to interrupt the Gemoconian president and embarrass everyone by acting as if she truly had a say-so about anything at all. Darmiya had to wrap her ankles together to refrain from stomping over to Lemdia and kicking her.

Dael's expression turned thunderous, which was uncommon, since everyone working for her normally went out of their way to do their best, except this unnerving woman. "Take a seat, Ms. Baslo. If you interrupt our president again, I'll have you escorted out of here."

Lemdia sat down, if a bit slowly, and glowered at Dael. Darmiya hoped this meant she wouldn't have to tangle with Lemdia any time soon. If she kept annoying Dael, Lemdia would find herself surveying locations for hover charging.

President Tylio merely shook her head, looking sorrowful for a fraction of a second. So, her command mask could slip. Darmiya supposed having the entire Exodus mission weighing on your shoulders for your entire presidency would do that to you. "Ms. Baslo, was it?" the president said in a low voice. "I have no idea what you've heard, or what you think you know, but I can deduce from your personal and quite offensive question that you have been jumping to conclusions, which I believe is contrary to what any accomplished scientist should do, yes?"

It delighted Darmiya to witness Lemdia blush profusely.

"The woman you so carelessly refer to as 'my changer' is a remarkable individual who has saved countless lives on more than one occasion, while putting herself in harm's way each time, I might add. The same goes for her sister, whom everyone aboard *Pathfinder* reveres for the self-sacrificing work she does for free. Yes, the Lindemay sisters are changers. Benevolent changers. If it wasn't for their powers, we wouldn't be here, and we wouldn't be aware of the malevolent changers my social anthropologist will brief you on here today. I'm told that each of you who is present here has level three or above security clearance. I'm not entirely sure that's enough." Tylio turned away from the microphone and murmured something to Dael, who nodded grimly. Looking back at the assembled crowd, the president straightened her back and winced in a barely visible way. "Admiral Caydoc agrees with me. I must ask everyone with a level-three security clearance to move to the conference room, where Commander KahSandra will brief you at the correct level."

Another woman, this one in an Oconodian uniform, rose and started walking toward the exit. "Follow me, please." Commander KahSandra waved the staff with lesser clearance to join her. Knowing she was being truly petty now, Darmiya had to hide a smile when she saw Lemdia walk among the others to the conference room.

"Your turn, Meija," Tylio said and smiled down at the first row, where Meija Solimar stood, pushing her unruly red hair out of her face. Only a few white streaks showed her age, and Darmiya could only stare at the stunning woman who had been part of this mission from the time *Pathfinder* existed only as an elaborate blueprint.

"Hello. I'm Meija Solimar, and I can't quite express how amazing it feels to have reached our new home. President Tylio asked me to summarize some of the knowledge we've gathered of the potentially dangerous changers. They made it aboard *Pathfinder* by using advanced technology to hide their genetic makeup. As the president said, a lot of what we know stems from information that the Lindemay sisters provided. I maintain we have only scratched the surface. After several terror attacks in which they used white garnet, they waited until we engaged the Alachleves in battle. Then the malevolent changers attempted to destroy an entire cube. They succeeded, to some degree. As we were realigning the cubes after complete separation, the changers put their plan in motion and created a vast explosion that left cube eighteen destroyed beyond repair." Meija's eyes darkened. "We lost so many people during that attack. Caya Lindemay was in the jumper tunnel and nearly lost her life, but thankfully she managed to get herself and a young man to safety. She had valuable information for the president and her cabinet and risked her life to convey it to us."

"Please, Caya. We need to hear the rest from you," President Tylio said, and nodded toward the podium.

Caya stood and approached the dais. She looked fragile and ethereal, her long, blond hair flowing around her as she stepped up to the microphone. Then she laughed, making everyone smile. The young woman totally charmed Darmiya.

"I'm sorry, but I need a box or something to stand on if I'm to speak into the microphone," Caya said, and laughed again.

"Here, ma'am," one of the presidential guards said and brought over an EM-kit case. "Will this do?"

"Perfect!" Caya stepped up on the case, and now she could reach the microphone. "As you heard, I'm Caya Lindemay. I'm a changer, but you needn't be afraid of me. My gifts are not violent, nor are they intrusive. Both my sister and I are getting better at switching our gifts on and off. I don't read people without their consent. Neither does Briar." Shifting slightly, Caya wrapped her small hands around the edges of the podium. She glanced at the president and took a deep breath. "There are more changers among the people arriving from Oconodos than you realize. And, yes, some of them are malevolent changers, which is unsettling, as we left our homeworld because we yearned for a life of peace and safety. The malevolent changers are highly organized. They exist in sleeper cells, and some are also divided up into groups, all led by a super-changer who possesses enormous powers. We don't know who this individual is—or even if it's a man or woman. Just before cube eighteen was destroyed, I learned from a group of friends that several benign, or benevolent, changers were aboard *Pathfinder*. Now, I hope to gather them here on Gemocon, enlist them, if you will, to help us weed out the malevolent ones and devise ways to protect ourselves."

A man in the first row raised his hand. "Did we undertake this journey, and carry out all this hard work, for nothing? We came here to get away from changers—no offense."

"None taken." Caya looked sorrowful, and Darmiya wondered what it was like for her when people appeared to either fear or loathe her, just because she carried the changer gene. Anyone from Oconodos could have the gene that brought out the mutation. Some showed signs of being changers as very small children; others didn't realize it until they were well into adulthood.

Caya lowered her head, and at first Darmiya didn't think the otherworldly looking woman would answer, but Caya raised her head, and her eyes seemed so transparent, they almost glowed. "No, your journey wasn't in vain. The situation on Oconodos could not be contained due to the sheer number of malevolent changers and the politics that kept benevolent changers, such as myself, from daring to live openly and honestly. I never went to school, I rarely left our house, and my sister worked tirelessly to support us and to homeschool me. When I revealed my identity aboard

Pathfinder, I experienced almost a repeat of my younger years. I was kept in protective custody with the best of intentions, but it was a matter of incarceration however you look at it. That is why I am so adamant about locating Briar's and my peers. We need to be transparent and make ourselves available to you, our fellow Gemoconians, and not hide. That only adds to the mystery—and potential conspiracy theories. Only by being approachable can we dedramatize our existence and work together to deal with potential threats from the malevolent super-changers and their followers."

At first the banquet hall was completely silent. Then one person began applauding, which made everyone else clap enthusiastically for a good minute. Caya blushed and held her hand out to the president. "Thank you. Thank you very much, but I'm not the one running our new homeworld." She motioned toward President Tylio. "This woman, she is the one who tirelessly has had nothing but the future of all of you on her mind and as her goal, for many years. We need to rally behind her when she begins to implement new laws, create new rules and regulations, and most of all, inspire the population to begin their new lives."

Impressed, Darmiya applauded again with everyone else. It was difficult not to become inspired by Caya, who now returned to sit next to her sister. When the president carefully nudged the EM-kit case aside to enter the podium, Darmiya noticed something so tender in the way she glanced at Caya. Had they become more than friends? Gossip had it that Thea Tylio had a new love interest. A recording of a speech Tylio had given shipwide after the Alachleve attack also suggested as much. It had been interrupted before Tylio had a chance to name the person, but it had seemed quite evident that her lover could be a woman.

"Admiral Caydoc will divide you all into interdisciplinary groups, where you will work toward solving this issue. We need all hands on deck until we have apprehended and tried these people. We did not travel for years to allow ourselves to even contemplate defeat. My assistants have provided you all with the in-depth information you will need. This conference, and all consequent meetings regarding this subject, are classified. You do not share what you learn with anyone other than the people in this room. If you have an individual in mind who might shed light on the matter at hand, take it up with Admiral Caydoc and nobody else." The president nodded toward Dael and resumed her seat on Caya's other side.

The men and women in the room looked around, as if trying to judge who they might be working with. Darmiya was uncertain if she would be in one of the groups, as she was infamous for working alone as of late.

Dael cleared her voice. "Group one will gather information and intel from the rest of you. Regard them as administrators of sorts. Some of them are from the advance team, others from *Pathfinder*. The same goes for the makeup of your groups. Group-one members will be Commander Aniwyn Seclan, Commander Adina Vantressa, Caya Lindemay, Briar Lindemay, Doctor Darmiya Do Voy, Doctor Calagan Do Voy, Lieutenant Nim Dodgmer, Commander Neenja KahSandra, Admiral Korrian Heigel, Chief Social Anthropologist Meija Solimar, Dalanja Bymento, and Vice President Jomay Bymento."

Darmiya looked at the faces around her in the banquet hall. Most of them appeared pleased, but some seemed confused or reluctant. It was a comprehensive list, with only three names from the advance team. Would anyone actually object? But so far nobody had openly done so, not counting Lemdia, who had been escorted out.

"Excuse me, Admiral Caydoc, but why so few of us, I mean, from the advance team?" a young lieutenant whose name Darmiya couldn't remember asked.

"Considering that we are one and the same people, and now when all two million of *us* are settling in, I don't think we need to divide us into 'us and them' anymore. I know it is tempting to do so, given that the advance team has worked tirelessly to prepare for these days. What matters is filling the positions with the right people for the right assignment. If you still feel you have any grievances, file them through the proper channels, please."

The lieutenant colored faintly. "No objections at all, sir. I was just wondering."

"Well, then." Dael gazed along the rows of people. "If you look at your personal tablets, you will find which group you belong to. The schedule will demand a lot of you, but I, for one, am certain you will meet any challenges head-on like you've always done. Any other questions?"

"Why are no ministers represented in the lead groups, except the vice president?" an older man asked. Darmiya recognized him as minister of infrastructure but couldn't recall his name either. "And what qualifications does his Gemosian wife have?" Now he spoke with a sneer on his face, which was reflected in his tone of voice.

"Minister Ylossa." Dael's voice hardened marginally, something Darmiya quickly realized was definitely not a good sign. Minister Ylossa might well find himself accompanying Lemdia in the time-out corner. "There is a good reason for this decision," Dael said. "As a high-ranking politician, you should realize why. All the ministers will have far too much on their plates when it comes to setting up your respective departments to take on something as time-consuming as this assignment." Dael narrowed her eyes, something Darmiya had learned she did quite deliberately when she wanted to drive a point home. "As for your comment regarding Dalanja Bymento, I'm sure it slipped your mind that she holds a law degree and worked successfully as a district attorney in her hometown on Gemosis before her husband ran for office."

Minister Ylossa looked as if he wanted to melt into the wooden flooring. He had perhaps hoped to stir the pot and sow seeds of doubt regarding the Gemosians, or perhaps he hoped to become part of group one. Darmiya found it curious that anyone would want more responsibility. Overwhelming amounts of it had worn her out and changed her from a happy, carefree young woman to a somber, brooding type running low on power.

"I suggest you seek out your fellow group members and plan for the initial meetings while we are all gathered here. Soon enough we will be neck deep in all the tasks at hand, and time will be a rare commodity." Dael nodded briefly and left the dais. She gazed around the room, found Darmiya, and waved her over.

"Do you have an ETA for my wife, Darmiya?" she asked, her voice low.

Darmiya checked her large tablet. "She is still two hours out, sir."

Dael's eyes darkened further. "She promised she'd be back by now. I think she needs a new timepiece."

"No use. She'll just ignore that one as well, sir." Darmiya smiled carefully. "Er, sir? Did you by any chance have the opportunity to speak to Fleet Admiral Caydoc before this meeting?" Darmiya shuffled her feet some, yet another nervous habit.

Dael had begun to look away but now snapped her eyes back to meet Darmiya's. "No? Should I have? Is she all right?"

"Yes, yes. Of course she is. It's just—there's been an unforeseen develop—"

"Darmiya! Come join us. I want to introduce you to—oh, sorry. Come over to us when you're done." Calagan had clearly spotted whom Darmiya was talking to and made an apologetic gesture.

"What unforeseen development?" Dael asked sternly.

Darmiya clenched both her hands behind her back as if that would give her strength. "There's no easy way to say this. It looks like Spinner's mother is alive—and she's here."

CHAPTER SIX

Pamas had not returned to the military headquarters since filling out the forms regarding her absent years. The ordeal of listing what had happened to her—and she confessed to herself that she had downplayed it—had gotten to her more than she thought it would.

Instead of attending the several information gatherings that the advance team had prepared for each camp, she kept to herself. She spent the first two days in her tent meditating. Using a technique taught to her by a fellow captive during two years when she was kept together with two other women, Pamas went deeper than usual, using her *kiminaya* spirit word to remain on a deep level. This technique had helped keep her alive, not to mention stay sane. So many times, she had been close to despair and ready to give up, or, worse, give in to Nestrocalder. The mere thought of the changer's name was enough to bring forward the pain and humiliation she had been subjected to. Submerging herself into the soft protection of meditation was what she needed. Pamas didn't care how long it took to find her bearings.

The locking mechanism on her tent had a privacy setting that kept track of how many times someone had tried to get her attention. The person calling could also enter their identity code, which made it possible for her to get back to them. So far, nobody except that persistent scientist, Darmiya, had called on her.

Pamas opened the small cooling unit and pulled out an emergency beverage. She downed it with ease, thirsty as always after a long session of meditation. It tasted bland, but she honestly didn't care about such things. It was good enough that the rations sustained her. She had survived on far less food for a very long time. Opening the tent flap, she spotted something waiting for her in her message unit. After she pressed her palm against it, she cautiously took the small message slips and a parcel and brought them back inside. As she guessed, the packaged contained her new communicator. Pamas looked suspiciously at it, ran the test sequence to make sure it worked, and then clipped it to her lapel. Opening the first of the slips, she pressed the sensor with her thumb.

"Hello, Lieutenant. Darmiya here. I'm stopping by to see how you're doing, but you have your privacy lock on. I can understand that you've gone through a lot and need to regroup. The thing is, I really need to talk to you. It's very important. You should have your new comm unit any day. Please page me."

Frowning at the urgency in Darmiya's voice, Pamas pressed the sensor on the second slip.

"So, still acting like a wounded silver hind? Well, I suppose I can understand. It's just that time's sort of running out here, and we need to talk to you. I mean, I do. I need to talk to you. Please get back to me as soon as you hear this."

Darmiya sounded frantic now, downright stressed.

Holding the third slip, tapping it indecisively against the palm of her left hand, Pamas shuddered. It had to do with Aniwyn. Or Pherry. Or both. It had to. What else could it be? Sighing, she opened the third message.

"Okay. I'm bringing some grade-four diamond spanners next time. I'm going to jail no doubt for breaking and entering, but if

that's what it takes to get you to notice my messages, then so be it. You're as impossible as your daughter can be. Do you know that? I always thought Spinner was the most stubborn woman I'd ever met—with a slightly self-destructive streak in her—but you seem to have that stubbornness as well. Let's just hope you're not as prone to getting yourself into dangerous situations. That would be unfortunate. I'm returning tomorrow. You better be up and awake, because I'm coming inside."

This message didn't sound upbeat or frantic. Instead, Darmiya seemed angry. No, furious.

Tapping her new communicator, Pamas heard the familiar set of clicks that showed it was ready to accept her commands.

"Lieutenant Pamas Seclan to Doctor Darmiya Do Voy."

Pamas counted to four, and then she could have sworn her communicator jumped into action on her lapel. "Really? Well, about bloody time! What have you been doing? I've been worried. I've been going—"

"Crazy. Yes. I could tell." Pamas picked up the blankets from the floor, folded them four times, and placed them on the bed. "What can I do for you, Doctor?"

"Oh, stop it. Call me Darmiya. And I thought that would be obvious. You are doing it. I only wanted you to get in touch with me before Spinner gets back. Her wife, Dael, knows about you. That you're back."

"What?" Pamas lost her grip on the last blanket, which fell back onto the floor. "Did you tell her?"

"I did. So did Helden. She needed to know so she can be there for Spinner when she learns the truth. I'm not sure how the Aniwyn you knew handled surprises, but my best friend Spinner hates them with a passion. She's going to be home tonight after an extended mission. No doubt, she's dying get together with Pherry and his family, but she'll learn of your miraculous return as well. I'm not sure how she's going to handle it. I mean, I can make a highly educated guess, but—" Darmiya stopped the rapid flow of words, clearly since she needed to breathe.

"Why does she need to know already? I have to get back on my feet and try to regain my military rank for real." Stressed again now, Pamas ran her hand through her messy hair.

"Come on, Pamas. The Caydocs know. They're loyal to a fault and are going to look out for Spinner's best interests, and that means her younger brother's as well. Dael isn't unsympathetic to what you've been through. Nor is Helden."

"Why, thank you. How reassuring. I couldn't care less what the military brass sympathizes with or not. The only ones I owe any explanations to are my son and daughter. Dael Caydoc may be my daughter-in-law, but that doesn't mean anything. Not really."

"Creator of all things, Pamas. Surely you're not that oblivious? I mean, you want to have a relationship with your children, right?" Darmiya sounded incredulous.

"Of course. That's what I said." Pamas began pacing back and forth on the narrow planks.

"I can tell you need some guidance, or you're going to screw everything up. For yourself, but also for Spinner. And Pherry, since he'll take his cue from Spinner, if I read the family dynamic right." Darmiya was silent for a moment. "We need to meet before Dael informs her wife about you. Helden won't tell Spinner, but Dael might think she has no choice."

Pamas had planned to meditate more later in the day, but her time had run out. "So, what do you suggest?" she asked curtly.

"We should make sure we're not overheard. Gossip on this planet is like a plasma storm. Much like on *Pathfinder*, I imagine," Darmiya added a huff. "I'm off duty in an hour. Why don't you come with me to my favorite spot in the hills north of the capital?"

"Very well."

"Oh, good." Darmiya sighed. "I'll pick you up by your gates in an hour then."

"All right. Fine. Seclan out." Sitting down on one of the stools, Pamas tried to stop her hands from shaking. Aniwyn was on her way back from an assignment, and it looked like Darmiya believed Pamas needed to meet her children tonight. It was—it was too soon!

She was aware of the irony of her reasoning. Almost twenty years of incarceration was an insanely long time. Of course she should want to throw herself into the embrace of her grown children, accomplished adults who probably had moved on after accepting that she was long dead. And not only that, but they probably also hated her for stranding them with their despotic father.

Grabbing her small toiletry bag and a towel, Pamas shoved the tent flap aside and stomped off to the common shower rooms. At least she had some time to make herself presentable.

For the first time, she found herself wishing she'd done something about the damn eyepatch.

Darmiya waited by the gates to the temporary residential area, pacing back and forth while she went over what she needed to convey to Pamas. The last few days had been insanely busy, and trying to reach out to Pamas had been frustrating. The third day, when she went to Pamas's tent and found it sealed once more, she feared the woman might have committed suicide. She had left the last note, knowing she would have to bring reinforcements if she had to leave a fourth one. When Pamas contacted her, Darmiya nearly wept, which in turn frightened her. What was it about this woman, apart from her being Spinner's mother, that got under her skin?

Darmiya's parents and brother had called her Butterfly when she was growing up, because her interests and infatuations were of the fleeting, temporary kind. Not that she was disloyal with her affections; it was merely that she fell in love easily with people, things, interests, and subjects. She would bounce from one person to another, adore them, pine for them, and then move on. She had a serious crush on Spinner when she first came across her in the downed spacecraft on Gemosis. Spinner was strong and brave, and, yes, flawed, and stunningly beautiful. Darmiya had tended to Spinner's wounds and then followed her like a lovesick pet until she realized Spinner was deeply and irrevocably in love with

Dael Caydoc. The knowledge had stung a little, but Darmiya's crush had quickly turned to friendship. She was surprised when the friendship grew to include Dael and her grandmother, as this wasn't her usual way of responding. Normally she would have moved on to a new person, or any new item or interest, to focus her affection on. Instead, the crush became something deeper and more real, which shocked and delighted her brother, who, up until then, had been her only constant.

"Doctor Do Voy? Darmiya?" Pamas's low, throaty voice broke through Darmiya's thoughts, making her spin around to face her.

"Pamas! There you are—and you look amazing." Knowing she was probably gaping, Darmiya tried to fathom that this stylish woman was the same bohemian-looking person that had stepped off cube eleven. She wore her dark hair in a severe twist at the nape of her neck, not trying to hide the eyepatch at all. She didn't wear any makeup, much like Spinner, but her features were sharp and chiseled where Spinner's were more youthfully rounded. According to her documentation, Pamas had been only eighteen when she had her first child, which would put her in her late forties now. As Darmiya stepped closer, she saw faint scarring on Pamas's skin, around her jawline, temples, and cutting through the eyebrow above her good eye. This disfiguration didn't diminish her stunning looks, but it made Darmiya's heart clench in sympathy when she imagined what Pamas might have been subjected to.

"Thank you." Pamas merely shook her head. "I'm here as requested, so where are we going?"

Darmiya nodded. "To a great place I found when I went on my first hike. I'm sure it won't be just mine for very long, as people are bound to expand into the hills to build dwellings and start their lives, but for now…it is mine." She smiled hopefully as she motioned for Pamas to follow her. "I thought you might like to try one of the hoverskids. This belongs to Calagan, my brother." She pulled the levers of both skids and gestured for Pamas to take the one with the taller stick.

Pamas stared at the hoverskid as if she thought it might explode at a mere touch. "I don't know how to operate one of these."

"It's really easy. I promise. Trust me, Pamas. If I can learn to ride it, you can too. I'm such a clumsy person, and you move like you're...not." Her cheeks burning at the last words, Darmiya stepped up on the dais of her skid. "Here. You stand on the platform like this. A gyroscope will keep you level. It's actually hard to deliberately fall if you only hold on to the stick." Darmiya held the tall stick lightly in her left hand. "This is how you steer. You push the stick, well, the lever, really, in the direction you want to go. The more you push it forward, the faster you go, and vice versa. You can stop quickly if you need to, but since you can't go much faster than forty kilometers an hour, you have time to brake. I never go quite that fast, as I normally use mine for shorter distances. But out in nature, it's fun to stretch the limits a bit." She smiled broadly. "I think you'll do great."

"Well, if I fall off and break my neck, a lot of problems might be solved." Pamas stepped onto the skid platform.

"What?" Darmiya stared at Pamas.

Pamas looked up at the sky for a few seconds, shaking her head. "A joke. Granted, a morbid one, but still, a joke, Darmiya."

"Oh. Right." A not-very-funny joke. Spinner must've inherited her dark sense of humor from her mother. "Ha-ha. Now, try to... yes, like that." Darmiya watched as Pamas tentatively pushed the stick forward, making the hoverskid rise twenty centimeters off the ground and slide forward. She attempted to back up slowly, and it didn't take long before she had circled Darmiya and her skid several times, each time faster than before.

"What an ingenious invention. Whoever came up with this, I'm impressed. And it makes me wonder why we didn't have them on Oconodos. It seems quite easy to make." Pamas stopped at Darmiya's side.

"It is sort of crude, I suppose," Darmiya said, "but that's what's brilliant when you don't have an abundance of resources but have to make do with what we brought with us aboard the advance ships."

"Of course."

Darmiya pointed to the trail leading off toward the northwest. "Follow me." She pushed her stick forward, feeling the hum of the hoverskid as its tiny reactor responded. Gliding along the path, they passed a lot of people at first, but as they approached the hills, the hikers became fewer, and Darmiya reveled in the beauty of the scenery around them.

The rounded hills were covered in soft, light-green grass for the most part. Every now and then they passed patches of flowers in all shades of blue and pink. Trees grew intermittently, and they weren't very tall, but dense with leaves and knotty branches. Darmiya had climbed them many times, as had many of the children who came with the advance team. Soon, the expert botanists would begin cataloging every single plant on Gemocon. Marine biologists and geologists would map the oceans, and the first farm started at an experimental level would expand, while others popped up all over the countryside when the farmers staked out new ground.

Right now, most of the scenery was virginal. It puzzled Darmiya why only benevolent wildlife and no humanoids inhabited this world. No doubt archeologists would scan every surface, and perhaps in time they would find that a civilization once existed here. The thought intrigued her, but right now, Darmiya enjoyed the fresh air, the beauty around her, and, yes, if she was completely truthful to herself, the woman just behind her.

Pamas ignited something in Darmiya that she hadn't felt since they arrived at Gemocon. It wasn't because she was Spinner's mother. Darmiya had sensed the strange connection long before Pamas had revealed her true identity. After feeling numb and withdrawn for months on end, Darmiya only had to talk to Pamas for a short while to experience a sense of being skinless.

Pulling up along a narrow path that only existed because Darmiya had hiked on foot there many times, she made sure Pamas was right behind her. When they reached the top of the grassy hill, Darmiya stopped and jumped off her hoverskid. "We're here." She looked at Pamas with a hint of apprehension. If Pamas couldn't see the beauty here where Darmiya found her bearings when everything else threatened to overwhelm her, it would truly hurt her.

❖

Pamas pulled the stick toward her, making the hoverskid stop. She was already fond of this simple means of transportation. Riding behind Darmiya, watching the young woman's curly black hair flutter in the wind, inhaling air so fresh it seemed to sparkle all the way into her lungs, Pamas was amazed at how relaxing this experience was.

Walking up to Darmiya, who looked oddly defensive, she took in the view. They were higher up than Pamas had realized, and she could see everything between them and the tall, snow-capped mountains in the distance. She found only one word for it.

"Breathtaking," Pamas whispered. "You found a one-in-a-million spot to call your own."

Darmiya sighed deeply and looked relieved. Had she worried how Pamas might react? Probably. Darmiya had something vulnerable about her that made Pamas believe it would be far too easy to snuff out her joy. "I'm glad you think so," Darmiya said.

"I may be missing an eye, but I have excellent vision in the other one," Pamas said laconically.

"Pamas!" Looking scandalized, Darmiya pivoted toward her.

"Well, it's true. And I'm grateful that you're showing me this place. I can see everything from here—or at least that's how it feels." She quickly identified the cube she had chosen to exit from, cube eleven, where it sat in the very center of what would become the capital of Gemocon. Roads stretched from the area where she had first met Darmiya, the arrival gate, and Pamas surmised that emergency vehicles would use them in the future. As far as she knew, some of the cube would be dismantled and serve as the main governmental building. Caydoc Park had been its main feature, along with the large stage where artists and musicians had performed during their long journey. The park stretched through the entire cube, and now that the top was coming off, the trees and grass in the park wouldn't need any of the photosynthesis lights any longer. In the stunningly fresh air, everything would grow naturally.

Farther to the east, cube eleven sat, surrounded by prebuilt roads that would accommodate emergency hovercars after they had touched down. The staff still residing in the cube would eventually have the opportunity to find new homes on the outside, like the rest of the Gemoconians, and then the hospital cube would expand to become a university for health-care students. No doubt, the hospital would expand as well.

The plains between the hills where they sat and the mountains in the distance would no doubt become filled with smaller communities and farms. Right now, Pamas saw the beautiful, almost golden, grass glistening in the sun. Some of the larger wildlife grazed at the far east, and she wondered what they looked like up close. Specks of color among the gold suggested the presence of wildflowers. A pang erupted in Pamas's chest when she remembered how Aniwyn had loved to pick flowers in the fields by the river behind their summer house on Oconodos. Even Pherry had enjoyed it, and Pamas had taught them how to bind wreaths to decorate the house and wear in their hair. She had saved some of the flowers they picked in a thick herbarium, but that, along with so much more, was lost to her.

"I'm glad you like it. It helps keep me sane when I have too much going on." Darmiya pointed at a large boulder beneath one of the trees. "We can sit here for a bit, if you like. I have some tea in my bag." She patted the small pouch hanging across her chest.

"Good idea. Thank you." Pamas found she really was thirsty after the ride up the hills. Sitting down on the boulder, she discovered it was barely big enough for both of them to fit but tried not to show how awkward she felt when Darmiya sat close to her. Accepting the foldable mug of hot tea, she sipped it carefully, relieved when she liked the taste of the sweetened beverage.

"Pamas. Listen. Spinner, I mean Aniwyn, gets back tonight. She has been on an excruciatingly long mission, and I think I know her well enough to say she's going to be torn between being excited to see Dael and infuriated that she was called away for this mission when the Exodus ship finally arrived here. She has talked about little else besides her younger brother these last few months. When we got the intel about the Alachleves' devastating attack, I think she experienced flashbacks from when they attacked the advance convoy. She and I, and several others, were on a scouting mission when the Alachleves attacked and we lost the *Mugdon*. Spinner blamed herself for not being there. She couldn't shake the feeling that she might have been able to make a difference."

"And we ran into the Alachleves' expanded sector, despite all your efforts to warn us about them via the buoy system. And Pherry and his family were aboard *Pathfinder*."

"And then cube eighteen was destroyed. She was frantic before she had confirmation that her brother and his family were safe. She knew they weren't living in that cube, but still. She started blaming herself that she hadn't persuaded Pherry to come with her on the *Espies Major*. She always thought it was too dangerous to bring him and his family aboard a ship that was going into the unknown. A pre-charted course did make more sense to them when they discussed it."

"I see." Pamas thought she knew what Darmiya was telling her. "You wish for me to stay away from both of them. I can understand that."

"What? No!" Darmiya placed a hand on Pamas's arm, squeezing it gently. "That's not it at all."

Confused, Pamas frowned, wanting to pull her arm away from Darmiya's grip. She wasn't used to being touched. Apart from the changer, Caya, the other day, the last person to touch her had fractured three of her fingers. "Then what do you mean?"

"Spinner has no idea you're alive. You were declared dead seven years after you left."

"I didn't leave. I was taken. I thought we had established that to be the truth." Feeling questioned again, Pamas did pull her arm away from Darmiya's hand.

"I'm sorry. Yes, we did establish that fact." Darmiya pushed her thick curls away from her face. "But Dael needs to tell her about you. Nobody can reach her as profoundly as Dael and her grandmother can. Helden used to know you. If she corroborates what Dael says, she may actually believe it."

"And then?" Pamas whispered.

"And then I bring you in. Once we clear that hurdle, she can help you reach out to Pherry and his family, if that's what you want."

"Of course that's what I want. It's just…you must realize that I'm not the mother they remember. I'm older. I'm damaged in more ways than one. I have to face the possibility that they might reject me on sight." Pamas rubbed her forehead and adjusted the eyepatch. "Pherry probably doesn't remember me. He was only eight, almost nine."

"He'll remember. I lost my mother when I was seven. I remember her very well." Darmiya wiped at a large tear hanging from her impossibly long lashes. "You're their mother, no matter what. Knowing Spinner, she may lash out from the pain she suffered while being without you, but she's as loyal as they come. When she learns of your ordeal, she'll come around."

What was it about this woman? Pamas shook her head as if that would clear it. Darmiya wasn't a changer. She was a Gemosian scientist, and without being an empath or an oracle, she seemed to be able to get under Pamas's skin and read her very accurately. "So, what you want from me is to take my cue from you—tonight?" Too fast. Too soon. Pamas was trembling again.

"Yes."

"I haven't finished my cycle of meditation yet. I have several days left to go. I could lose my equilibrium and screw everything up." Pamas knew her equilibrium was far away right now. She also doubted she had enough energy left to ride the hoverskid back to the camp, let alone try to make a good impression on her children.

"You'll be fine. I'll be there. You know me by now. I'm easy to read. Some perceive me as shallow. Annoying, but harmless, sort of." Darmiya smiled, but her eyes, the mere movement of her lips, and her voice were flat.

"Yes, I do believe I'm getting to know you." Pamas pinched herself to stop hyperventilating. "And you are by no means shallow. Harmless? Depends on what you read into that word. If they mean you're the sort who wouldn't willingly harm anyone, then I agree. If instead they suggest you're harmless as in meek or uninteresting—then I don't." Pamas was surprised how much focusing on Darmiya seemed to ground her. Her tremors had lessened, and she wasn't gasping as much for air.

"Really?" Darmiya's dark eyes grew even bigger. "I didn't think you noticed me at all."

"Hard not to. You're very stubborn." Pamas shook her head. "Which is mostly a good trait."

"Ha. Well, let me tell you what I had in mind, exactly—"

A large, sharp noise rolled up toward them from the capital area. Pamas stood, pulling Darmiya with her. She had heard this sound too many times on Oconodos. Explosions. Bombs. Her military training had taught her to recognize missiles and mortars. You never knew what was in the damn things. They were at a safe distance if the explosion came from a clean substance, but if someone had put any type of garnet into it, they could still be affected. "Come on, Darmiya! We need to get going!" Yanking at Darmiya, who simply stared in shock at the cloud forming below them, Pamas rushed toward the hoverskids.

CHAPTER SEVEN

Darmiya shoved the stick on her hoverskid forward so hard, she feared it might break. All she could think about were her friends and colleagues down in the capital. And the children! In front of her, Pamas drove the skid as if she had trained for months, almost touching the ground when she made sharp turns along the winding path. The gyroscope righted her, but Darmiya was afraid of what could happen if it malfunctioned.

Another explosion erupted as they closed in on the first road leading toward the center of the capital. It came from farther away.

"Not cube eleven again!" Darmiya pulled up alongside Pamas. "We need to get to headquarters." She had to scream to make herself heard over the wind that carried the sound of emergency klaxons from below.

"You go to headquarters. I need to find Pherry." Turning the lever far too much to the left, Pamas still managed to glide around the next hill as if she were glued to the dais.

"No! That's impossible. It's bound to be mayhem everywhere. Help us organize search-and-rescue instead. That way you can find Pherry and truly help him as well. Please, Pamas!" Clinging to her stick, Darmiya cast an imploring glance at Pamas. "Please!"

"Damn it. Are you always right like this?" Pamas growled the words but maneuvered her skid closer to Darmiya. "What makes you think they'll even let me help?"

"Because Admiral Caydoc trusts me." Darmiya hadn't had time in the hills to get into her plan for how Pamas could approach Spinner. Dael and Helden agreed with her that Spinner needed to get to know Pamas, at least to some degree, before she found out the woman was her mother. Dael had concluded via DNA and through the questionnaire and Helden's testimony that Pamas was who she claimed to be. Another thing she hadn't taken up with Pamas was the very valid fear that Spinner's mother could easily have been turned while being at the changers' mercy for so many years. That aside, Pamas had been a lieutenant in the fleet, possessed knowledge about how to deal with disaster, and having her close would make it possible for Darmiya to keep an eye on her.

When they reached the road leading up to the military head-quarters, Darmiya recognized the organized chaos that showed everyone was at their duty station. Having been aboard the advance ships while they were faced with one disaster after another, Darmiya knew what might look like complete pandemonium was not when it came to the military. She hurried up the steps with Pamas right behind her, searching for any of her commanding officers. She spotted Dael with some of the brass from *Pathfinder*, as well as Korrian Heigel and Commander Vantressa. Running over to them, she was glad to see that they were physically all right.

"How can we help, sir?" Darmiya asked. Privately she was on a first-name basis with Dael, but naturally not when it came to official business.

"Darmiya. Thank the Creator you're all right." Dael nodded toward Pamas. "Lieutenant Seclan. From now on, until you either resign or are relieved of your rank for some reason, you are back on active duty. You report directly to me until you learn otherwise."

"Understood, sir." Pamas saluted. "I will replicate a uniform later."

"Good." Dael returned her attention to Darmiya. "To alleviate your fears, Calagan is fine. I saw him two minutes ago, when he headed toward his laboratory. The first explosion tore the ceiling off the new commercial area. Fortunately, that part has not been officially opened yet. Casualties consist of construction workers and some merchants that were starting to set up shop in there." She cleared her throat. "The second explosion was smaller, but as far as we can tell, it caused more devastation as it hit the entrance to cube eleven."

"No." Darmiya clenched her hands. "Commander Vantressa? Your partner, Briar?"

"I don't know yet," Adina said. "I have to get there to find her and Caya. They were both there today, working at their clinic."

Darmiya knew what this meant. Caya was close to the president. Taking her out with a terrorist attack would score points for the people behind it. A lot of people would rally behind the idea of getting rid of stowaway changers, no matter how well-connected they were.

"That's where we're needed then." Darmiya pointed toward the building next to the headquarters. "Let's get some EM-kits and then head over there. We'll help you locate your partner and her sister if need be, Commander."

Pamas had already started moving toward the storage unit while listening to Darmiya. Together, they pulled on double sets of EM-kits.

"We need protective gear." Darmiya pulled open a crate and removed three white parcels. "Here. Not sure if we'll have to use them, but it never hurts to be prepared." She tucked hers into the side pocket of one of her EM-kits.

"Come on. I have a hovercar ready." Vantressa pointed at the sleek vehicle already hovering by the side of the road.

They threw themselves into the car, Vantressa taking the driver's seat. Pulling at the levers, she skillfully rose to maximum travel height and turned it toward cube eleven. Acrid smoke filled the air and Darmiya coughed.

"We need masks," Pamas said, clearing her throat.

"Open the protective-gear package. You have one for just your face, and the other is part of the suit." Darmiya opened hers and pulled on a thin, transparent mask. It soothed her stinging throat immediately, and she could take credit for some of that, having invented the balm-like agent infused into the filter.

"Thank the Creator," Pamas said after drawing in some cleansed air. "That helped." She turned to Vantressa. "What can we expect, Commander?"

"Doctor Do Voy knows more regarding that than I do." Vantressa tore at the levers, pushing the hovercar to its limit.

Darmiya nodded. "Injured staff, patients, and visitors. Worried people wanting to enter to save their loved ones, demanding information, and then of course the residents that still live in the cube, which is mostly hospital staff."

"And we shouldn't disregard the fact that the perpetrators might still be present, ready to deploy more explosives." Pressing the pedals, Vantressa made the car bank and turn to land on the side of the cube where the wind blew the potentially poisonous or corrosive smoke away from them. Stepping out, she rushed to the storage area in the back and pulled out a small crate. She opened it by pressing her thumbs against the locking mechanism, then removed a sidearm and a harness with a holster. "Here, Lieutenant. I can't have you go in there unarmed. Do you have any proof of your identity yet?"

"No, sir. Not yet." Pamas looked serious. "I'll have to take my chances that none of my colleagues shoot me on sight."

Vantressa sighed. "Just stay close to me or Doctor Do Voy."

They moved out, Pamas walking close to Darmiya. "Are you armed?"

Darmiya nodded grimly and patted her hip. "Admiral Caydoc sent out a general order that even we civilians should wear at least a sidearm set on light stun once the *Pathfinder* cubes had landed. It's small, but it does the job if required."

They approached with caution, trying not to get in the way of the rescue personnel.

"Commander! Over here!" a voice called out from the left side of the main entrance. "You can pass through here without risking anything falling from the ceiling." Darmiya recognized Commander KahSandra, the officer that had escorted the people without high-enough clearance the other evening. Dusty and with a torn jacket, she wore a mask and was directing men and women carrying stretchers into the cube rather than out.

"Aren't we evacuating?" Pamas asked.

"The hospital is intact and fully operational as far as we can tell this shortly after the explosion. Besides, we have nowhere to evacuate to. The other *Pathfinder* hospitals are on cubes too far from here without a jumper system available. They're setting up triage in the square outside the main emergency entrance."

"Good job, Commander. You seem to have this task well in hand. Page me if you run into any technological issues. Where was the center of the explosion?"

"Over there. By the entrance leading to the gate. They were working on taking down the gate, as everyone in this cube has been scanned and approved. I was here on a private errand. First we heard the explosion coming from the commercial area, and while we were getting ready to accept casualties, another explosion hit here. Smaller, I hear, but with more people present."

"I'm going to make sure my staff is on top of it all, and then I have to locate the Lindemay sisters."

"Damn, sir. I wasn't aware they had their clinic open today. That's on the second deck, though. They ought to be fine if they were up there."

Vantressa nodded curtly. "That's what I'm hoping for."

As they got inside, the scope of the explosion became clear to Darmiya. She stared in horror at the wounded people lying scattered as if tossed around the area by a giant's hand. It took her only a few moments to see the same pattern as back at the military headquarters. Organized chaos where medical professionals did what they were trained to do—saving lives.

Vantressa located some of her staff and rattled off questions and orders. In the meantime, Pamas helped place the wounded on stretchers. Darmiya found a water fountain that was still operational and began filling containers. Handing them out to the wounded still waiting to be seen, she also gave them soft towels from a nearby restroom to wipe away the dust that covered their skin.

Vantressa came over "All right. I'm ready to try for deck two. You two sure didn't need telling what to do. Good job. Follow me. Seclan, you take up the rear, all right?"

Darmiya wanted to say she didn't need protection, but this was not unusual among her friends and acquaintances. They saw her as cute and helpless, since her persona was bouncy and extroverted. That, together with her looks, made people assume she was frail and vulnerable. This wasn't the time to argue, but she promised herself that at least Pamas needed to know that Darmiya was completely able to fend for herself.

The stairwell wasn't as dusty, but some of the steps had bent when the bulkhead shifted during the blast. They hurried up the stairs, clinging to the outer railing, and after climbing along a gaping hole where three steps were missing, they reached the door to deck two. The automatic-opening feature wasn't functioning. Vantressa opened a hatch next to the door and took out a square item that Darmiya recognized from *Espies Major*. It was a suction device that allowed the user to push or pull a sliding door open in instances such as this.

Vantressa yanked at the suction handle, but the door didn't budge. She pressed a button that extended the handle and nodded to Pamas. "Give me a hand, Lieutenant."

Being the taller of the two of them, Pamas grabbed ahold of the top part of the handle and braced herself with her foot against the doorframe. Slowly, and with an ear-splitting, squeaky noise, the door began to shift. When the opening was ten centimeters, Darmiya placed her foot against it, and with her back against the wall, she pushed with all her strength. The door finally gave in completely and hit the opposite doorframe with a thud. Darmiya lost her balance and ended up on the floor.

"Darmiya! Are you all right?" Pamas let go of the handle and knelt next to Darmiya, who felt incredibly silly for having bruised her buttocks. It hurt like hell, but no way was she going to admit that in front of the other two.

"I'm...um...I'm fine." Darmiya accepted Pamas's hand and found herself hauled off the floor and into the other woman's steady grip. "Only my pride got bruised." And her ass. Darmiya wanted to scream when she took a step forward and felt her tailbone object.

"You certain? You are quite pale, Doctor," Vantressa asked, sounding concerned.

"Oh, for heaven's sake. First, call me Darmiya. Secondly, let's focus on what's important here. Terrorists. Explosions. And your partner." *And leave my ass alone.*

"All right, Darmiya. I'm Adina. This way." Adina moved lithely through the corridor that seemed untouched by the explosion. She kept scanning the area and often checked the bulkhead with her hands. "Keep your masks on. I'm not sure, but something's not quite right with my readings."

"Well, there was an explosion, after all," Darmiya muttered, barely refraining from rubbing her sore behind.

"Apart from that. Yes, some dust particles, but it's more what I don't see that worries me. Let's keep moving. The Lindemay Clinic is over here. They just expanded into two more sections." Adina sounded calm, but the throbbing vein at her temple spoke of frayed nerves. "Here we are."

"Is this door jammed, too?" Pamas waved, clearly trying to make the sensor wake up and open the door, but to no avail.

"Looks like it, unless it's locked, but then the sign with information of their opening hours would light up here." Adina pointed at a screen to the left of the door. She then banged on the door. "Briar? Caya? You in there?"

A muted cry had them all on edge. Adina pulled her sidearm, and so did Pamas and Darmiya.

"Briar?" Adina slapped her communicator, but it merely gave a raspy, staticky noise. She opened a similar hatch as before and pulled out yet another suction device. "Briar, can you hear me?"

"Adina?" a muted voice called out from the other side. "We can't get the door open, and Caya is injured."

"Damn," Adina whispered. "Have you tried the suction opener?"

"Yes, but I'm not strong enough," Briar said from the other side. "...pressure...bleeding badly..."

"Oh, this isn't good." Darmiya tried her communicator but had the same discouraging result as Adina.

Pamas and Adina pushed at the suction handle, but this door didn't even move a millimeter. Darmiya could see how stressed Adina was. Pale, with beads of sweat forming on her forehead and upper lip, she tore so hard at the handle, Darmiya feared she might dislocate a joint—or several.

Darmiya began to feel dizzy. She stumbled and pressed her palms against the wall. Nausea made her stomach roll, and she closed her eyes to try to keep the world from spinning. "Hey. What's going on?" Scared now at how her words slurred, she slid down onto the floor. The contact hurt her already sore buttocks, but now a pounding headache had started just inside her temples, and it drowned out every other sensation. "P-Pamasch...? Pam...P..." Darmiya tried to alert Pamas, but her tongue wouldn't obey. Gentle hands lowered her onto the floor, or maybe she fell? It really didn't matter, as everything was fading away.

CHAPTER EIGHT

Pamas saw Darmiya go down and let go of the lever. Kneeling, she caught Darmiya's face between her hands. "Darmiya?" Pamas leaned in closer, scanning the grayish pale face before her. "Damn. Her face mask has slipped." Pamas adjusted the mask and glanced up at Adina in horror. "What the hell did these fuckers use?"

"I have no idea. The people who might sense what's going on are locked behind the damn door." She smacked it with her palm, grimacing at the pain it caused her hand.

"Darmiya? Can you hear me? Say something."

"So nauseous. Don't want...throw up on you..."

Pamas shook her head. "Don't worry about that. Just keep breathing. We'll get help for you." She turned to Adina, who was working at the wiring behind the box holding the suction device. "I need to get help. I'll take Darmiya down to the emergency unit and try to grab some of your staff and a physician. If they hear the Red Angel is in trouble, they'll listen to me."

"All right. Hurry. I'll work on the wiring, but it looks as if something fried it to a crisp."

"Come on, Darmiya." Pamas pulled her up and lifted her with one hand behind her back and the other under her knees. Hoisting the petite woman for a better grip, Pamas hurried to the staircase they came from. The broken steps looked impossible to maneuver.

She needed to hold on to the railing with one hand and better see where she was stepping.

Shifting Darmiya in her arms, pressing her slumped body gently against the bulkhead for a moment, Pamas bent down and slipped in under Darmiya to allow for the rescue hold that would allow her to keep one hand free. Pamas secured her grasp of Darmiya's left wrist and ankle against her own upper chest and clung to the railing with her other hand. Slowly she placed one foot in front of the other, praying to the Creator that she wouldn't trip.

With each successful step, Pamas glanced over at Darmiya's face to make sure the mask was still in place and that she was breathing. "You reckless girl," Pamas muttered. "So intent on helping others and then you do this to yourself. What the hell did you inhale?"

"N-not my inten...tion..." Darmiya whispered and moved her head against Pamas's shoulder. Her locks tumbled down, reaching all the way to Pamas's elbow. "Accident."

"Of course it was an accident." Pamas was furious and had to restrain herself. Good people got caught in proverbial crossfire all the time. Why did it gut her so much when it was Darmiya? Pamas shut up her inner voice before it started listing all the ways that Darmiya had penetrated her defenses.

"Don't trip. Weird steps." Darmiya was slurring even worse now. "You...hurt enough..."

Pamas groaned. Even now, while potentially dying, Darmiya thought of Pamas's safety.

"Just hold on, Dar," Pamas murmured and commenced their descent. "Focus on breathing, and I'll get you down to the doctors. They'll take good care of you." They'd better. Pamas hadn't approached any physicians regarding her old injuries, as she didn't put much trust in people of any category. When it came to doctors, the last one she had been subjected to had been another of Nestrocalder's prisoners who was only too ready to do the changer's biddings. The physician, a middle-aged man, had kept Pamas and the other captives from dying, but hardly lived up to the sacred oath each medical professional took when they graduated.

Pamas's legs trembled now from Darmiya's weight. She had to stop and breathe through her mask several times as small black dots swam into her field of vision. Was the filter in her mask failing? She couldn't allow herself to faint in the stairwell, or they would both perish before help found them.

"You still with me, Dar?" Pamas asked, out of breath and desperate to know the woman slung over her shoulders hadn't fallen into a deep coma, or worse.

"Here."

"We have about ten steps left. Then we just have to get through the doors to find you some help." Pamas coughed. "Can you help me count?"

"Sure. One." Darmiya's tremulous voice still made Pamas smile at how willing the other woman was, despite her precarious condition.

"Excellent. Two," Pamas said.

"Three...four...five..." Darmiya counted, sounding weaker with each step. "Six...sch-scheven...-ght..." Giving a gurgling sound, Darmiya had clearly stopped breathing.

Risking everything, Pamas took the last three steps in one big leap and slapped the sensor on the wall. Here, the door opened obediently, and Pamas hurried through it while calling out.

"I need a doctor here! She's not breathing. Help us!" She sank to her knees among the rubble but didn't allow Darmiya to slide all the way down to the floor. Whatever was in the air could be on all the sharp bits and pieces of bulkhead and other items. If something potentially contaminated pierced Darmiya's skin, who knew what that could do to her.

Two women rushed toward them. "Here. Let us take her."

"This is Doctor Darmiya Do Voy, one of the advance-team members from Gemosis." Pamas slumped back and would have sat down on the deck, but the other woman caught her. "Madam. That's not safe. Until we know, please stay off the ground. In fact, go outside and get some fresh air and then exchange your facemask. Its sensor is showing you don't have much of the filtering agent left."

So, she had guessed right. "I'll do that, but first, the Lindemay sisters are trapped on deck two, and one of them is injured. The door won't open. Commander Vantressa is up there attempting to get to them, but she and I donned our masks at the same time..."

"Both the sisters?" The woman pulling Darmiya over on a hover gurney paled as she placed an automatic respiration unit over Darmiya's face, before reaching for her communicator. "Damn. I keep forgetting the coms don't work. Madam—"

"Lieutenant Seclan, please." To skip unnecessary explaining, Pamas merely gave her rank.

"Lieutenant? What a relief. You need to grab the highest-ranking officer you can find outside and have them let the president know. Then you have to organize a rescue team."

As if her old training hit her all at once, Pamas nodded briskly and got onto her feet, pushing away from the counter she had leaned on carefully. "Will do. Where are you taking Doctor Do Voy?" Pamas wanted to be sure she could find Darmiya later.

"IDB4. We're moving as many patients on the lower decks that we find to the intensive department. The engineering team found ways to open bulkhead plating there and set up fans."

"All right." Stroking Darmiya's pale hand once, she leaned down, her lips so close to Darmiya's ear, they were nearly touching. "You keep fighting. I know you can." Pamas straightened and strode out of cube eleven's entrance, tearing the mask from her face as soon as she spotted others without them. Inhaling deeply a few times, she was relieved to feel the burning sensation in her throat diminish immediately.

Pamas took in the situation around her. As before, a multitude of people milled around her, each on a mission to do their job. A makeshift command center had been erected about seventy meters from the cube. Around it, large natural boulders protected the people inside. Pamas strode across the uneven ground toward the center but was met with raised weapons held by two burly soldiers at the entrance.

"My name is Lieutenant Seclan. I'm in civilian clothes. I need to brief Admiral Caydoc or whoever is the highest-ranking officer present."

"Seclan?" The soldier frowned. "You're not the CAG." He shook his head. "I can't let you through without ID, sir."

"I realize that. Scan me, Ensign, and be quick about it. You don't want to be the one that held me up if I don't find any of the brass to deliver my report." How odd. Her command voice, so second nature to her twenty years ago, came back to her effortlessly, and it clearly made an impression on the ensign.

"All right, sir. Place your palm here. You will feel a sting as this reads DNA as well as palmprints. Saves time."

Pamas pressed her palm against the cold surface of the box the ensign produced. Tiny pins pricked her skin, making her wince. "Sting" wasn't the word she'd choose. It felt more like it eviscerated her hand. The ensign read the result, which seemed instant, straightened, and saluted. "Lieutenant. I apologize from holding you back." The other ensign repeated the salute but didn't open his mouth.

"No problem. You're just doing your job, Ensign...Dallope," Pamas said after glancing at his nametag. She entered the command center, and at first she didn't attract any attention. She scanned the tent-covered area and quickly determined that the circular desk in the center was the hub around which everything revolved. It was covered with technology, and five ensigns worked the console and spoke into their communicators simultaneously. Behind the round desk were two rows of rectangular desks where digital maps and screens fought for space. Pamas stepped up to yet another ensign, this one female and even more intimidating than the guys at the gate.

"What can I do for you, madam?" the ensign asked shortly. "And no civilians are allowed—"

"I'll take it from here, Ensign," a voice said from behind. Pamas turned quickly, her hand on the hidden sidearm for a moment until she recognized Admiral Korrian Heigel.

"Sir!" Hand to chin, Pamas stood at attention next to the ensign, who did the same.

"At ease, both of you. No time for that." Admiral Heigel shook her head. "Report, Lieutenant." She motioned for Pamas to talk.

"As you know, we're looking at some poisonous agent, sir. The Lindemay sisters are trapped in the midst of it on deck two. Commander Vantressa is up there trying to break through the door to get to them. Doctor Do Voy's protective mask was compromised, and she's in critical condition—"

"What? Darmiya is caught up in this?" another female voice broke in. "How the hell did she end up near cube eleven?"

Pamas turned slowly, certain she would fall dead to the ground any second, as she couldn't feel her heart beat. Instead she heard nothing, only complete silence around her as she turned to look at the woman who had just spoken.

In front of her, dressed in the Oconodian fleet uniform, all gray and with gold and multicolor insignias and ribbons, stood a dark-skinned woman with curly, short hair and dark, golden-brown eyes. Pamas would have recognized her anywhere. With her hands clasped behind her back, she forced herself to sound calm and collected as she began to brief her daughter.

CHAPTER NINE

S he was going to faint after she delivered her report. Pamas stood rigid before Aniwyn, her daughter who now outranked her. She wanted to commit every single one of Aniwyn's features to memory and keep them in her mind like a computer file. Aniwyn had changed from a scrawny, all-elbows kind of girl to a tall, wiry woman with striking features. Pamas couldn't get enough of looking at her.

"I need to go to Darmiya once I've met up with my wife." Aniwyn slapped her left palm with the gloves in her right hand. "I should never have accepted going on an extended mission on the other side of the fucking planet when *Pathfinder* was in orbit." She was talking to Korrian. "And since when do we allow civilians into our emergency command centers?" She nodded toward Seclan. "Even if, in this case, this woman seems to have helped rescue Darmiya."

"This woman is a newly reinstated lieutenant in the fleet, Commander," Korrian said lightly. "She hasn't had the chance to procure any uniforms, as the attack came out of nowhere, as attacks tend to do."

"Ah. I see." She didn't go any further into the matter but tapped her communicator. "Spinner to Admiral Caydoc." Only a faint static noise came through. "Damn, are we still not able to transmit via communicators?"

"It's among our highest priorities, Commander." Admiral Heigel spoke solemnly. "Taking care of our wounded and finding out what was in the explosions, and who is responsible, are equally important."

"I hear you, Admiral. It's just—until *Pathfinder* landed its cubes, we haven't had to deal with any of this. Now everything seems to be happening at once." Aniwyn sighed. "I'm not going to be of much use here, though. I'll grab some protective gear and go find out about Darmiya. Afterward I'll pop over to headquarters and see if they have new orders for me. And before you point out I should do it in the opposite order, Admiral, I'm well aware of that. I just choose to ignore it."

"I wasn't going to say anything since you're not under my command, but Caydoc's." Admiral Heigel shook her head. "She won't appreciate being kept waiting."

"If I could let her know, I would." Aniwyn frowned. "I just have to find out about Darmiya." She rubbed her neck, looking torn.

"Excuse me, sir," Pamas heard herself say. "Why not send a messenger? I think that's what we need to do anyway, since the commlinks are still randomly affected."

"Now, why didn't we think of that?" Admiral Heigel shook her head. "Good thinking, Lieutenant. I can tell we need some logical and low-tech thinking around here."

"Yeah, why didn't we think of that?" Aniwyn seconded and smiled wryly toward Pamas, who had to fight back tears. She had lived for the memory of such visions as her children smiling. "You are the one who knows where Darmiya is, right?" Aniwyn asked.

"Yes. In the IDB4—"

"No. I want you to take me to her." Aniwyn turned to the ensign at the main desk. "Send someone to Admiral Dael Caydoc at headquarters. Tell her Commander Seclan is all right and that I need to ascertain the situation in the hospital in cube eleven. I will contact her as soon as it is doable over the commlink or in person."

"Aye, sir." The young woman saluted and then waved a young man over.

"Let's go, Lieutenant." Aniwyn motioned for Pamas to join her. She walked through the multitude of rescue workers and law-enforcement officers, lithely weaving back and forth to avoid colliding with any of them. Pamas, who still struggled with the surreal sensation of feeling shell-shocked, moved in Aniwyn's path just behind her.

As they reached the makeshift gate set up at the safety perimeter, Pamas stopped. "Commander Seclan? You can't walk inside without protective gear, remember? I realize you want to find Darmiya, but if you go in without at least a mask on, you won't last very long."

"Damn, I forgot. I'm honestly running a bit low on sleep. Thanks, Lieutenant. Good call."

"No problem, sir. Here you go." Pamas handed Aniwyn a mask and then donned one as well. "The first symptoms are headache and feeling disoriented and slurring words."

"Got it. I'll keep an eye on you, and you do the same for me."

"Aye, sir." Oh, yes, she would. Pamas would not let anything happen to her daughter now that she had found her. So far, Aniwyn hadn't asked her name, and she hoped she wouldn't do that—not just yet. If she did ask, Pamas wouldn't lie to her, but for now she didn't want to add to Aniwyn's problems. Already aware that Aniwyn and Darmiya were best friends, Pamas understood how worried her daughter must be.

"You go first, as you're the one who knows the cube system." Aniwyn signaled for Pamas to walk through the open doors ahead of her. Before they entered, Aniwyn looked up at the exterior of cube eleven. "I see they've begun airing out the entire ship the old-fashioned way."

Glancing up, Pamas nodded. "Yes. The attack screwed up the ventilation system. They needed to break open the hull where Admiral Heigel and her engineers used special plating meant to be removed and replaced with windows once the cube had landed."

"Very clever."

As they stepped inside, Pamas noticed that the hospital staff had managed to empty the foyer of patients and move them up a few decks. She stopped at an orientation screen, but its image was flickering so badly, she could barely read the text or follow the marked paths to different units. She had hoped she could send Aniwyn up to Darmiya immediately. Sooner or later, someone would call her Seclan or Pamas, which was bound to spark new questions. More important than that, she needed to go check on the Lindemay sisters and Adina.

"Lieutenant! You're all right." As if conjured up from Pamas's thoughts, Adina showed up at her side. "I was getting worried when I couldn't find you. Where's Darmiya?"

"We're just going up to see her and find out. This is Commander Seclan from the advance team." Pamas hoped she sounded like a plausible subordinate and that Adina would notice that neither she nor Aniwyn showed any evidence of having had any sort of reunion, emotional or otherwise. "Commander Seclan, this is *Pathfinder*'s chief engineer, Commander Vantressa."

Adina blinked twice, clearly trying to decipher what was being said, or not, as it were. "The very famous CAG of the *Espies Major*. I'm honored." She saluted, which in turn made Aniwyn look confused.

"Please, sir," Aniwyn said. "Call me CAG or Spinner. All this sticking to protocol when we have a situation and our friends and family are wounded gives me a headache. You too, Lieutenant."

"Thank you, sir. Eh...Spinner."

"What do we call you then, in private?" Spinner had begun walking down the corridor toward the main desk farther in.

"P-Pam. Pam is fine, sir." It was a nickname nobody had called her since she was a cadet at the fleet academy, but it would have to do for now.

"Pam it is, then."

"How are your partner and her sister?" Pamas asked Adina, thinking it couldn't be too bad when she was here accompanying them rather than staying with them.

"They're doing okay. Briar is fine. She's back at work at the hospital. Actually, she offered her services to the intensive department bay. Caya had to be admitted for observation, and now everyone is holding their breath as she sent a messenger to the president's offices about her ordeal. At least her head injury wasn't as bad as we feared. Still, the president won't take this in stride."

"Oh, I can only imagine." Spinner shook her head. "It's the biggest official secret around how much the president loves this girl."

Adina merely nodded. "That's an understatement."

Pamas made a beeline for the main desk area, where two administrators were using both their computer consoles and pen and paper. "Commanders Seclan and Vantressa to check on Doctor Darmiya Do Voy, who was admitted about an hour ago to the intensive-care department."

The man closest to her glanced up, looking quite unimpressed until he spotted the high-ranking officers behind Pamas. "Yes, of course. Certainly." He tapped a few commands into the computer, swore under his breath, and pulled out a large notebook. "Do Voy, you said? Ah, yes. She's still there. IDB4. I'm afraid you must use the stairs for now. Deck four. Nurses in that unit will know where she is."

"Thank you." Striding back to Adina and Spinner, Pamas kept her focus on finding Darmiya. If she dived too much into the fact she was standing right next to her daughter, she would lose it. This was not how she had envisioned their reunion. She never could have imagined being on an assignment of sorts with the daughter she feared she might never see again. And yet—here they were. "Deck four. And we have to use the stairs."

"I'm going to leave you to it," Adina said. "I need to round up my subordinates and have them report back to me. We have to find out what foreign agent has done this."

"Good luck, Commander," Spinner said and saluted. Pamas did the same, even if she was out of uniform still.

As they made their way up the stairwell, Pamas was relieved to see that it was not in as bad a shape as the one she had been forced to carry Darmiya in. The steps here were complete and not broken, though some of the lights were out. At deck four, the door had been removed.

"They must have had to move patients through the stairwell," Pamas murmured.

"I suppose even if some elevators are working, it's too risky. Getting stuck with someone in critical condition in an elevator is a nightmare."

The fourth deck would have looked untouched by the explosion but for the presidential guards outside one door and the lights going on and off at random.

"The presidential guard," Pamas said. "That must mean Caya Lindemay is being kept for observation on this deck as well." She stopped a nurse carrying a tray with instruments. "Excuse me. Doctor Darmiya Do Voy, please."

The nurse looked blank for a moment, but then she brightened. "Ah, yes. She's in the room next to the one being guarded over there. She's still unconscious, but Doctor Tiener managed to filter the foreign agent from her system. Now we just have to wait until she wakes up."

"And when will that be?" Spinner asked darkly. "And is she just in there by herself or…?"

"Of course not. A nurse is monitoring her at all times. Our surveillance system keeps malfunctioning, so until that is fixed, we're going to have to do it in person." The nurse didn't seem upset at all by the harshness in Spinner's voice.

"Thank you," Pamas said and walked ahead of Spinner toward Darmiya's door. The guards outside Caya Lindemay's room went rigid as they approached. When Spinner and Pamas passed and opened the door to the next one, they relaxed marginally.

Someone had managed to open the bulkhead and slide in a glass plating. The room was bright from natural daylight. In the center of the room sat a hospital bed. The woman in the bed was as white as the bed linen, which made Pamas's heart stop beating, only to change its mind and begin racing so fast it hurt.

"Darmiya," Spinner said and rounded the bed. The young nurse sitting on a stool on the other side of the bed got up and waved Pamas over. "Doctor Do Voy is resting comfortably. I even saw her stir a few times recently. If you plan to visit with her for a while, I'll go out and assist my colleagues. Just grab one of us when you need to leave. She shouldn't be alone in here when she wakes up."

Grateful to the nurse for saying "when" and not "if" Darmiya woke up, Pamas swallowed hard and nodded. "Thank you. She won't."

Spinner stroked the unruly, dusty locks from Darmiya's forehead. "Are you awake inside that brilliant mind of yours, Darmiya? Wake up and look at me. Or at Pam, your new friend. We want you back with us, all right? I'm going to have to find Calagan and bring him here, and you know, if you're not awake when he gets here, he's going to cause such a scene." Wiping at an errant tear, Spinner gave a watery smile. "He adores you. We all do."

Pamas wanted to say out loud that she too cared for this friendly, amazing young woman. Seeing Spinner next to Darmiya also emphasized the immense difference in how she felt about the two. Pamas loved her daughter with every cell in her system. She would die for her without even contemplating it very much. As for Darmiya, she had confusing feelings for her as well, but vastly different from those she harbored for her daughter. There was nothing maternal in the way she regarded Darmiya, not at all.

Spinner took the stool the nurse had used, and Pamas pulled up a visitor's chair. Sitting on either side of the bed, watching the sun grow larger as it sank toward the horizon and its color turned to golden, Pamas looked back and forth between Darmiya and Spinner. After her daughter had asked her to call her Spinner when in private, she had made a real effort to do so, even in her head. Clearly the call sign meant a lot. If it was like Pamas remembered, call signs were your identity when used among your peers, even more so than your given name. "Spinner" suited the mercurial woman.

Pamas realized that when Darmiya woke up, she would have to tell Spinner who she was. She wasn't at all surprised that her daughter didn't recognize her. Scarred, and with an eyepatch, and more or less being back from the dead…it all worked against her. Why would Spinner even look for her mother in a stranger?

Squeezing Darmiya's hand lightly, she thought perhaps she should do it right away, before the woman between them came to. Her stomach twisted as if squeezed by icy hands. Spinner might react in several different ways. Clearly, she could choose not to believe Pamas. She could also be thrilled and happy that her mother wasn't dead. The next, and most likely reaction, was that Spinner would be furious, feel betrayed still, and do her best to turn Pherry against Pamas. And yes, Spinner might be completely indifferent because she had moved on.

"I'm going stir-crazy in here, but I can't leave her. I have no specific assignment now that I'm home from a long mission. Darmiya has been there for me so many times, and her brother as well, that I can't even contemplate letting her fend for herself. You just don't abandon people!"

Pamas trembled now. She was never going to get through to this amazing woman that was her daughter. Her beautiful, headstrong, brave child that had grown up to hold such a high position when it came to rescuing their people.

A loud bang from the corridor made Spinner and Pamas jump. A few more bangs were followed by a female voice yelling something intelligible. Spinner tiptoed to the door and opened it a centimeter.

"Damn. Isn't that the president's former husband?"

Pamas hurried over to the door and glanced through the narrow crack. "Sure is. What's he doing here? Is he trying to see Caya Lindemay?"

"I'm not sure. I read the president's brief after the divorce. He was horrible to her." Spinner's eyes were almost black. "Abusive husbands…I hate them with a passion."

She would, Pamas thought. The only reason she wasn't haunted by her own husband's abuse was that she had lived through several layers of hell after she was taken.

"I need to find out what's going on. Those guards are on duty looking after the woman who holds Tylio's heart. Her former husband will get himself killed if he doesn't back off. You stay with Darmiya."

"No. You need me to go with you. If he's as unstable as the rumor mill has it, he might see your uniform and think you're with her. You know. Just another minion. I look like a civilian. Harmless."

"Hmm. Not as harmless as you might think, but all right. Let's push her bed out of sight from the door." Spinner hurried over to Darmiya, and together they pushed the bed to the far-right wall. Drawing their sidearms, Spinner once again looked out through the door. "He's still there, arguing with one of the guards. For the love of the Creator. Both presidential guards have their hands on their weapons."

Pamas knew it was her turn. She nudged Spinner aside and ducked out through the door after tucking her weapon into the back of her trousers. Walking toward the guards, she scowled and hoped her expression didn't look too exaggerated.

"What the hell's going on? My friend's unconscious in there, and you guys are carrying on like the Creator needs waking up. Can you at least show some consideration?"

Hadler Tylio, former presidential spouse, turned to look at the no-doubt unwelcome interruption. "Who the hell are you?" he said, a faint slur giving away his inebriation. "I'm going in to obtain evidence against the woman in this room. She's the one responsible for this explosion, like she's been from day one, even if my wife has refused to...to see it."

"I don't care if it's the Creator in there. As long as you take the sound down a peg or two. My friend is very sick—"

"Put the blame where it belongs. On her!" Stabbing a shaking index finger toward the door, Hadler Tylio drew his narrow lips into an ugly sneer. "In the eyes of the true Oconodians, I will always be the presidential spouse."

"I have no idea what true Oconodians you're talking about, but these two guards are not buying that. They serve the president and take their orders from her alone. If they're guarding someone on her behalf, they're authorized to drop you—sir." Pamas stepped into Hadler Tylio's comfort zone. "And since the woman in there apparently means a lot to the president, I wouldn't bet that their weapons are set on mild stun." Pamas shrugged.

"You insolent—"

"Step away, Hadler," a stern alto voice said quietly. "What are you doing here?"

Hadler Tylio pivoted, turning toward the blond woman behind him. "Ah. Gassinthea."

Pamas snapped to attention. The president's charisma was palpable. Right this instant, she was more intimidating than charismatic. "I don't care to repeat myself. Why, Hadler?"

"You know why. We've arrived. Terrorists are at large, and your barely housebroken changer is at the center of things, as usual."

Pamas gasped inwardly but remained where she was, ready to drop the former spouse if need be.

"You sound as delusional as always," the president said. "Step aside." Walking straight toward Hadler, President Tylio was clearly not going to veer off. As she was right in front of Hadler, he raised his hand, and that's when Pamas responded. Acting fast without second-guessing herself had kept her alive. This time, her method meant the former presidential spouse ended up on his back on the deck with a resounding thud.

"Thank you." The president stepped over the man and continued into the room where Caya was located without even looking at him.

"Damn. You act fast when you need to." Spinner came up to Pamas. She motioned to the guards by the door to help the wheezing man up. "Brush him off and send him on his way. He's not wanted anywhere near Caya Lindemay or the president. Next time, and trust me on this one, you need to apprehend him and throw him into the closest brig. Understood?"

Pamas thought the guards would object, as Spinner wasn't their commanding officer, but they merely nodded. "Yes, sir."

The door opened again, and a slightly flustered president poked her head out. "Caya wants to talk to the two of you." She pointed at Spinner and Pamas. "I have no idea why, but she's adamant about it, so…" Shrugging, she waved for them to step forward.

Pamas knew then that she was in trouble. After reading her so accurately, Caya knew far too much about her. This would not end well. She just knew it. "I should go back to Darmiya and keep her company. She's alone and—"

President Tylio waved over someone from her entourage, who had until now kept away from the drama. "Find a nurse to watch over Doctor Do Voy." Turning back to the sisters, she jerked her chin impatiently toward the room. They followed her instantly.

Caya sat propped up in bed and looked quite well, considering she had a concussion. "There you are again, Lieutenant." She held out both hands to Pamas, who had to take them, or it would seem very strange to the other two. "I have worried that reading you may have put you off, or even caused you to put the blame on someone else for letting it happen. I'm glad to see you are still in Darmiya's vicinity. She's going to need you."

"She'll be all right?" Pamas whispered.

"Yes." Looking paler now, Caya sank back into the pillows propped against the elevated top end of the bed.

"Darling, you should rest. Even my being here is too much for you." President Tylio brushed a thick tress of Caya's long hair away from her face.

"I'm okay. Largely because of the lieutenant here." Caya nodded at Pamas. "She managed to send help to Adina, who got us out of our clinic in time. Our masks were becoming depleted of their filtering agent, little by little."

"Then I'm in your debt, Lieutenant—?"

Pamas opened her mouth to speak but closed it again as panic rose into an inferno in her head. Her heart thundered, and sweat broke free on her forehead.

"Yes, what is your last name? I don't think they formally introduced us over at the emergency command center. Not that there was time." Spinner shifted her gaze to the president and Caya. "It's an honor to meet you, Madam President, Ms. Lindemay. I'm Commander Aniwyn Seclan, call sign Spinner."

"Go ahead," Caya said, smiling gently at Pamas. "It'll be all right."

"What does she mean?" Spinner asked, quietly. "Wha-what the hell's going on?" Spinner looked bemusedly at Pamas.

Swallowing hard, Pamas jutted her chin out and stood even straighter. "I apologize for the confusion, Madam President, Commander Seclan. My name is Lieutenant Pamas Seclan, and I returned to active duty today after being incarcerated by malevolent changers for close to twenty years." She couldn't face Spinner, and though she strained her hearing, she couldn't detect even a minute gasp from Spinner's direction.

"Seclan? Any relation?" President Tylio stepped closer, frowning now.

"Yes." Pamas knew this was one time when she couldn't prioritize the president. Instead she looked at Spinner, pleading with the expression in her one good eye. "Spinner doesn't know it, but I'm...I'm..."

Spinner's throat worked spasmodically. She opened and closed her mouth several times before she made any sounds. Then her dark eyes hardened. "It appears that Pam, Lieutenant Seclan, claims to be my mother." She turned around and headed for the door. "Excuse me. Darmiya needs me."

Pamas wanted to go with Spinner and be there for Darmiya, but she sensed she wasn't welcome. Knowing everything she'd read about Spinner by heart, she feared she would never be.

CHAPTER TEN

Darmiya opened her eyes. Not slowly or with hesitation, but with the impatience that was part of her personality. At first, the room seemed empty around her. Medical equipment and technology suggested she was in the hospital. On cube eleven? They didn't have any sick bays like these at the local medical center on Gemocon. Only when *Pathfinder* would land—no, wait. Had landed. Every single one of the twenty cubes had landed successfully at their given coordinates, including cube eleven, which contained the university hospital—and the best medical personnel that the two former homeworlds could offer.

"Hello?" Darmiya's throat hurt, but she could still speak. What a relief. Sometimes when nightmares plagued Darmiya's sleep, she would dream that her voice was stolen from her. As she liked to talk and debate, that would be a horrible thing.

"I'm here, sweetie." A familiar face, Spinner's, hovered above her, smiling. "So good to see those violet eyes of yours. How are you feeling?"

"Sore. Tired. What happened?" Darmiya tried to remember, but everything after leaving the Emergency Command Center was a blur. "The explosion? We went to investigate?" she asked, extrapolating from her fragmented memories.

"You did."

"I went with…where is…?" Though she stopped herself in time, Darmiya could tell, despite her aching head, that Spinner knew. "Where is Pamas?"

"So, you're on a first-name basis with the woman posing as Pamas Seclan?" Continuing to speak softly, probably telling herself that Darmiya was still rather sick, Spinner shoved a hand through her wild curls.

"Not claiming to be, Spinner," Darmiya said and coughed. "Her identity has been verified, and she's regained her commission on Dael's orders."

"Dael's orders? Dael knows?" Looking furious, Spinner clenched her hands. "Why the hell am I the last to find out?"

"Because you were on assignment, you fool," Darmiya said weakly, trembling now. She loved Spinner, she truly did, and she knew how shocking this must be for her, but she wasn't in very good shape to deal with this fury before her. "How did you find out about her?" Darmiya found it hard to believe that Pamas had just blurted it out the first time she met her daughter after so many years.

"It came up when we ran into the president. The woman next door, one of the changers, Caya Lindemay." Spinner stroked Darmiya's hair, suddenly looking remorseful. "She seemed to know that woman from some vision. It was rather confusing."

"Ah. That explains things. Sort of. I have vague memories of trying to help Adina get Caya and Briar—Briar is Adina's partner—out of a room where the lock…something was wrong with the lock. Then everything hurt and I must've passed out. Wait. I think Pamas carried me down the stairs. She saved my life." Rubbing her temples with both hands, Darmiya coughed again.

"Let me page the nurse," Spinner said, reaching for the alarm buzzer.

"No. No. I'm all right. Just a bit of a scratchy throat."

"I can tell you're a fighter, but the staff should be made aware you're conscious, Doctor Do Voy," an unknown voice said from the door. Darmiya shifted to look past Spinner and saw the president standing there with a young woman in a hoverchair. There was no sign of Pamas.

"Madam President," Darmiya blurted and felt she should stand, or at least sit up straight, but instead coughed again. How undignified.

"May we come in? Caya here was getting quite worked up. She insists on seeing you."

"Of course, Madam President." Darmiya waved for them to enter. "How are you, Caya?"

"Concussed, but all right. And you? I know you inhaled some of the foreign agent when you tried to help my sister and me. I'm so sorry you were injured." Caya reached for Darmiya's hand. When Darmiya hesitated for a moment, she smiled. "I won't read you unless you explicitly tell me it's all right. I give you my word."

"Very well. I really don't mind you reading me, as you put it, but I do have top security clearance, and I'm not aware if you do." Shrugging helplessly, Darmiya glanced over to the president, who stood behind Caya looking concerned.

"The reading would be mostly for your benefit, Commander Seclan," Caya said. "I could link you with me, and you could see that Darmiya is telling the truth."

"I already realize that Darmiya is telling the truth, Caya." Spinner's lips were narrow and white. "I've known her for a long time now, and she's my best friend. She wouldn't lie to me. That said, I have no idea what the woman posing as my dead mother... what her agenda is. I will, however, figure it out."

"I can help with that, if you allow," Caya said.

"I've heard of your remarkable gifts, but there's no need for you to jeopardize your health, Ms. Lindemay. I organized a memorial service for my mother more than ten years ago. I had to do it on my own since my father couldn't be bothered. I stood there next to my brother Pherry and said good-bye to an empty burial vessel. I chose the program, the music, everything. I knew how my mother would have wanted it to be, so that's what I did. Because I knew my mother, damn it! Don't you think I would recognize her if she were truly here? That imposter is trying to take my mother's place—" Spinner's voice faltered and she clung to Darmiya's hand. "I have no clue what her true agenda is. For all I know, she could be a malevolent changer, someone from a terrorist cell. And where is she now, by the way?"

The president looked uncomfortable. "Lieutenant Seclan decided to return to the Emergency Command Center to report. I think she felt her presence was complicating things right now."

Darmiya's heart ached for Spinner and Pamas. They had lost so much. If she could only reach Spinner and make her see that though twenty some years had gone by, at least she and her mother would have the rest of their lives together. Lowering her voice, she tried not to cough. "Spinner, sweetie. We know you had to have the burial ceremony because everyone assumed she was dead. But if you listen to Pamas's story and examine the DNA and compare it to yours, you'll find we're telling you the truth. You know me so well. You just said so yourself. We're best friends, and I would never tell you something like this if I wasn't sure. I would never, ever be that cruel."

Spinner breathed heavily, on the verge of hyperventilating where she stood clinging to Darmiya's hand. "I...I just can't..."

"If I may add my voice to this matter, Spinner—if I may call you that—I can assure you that Caya's gifts are absolute. She's a true oracle and her sister is an empath. Neither of them is fooled when they enter someone else's mind. I trust them implicitly, and surely you wouldn't consider your president to be easily fooled?" President Tylio looked with sympathy at Spinner, and Darmiya nearly had an out-of-body experience seeing the Gemoconian president go out of her way to reassure Spinner.

"My mother is dead." Spinner whispered the words over and over as tears clung to her long lashes. Losing their grip on the long strands, they ran down her cheeks. "At first, we thought she abandoned us, Pherry and I. Once she was declared dead, it was easier in a sense. As hard as it is to lose a parent, knowing she didn't abandon us was marginally better."

"May I read you, Spinner? Not super deeply or invasively, but just regarding this?" Caya eyed Spinner carefully. Darmiya nodded encouragingly at her friend. Spinner could be so stubborn and found it nearly impossible to ask for help.

"All right. If I say stop, you stop."

"Of course." Gently placing her hand on Spinner's, Caya tilted her head as she closed her eyes. She had to place the other hand on Darmiya's shoulder, most likely not to lose her balance as she reached for Spinner.

"Oh. I can't say how sorry I am, Spinner. He was a deeply troubled man, your father. Trying to balance caring for your brother and keeping him out of harm's way is too much for such a young girl."

"Creator..." Spinner pressed her lips together.

"And you missed your mother terribly for years. You waited for her to come back, take you and your brother away from the man who resented you for being so much like her. Every birthday, every Creator's Day, you thought this was the day she would return. When she didn't, and when she was pronounced dead, you thought you'd lost a precious part of yourself." Caya slumped against the left armrest for a moment. "Oh, dear Creator."

"What's wrong, darling?" Thea cupped Caya's shoulders.

"I'm receiving mixed emotions, mixed signals, Thea. This is so bad, so incredibly horrible." Looking up, Caya's transparent turquoise eyes filled with tears. "I was watching a scene where Darmiya interacted with Pamas Seclan, and I must have let more of Darmiya into the reading. I suddenly saw what was in her lungs earlier. In her entire system." Caya tried to get on her feet. "We need to contact the military and the cabinet."

"What's going on?" Darmiya sat up straight. "What's in my system?" She trembled and felt Spinner hold on to her to keep from falling out of the hospital bed.

Caya shook her head. "You're not in danger anymore, Darmiya. What was in your body is no longer causing you problems, and you will recover."

"Stop stalling," Darmiya said, her voice stern now. "If it's a matter of security clearance, both Skinner and I are privy to the highest level. You can confirm this with Admiral Caydoc." Furious now, Darmiya was ready to fight them, no matter that one of her visitors was the president herself.

"Caya. I'll have my assistants call an emergency meeting at the headquarters, but then I think Darmiya and Spinner need to know what you saw." President Tylio spoke quietly, but Darmiya saw how Caya slowly relaxed. Perhaps being inundated with all the impressions and personal secrets was as strenuous as it looked for the young oracle.

"All right," Caya whispered. She waited until the president returned to Darmiya's room. "When I inadvertently reached within Darmiya, I was pulled in toward her core. I've never experienced anything like that, I swear. Then I saw everything as if in an electron microscope. Every little particle. And there it was, what Adina showed me and Briar when we were afraid the terrorists might have gotten their hands on worse things than white garnet." Caya turned her pale face up toward the president. "I know now what they used to dirty the explosion." She swallowed hard. "The outer shell of black-garnet molecules."

Darmiya gasped, snapping her head around to face Spinner, who had gone as pale as Caya. "Black garnet. That's the worst news possible, Spinner."

"Even I know that. We need to tell Dael." Spinner cleared her throat. "And the woman who claims to be my mother, Pam, I heard her coughing quite a bit. Can she be worse off than we think?" The dread in her voice was obvious.

"I don't think so. I inhaled more than she did, much more, as my mask slipped almost off. If I'm all right, she is too." Darmiya swung her legs over the edge of the bed but had to hold on hard to Spinner. "Oh, damn, I'm really very dizzy. How annoying. I'll need one of those hoverchairs, Spinner."

"You need to remain—"

Oh, no. None of that. "If you're going to tell me to stay in bed, I'm going to scream. This is partly my area of expertise. I need to help devise a method to scan for black garnet in a safe way. In the meantime, I think it would be highly useful to those worse off than me in this unit if Caya could find the energy to read their systems. Perhaps it might help the physicians treat them." Darmiya might not be an empath or an oracle, but she could clearly see that Caya would go beyond the call of duty to help people.

"Will that be safe for her?" the president asked, looking up from a large tablet.

"I don't see why not. Whatever residual black-garnet shells are inside these unfortunate patients aren't airborne. And as long as she uses a mask when in rooms without windows, such as this one that has been aired out, the risk is virtually zero." Darmiya pressed the sensor on her bedframe. "Now. I need to get dressed, and I'd rather have one of the nurses assist me. Once I'm ready to go, Spinner or one of the presidential guards can escort me to headquarters."

"I'm taking you." Spinner sounded grave, and her dark eyes were opaque in a way that Darmiya recognized.

"You may have more important things to do. That's all I mean." Darmiya tilted her head. "Such as catching up with your mother before she thinks you hate her." Realizing her words were harsh, she forced herself not to cringe. This was sometimes the only way to get through to the headstrong woman before her. Sort like ripping off a bandage in one determined yank.

"I can't believe you said that." Spinner swallowed. "I could never hate—"

"Darmiya!" A young man, barely recognizable as Darmiya's brother Calagan, fought his way halfway through the door. "Let go of me!"

"The president of Gemocon is present in this room, and thus, only people with the proper credentials are allowed entry." The presidential guards struggled to hold the wiry young man back.

"It's only my brother." Darmiya clasped her forehead. "Hold on, Cal. I'm just going to change clothes. If you'll just calm down for a damned minute, Spinner will tell you what's going on."

"Come on, Cal. She's all right now and will come with us to headquarters." Spinner placed her arm around Calagan's shoulders. "Don't make such a fuss that the guards throw you in the brig. We need all hands on deck as it is, especially people with brains like yours and Darmiya's."

"I was on a mission in the southern hemisphere when we heard about the explosions. I think I broke a record getting the shuttle back here." Calagan's voice was trembling, and Darmiya knew that had he lost her, his only living family member, he would have been devastated.

"We'll leave you to get sorted. I'm taking Caya to the guards to make sure she's protected when scanning some of the other patients." President Tylio walked closer to Darmiya, extending a hand. "Since I believe we're going to work very closely with you, and with that young man out there, I think you should call me Thea when we're not in public."

Gaping now, Darmiya was certain she looked like an idiot. "Um. Really? I mean, oh, dear. Thank you, Madam Pres—I mean, um, Thea."

"She had the same effect on me when I first met her, if that's any consolation," Caya said, smiling broadly. "I was such a fan, I think I forgot my own name in the process."

"Well, yes. I can understand that." And Darmiya truly could. Thea was beyond charismatic. Her persona seemed to wrap around you and fill the entire room at the same time. Caya was a formidable woman in her own right, just as strong and with an exceptional aura around her. Darmiya wasn't sure how she knew, but she was certain that together, these two women could do anything.

Perhaps she focused on Caya and Thea to avoid thinking about Pamas.

The nurse helped Darmiya change into her recycled clothes, now clean and fresh again, and onto the hoverchair. She had never used one and took a few moments to familiarize herself with the controls. Thanking the nurse, she took a deep breath and maneuvered the chair out the door to Spinner and Calagan.

"You ready, sis?" Calagan looked concerned. "You're awfully pale."

"I'm fine." Darmiya was getting tired of the constant worrying and questions about her well-being. And it wasn't just today. For the last few months, people had commented on how unlike her usual exuberant self she was, and it was driving her crazy. "Let's get back to the ECC. The nurse gave me a copy of all my tests and those done on the other patients on this ward. Caya is doing her type of scanning, which should help. If we can pinpoint exactly where people were located when the explosions occurred, we stand a better chance of extrapolating how the black-garnet shells were dispersed."

"How can that help us?" Spinner hurried along next to the hoverchair. "And does this chair you're in manage stairs?"

"It has a step setting, so I hope so. I take it the elevators aren't reliable yet?" Darmiya grimaced, hoping she wouldn't plummet down to deck one and break every bone in her body.

"Oh, damn. Calagan and I have to hold on to it." Spinner opened the door to the stairwell, and Darmiya pushed the sensor that allowed the hoverchair to detect the steps in front of them.

"As for your first question, finding the pattern in how the black-garnet shells dispersed will help us look for remnants, even on a molecular level. People like me haven't inhaled all of it."

"And after we have collected samples, we can learn how to scan for it." Calagan spoke quietly as he walked behind the slowly descending hoverchair. "And hopefully we won't find any actual black garnet through our scans."

Darmiya shook her head. That would be the ultimate nightmare scenario. Black garnet was the most dangerous substance known to humankind. White garnet was often used in controlled blasts. Red garnet, more volatile and unstable, had caused of destruction of Gemosis, her and Calagan's home planet. Reckless miners on their moon had used it, not realizing the disastrous effects when the red garnet encountered frozen water. The entire moon had exploded in large chunks, causing earthquakes, tsunamis, and volcanic eruptions. Within less than a day, Gemosis was uninhabitable, and only 100,000 Gemosians were left from the millions on the planet.

As if red garnet wasn't bad enough, black garnet was the ultimate weapon of mass destruction. Or would be if someone could figure out a way to safely harness it. Theoretically, you could handle black garnet safely in an anaerobic environment, but one single oxygen molecule could cause a chain reaction. And the substance was even more dangerous because it wasn't visible to the naked eye. It didn't reflect light, not even against a white background. If Caya was right, and the shells from the black-garnet tubes had been used, they might be on their way to a scientific breakthrough that any scientist would sacrifice every one of their limbs to put their name to.

Darmiya was not, and had never been, interested in fame. The fact that she and Calagan had been household names on Gemosis before the disaster had tormented her. Their brilliant minds, combined with the fact they were good-looking young people, had been like gold for the press. The university they worked for had capitalized on their fame and used them as poster children for obtaining grants.

Despite her bubbly personality, Darmiya was very private and didn't let strangers into her inner circle easily. Perhaps finding Spinner's crashed aircraft and helping Calagan rescue her had bypassed Darmiya's normal vetting process. Her mind drifted to Pamas and the fact that the same seemed to apply to Spinner's mother. Darmiya worried for Pamas, knowing how fragile she was after her many years in captivity. What if Pamas thought that Spinner would never accept her? Would she keep trying or approach Pherry and hope for the best? From what Spinner had told Darmiya, Pherry looked up to his older sister and took his cue from her. It wouldn't go well for Pamas if Spinner couldn't accept what had happened to their mother.

Finally, they reached deck one, and Darmiya could speed up the hoverchair. As they hurried across the field toward the ECC, she prayed to the Creator that nobody else would get hurt. Most of all, she feared that someone, somewhere, had black garnet at their disposal and was prepared to use it. But why were the terrorists doing this to their fellow Gemoconians? Their survival on this planet depended on their all working together. If they destroyed this world, there would be no going back, literally.

"Go back?" Her mind reeling, Darmiya lost her grip of the sensors, nearly stalling the hoverchair.

"Hey, careful!" Calagan grabbed Darmiya by the shoulder and kept her in her seat. "Slow down, will you?"

"Sorry." Her heart pounding, Darmiya began to attack her embryo of a theory from all sides, trying to determine if it was probable. The more she thought about it, the less unlikely it seemed, but she was also aware that the black-garnet shells she had inhaled could still affect her mind negatively.

Darmiya needed to sit down and discuss this idea, and she could think of the one person who had more experience with malevolent changers than anyone else on Gemocon.

Pamas.

CHAPTER ELEVEN

Pamas regarded her reflection impassively. She had expected the image of her in uniform would take her back, but instead she felt numb. She was wearing what the fleet referred to as a battle-ready uniform for on-planet use: a blue-gray coverall, not unlike a flight suit, with a tall collar where her rank insignia sat, a round cap with a foldable screen against sunlight, and black, battle-ready boots that reached halfway up her calves. A harness attached to the belt held her ammunition and sidearm, several utility packages, and an EM-kit.

She adjusted the mandatory scarf, which apart from keeping her warm could also be used to collect rainwater or, if doused with the content of a bottle marked #2 in one of her utility packs, used to set fractured limbs. If she instead poured the contents of bottle #3, she could use it to temporarily stop hemorrhaging. It was strong enough to serve as a makeshift gurney when combined with two other scarves and some branches. She was proud of her invention.

Checking her chronometer, Pamas saw it was time to join her colleagues in the ECC. The last thing she needed to add to her uniform was her nametag. She slapped it onto the flap of her right breast pocket. Looking in the mirror once more, she shuddered. The last time she had seen herself looking like this was when she left to organize the last part of her and the children's escape. She'd had to drive the hovercar to the spaceport and report to then-Captain

Caydoc. Together, they would finalize the itinerary that would take Pamas, Aniwyn, and Pherry off-world. Instead, the last thing she remembered was how two people had darted toward her hovercar from the sky, looking impossibly like they were flying. A third individual seemed engulfed in blue flames and held a spinning, blue-white flame between their hands. The next thing Pamas knew, she woke up in a damp bunker in a humid jungle.

Straightening the string that held her eyepatch in place, Pamas strode out of the restroom where she had changed clothes. She didn't look back at the clothes she had worn before. The Pamas who had lived as a barely alive captive no longer existed. The previous Pamas, the woman who had been prepared to leave everything behind to save herself and her children, was also gone. Spinner would not accept her; that much was clear. And, knowing what she did of her son, he would follow his sister's lead. If Spinner hated her mother and thought Pamas was an imposter, so would Pherry. At least in this uniform, on this planet, she could do her job. Perhaps she could be useful to someone.

The vision of Darmiya's pale face flickered through her mind, and Pamas tried to push the image away. Thinking about the young woman wouldn't help her perform her job better. She couldn't brush aside the warmth and understanding, and yes, the nonjudgmental attitude that Darmiya had showed her. Pamas yearned for the odd comfort Darmiya's presence gave her. Pamas scolded herself. How selfish she was. The Gemoconian people were under attack, and all she could think of was her own petty circumstances. People were dead or dying from whatever the explosions had dispersed. Enough of this self-indulgent moping.

She reached the hub in the middle of the ECC and found Admiral Korrian Heigel there with several of her engineers. Next to Heigel stood Admiral Caydoc, the younger one.

Pamas stood at attention and saluted. "Lieutenant Seclan reporting for duty, sir."

Dael glanced up and winced visibly. "It'll take me a while to get used to having yet another Seclan part of this mission. As you were, Lieutenant. And we need to see about your rank. Depending on what my grandmother has to say, I expect to promote you once we take care of this ordeal."

"Appreciated, sir." Pamas didn't let it show, but she was shocked. For them to accept her being back was amazing, but contemplating a promotion? That was unexpected, to say the least.

"Pamas! I hardly recognized you." Darmiya's voice made Pamas jump despite her strong hold on herself. Turning around, she saw Darmiya sitting in a hoverchair. Behind her, oh, Creator, stood Spinner, looking at Pamas as if a weapon set on heavy stun had hit her.

"Creator," whispered Spinner hoarsely. "It really is you."

Pamas blinked. "What? I mean, excuse me, sir. I didn't hear you correctly." Or she didn't think she did. She trembled and clasped her hands hard behind her back.

"It is you. Now, when I see you in uniform, with your cap and scarf...and your hair tied back like that. Exactly like she—you—wore it. It is you."

Everyone around the round desk quieted. Admiral Caydoc walked over to Spinner and placed a hand at the small of her back. "Yes, darling," she said quietly. "It is her. I have confirmed it, and though I realize how unfathomable this must seem to you, and how difficult, it is her."

"It's insane." Spinner shook her head. "And I'm having problems dealing with this revelation."

"I have a suggestion," Pamas heard herself say. She hadn't planned to tell anyone about her situation, but it was clear that they needed to address this development in some way in order to get back to work. "I know who I am. The admirals, some other high-ranking members of the military, and President Tylio know who I am. My own daughter is starting to see the truth, but nobody can expect her to be emotionally ready for this. I suggest we table my having-returned-from-the-dead thing. Once we have the situation under control, my children and I can sort out our private business." Pamas stood at attention and saluted.

Admiral Heigel nodded approvingly. "That's the best suggestion yet. That all right with you, Commander Seclan?"

"Please. Call me Spinner. It'll confuse us to tears otherwise." Spinner smiled crookedly, but the pain behind her expression was turning it into more of a grimace.

"Hear, hear," Dael said and quickly ran the back of her knuckles along Spinner's cheek. "Having had similar name issues when my grandmother was on active duty, I understand."

Darmiya placed her chair next to Pamas. "You're amazing. You know that?"

Her heart wobbled between two beats as Pamas felt Darmiya squeeze her left hand. "And you are prone to exaggeration." She made sure to smile, albeit faintly, at Darmiya to make sure she knew she had spoken facetiously.

A thick drape made of some porous material was lowered around the main desk area, shielding them from the surrounding ECC officers and their workstations. Pamas had seen these drapes many times in the past and knew they kept everything that was handled inside completely confidential.

"Normally, we would be at headquarters, discussing this development from all angles in the conference room, but we don't have time for that." Dael spoke quickly. "Thanks to Caya Lindemay, we now have more information than we could have hoped for. Apparently, the people responsible for these explosions have access to some form of black garnet. We know it is a highly volatile substance, and that's why we all hope they have merely the husks, or shells, surrounding the actual active part of the black garnet. If we're wrong and they have the actual substance, we could see the destruction of a city-to-be or the devastation of an entire continent. It could make large parts of this amazing planet uninhabitable. That would be catastrophic. We couldn't move as many people as we just did, that fast, and finding a new world yet again would seem like a horrible, undoable feat for all of us. We need to apprehend and try the culprits who did this and caused so much pain and suffering aboard *Pathfinder*."

"I keep receiving new information on my tablet from all kinds of sources." Darmiya held up her tablet for emphasis. "I'm getting it from engineers, chemists, physicians, military personnel, and the public."

"Anything you can share with us that stands out to you, Darmiya?" Dael asked and moved a transparent screen for her aide de camp to take notes if required.

"Absolutely," Darmiya said and attempted to stand, but failed utterly. Pamas caught her just before she fell off the chair.

"Do remain seated," Dael said, looking alarmed. "Calagan can read your notes if you're not up for it."

"I'll just sit and read. I'm fine." Jutting forward a stubborn chin, Darmiya tapped her tablet and scrolled through the massive amount of information. "I'm not going to repeat what I am sure you have all been briefed on. In fact, I'm working on a theory that looks really promising, and I wanted to take a minute to get your feedback on it, especially from Admiral Heigel and Commander Vantressa."

"Go ahead." Heigel nodded.

Pamas had known Darmiya must be a brilliant woman since she had top security clearance and roamed the halls of the military headquarters as if she grew up there. Still, to hear her go over her notes and then talk about her theory, Pamas knew this young woman had to be among the most gifted scientists alive.

"One problem, of many, with black garnet is that we cannot scan for it. No sensors, no matter how finely we calibrate them, can detect something that doesn't reflect light or give off any trace elements. At least, this was true until Caya Lindemay sensed its presence in my system—even after it was gone. She possesses gifts that top even the most state-of-the-art instruments and only had to touch me—and this was through Spinner, mind you. She kept her hands on Spinner, who was holding on to me. Now Ms. Lindemay is doing the same with other patients in the IDB, but directly this time. From what I have found out, she can describe what they used down to the atomic level. It's unbelievably amazing."

"Unbelievable might be the operative word," a general said curtly. "I represent the ground forces that are setting up their branch headquarters and habitats on the southwest plains close to cube seventeen." He nodded solemnly, as if to establish how much weight he carried within his military branch. "The thing is, most of you are new to Caya Lindemay and her changer sister. We on *Pathfinder* have lived with their presence and seen a most unhealthy fan base for these girls develop over time. They even have a clinic where they claim to read people's thoughts and treat all kinds of maladies. I would take Caya Lindemay's notes with a healthy dose of common sense."

Pamas blinked at the man who so clearly had gone against what the president and so many other high-ranking and prestigious individuals held to be true. Pamas knew from the short reading the sisters had done of her that they were not fakes. Then again, she couldn't say just how powerful their gifts were.

"Excuse me, General," Dael said mildly. "Do you debate the fact that the Lindemay sisters, together with Commander Vantressa, Admiral Heigel, and Meija Solimar, saved *Pathfinder*'s passengers on several occasions while you were en route to Gemocon?"

"Ahem. Well. No. Far be it from me to debate facts. But what the Lindemay sisters claim to be able to do, and what is verifiable truth, are entirely different."

Pamas wanted to smack the cranky old man over his bald head. He was a lot older than her husband, but so much of his condescending tone was the same. Pamas set her jaw and clenched her teeth.

"I'm sure we'll have reason to discuss the Lindemays' way of doing things, but for now, we don't have time to bicker. If Darmiya's plan or theory is sound and doable from a scientific point of view, we must act. What we cannot do," Dael spat, "is to sit around the campfire and debate day in and day out while the enemy sit around *their* campfire and plot against us." Dael's voice was a low growl that made everyone present straighten.

Admiral Heigel looked pensively at the general. "Sir, I think we can safely say that I'm not easily fooled, and I know for a *fact* that Caya and Briar are who they say they are and possess gifts that keep growing exponentially each time they use them. Continue, Darmiya."

"Thank you, sir." Darmiya leaned against her armrests, and Pamas stealthily shifted to support her shoulder. "We now know more about the black-garnet shells, and I am working on ways to calibrate sensors, but that's not the most important part."

Pamas scanned the circle of spectators near the circular desk, watching closely how they were all absorbing Darmiya's information. The ones belonging to the advance team looked like they were used to taking Darmiya's words as truth, while the ones from *Pathfinder* who didn't know the brilliant woman appeared puzzled. The situation was pretty much reversed if you compared how the different crews responded to the Lindemay sisters.

"Go on, Dar," Pamas said, pressing herself more firmly against Darmiya, who had begun to slump.

"Bear with me, all right?" Darmiya was trembling and put her tablet down. Pamas suspected she didn't want the others to notice. "When I began getting information from Caya, relayed by the guards placed to protect her, I saw a pattern. It all made sense. She could detect subtle differences in how the black-garnet shells had affected their physiology. I had an idea that this might be significant. On my way over here, I began comparing it with other data related to the explosion. The guards who came to the victims' rescue marked on a tablet grid where they found them and what position they were in. Perhaps it was just happenstance that one of the guards had the idea this might matter in a law-enforcement investigation later. As I see it, it does. The shells within each patient that the blast knocked over were aligned in the same direction. This fact tells me two things. I know how to begin calibrating the scanners, and I can use Caya's information as a template. But there is more." Pamas could tell that Darmiya was eager now to explain. She tried again to stand up but failed, and tears of clear frustration rose in her eyes. "Damn. I need the grid board over there. The one that overlaps the map of the territory."

Pamas didn't wait for permission. She pushed the hoverchair over to the grid board and elevated the chair so Darmiya could remain seated and still reach it.

"We are here." Darmiya drew a red circle where the ECC was located on the map. "Here's cube eleven. Here, by the doors, is the epicenter of the blast. The victims were located throughout the lobby. It took only minutes for the hospital's emergency staff to reach them and begin triaging. As I mentioned, the guards marked their location into a grid pattern. Like this." She placed a computer chip against a sensor, and a set of glowing lines showed the victims and the direction they were found in. "Red dots signify their heads, blue dots their feet. Now, let me show you Caya's information regarding how the shells aligned within each one's body—something she could determine even with those of us who had evacuated the shells from our bodies already. Her gifts are truly remarkable." Placing another computer chip into a vacant slot, Darmiya leaned back, breathing hard. "Damn, it hurts," she whispered to Pamas. "I hope they get it. I don't think I have enough energy to explain this twice."

Pamas was ready to shoot anyone who didn't catch on right away.

"Look at that," Adina said, her eyes wide. "Same direction, in every instance."

"But you weren't there during the explosion. How does this work in your case, Darmiya?" Dael asked.

"After reading through the data, I pondered that question all the way over here." Darmiya steadied herself against Pamas, who now slipped a hand behind the shivering woman and grabbed hold of her shirt to keep her from sliding off the chair. Darmiya needed to lie down again. Spinner had obviously reached the same conclusion and now stood by Darmiya's other side. She glanced at Pamas and nodded briefly.

"It was actually that fact that gave me the idea. I wasn't part of the blast but inhaled a smaller amount when my mask was compromised. Caya couldn't figure it out, since she wasn't quite sure what she was seeing. The shells in me were fewer in number and aligned vertically."

"How do you mean?" Dael looked at the grid on the large screen.

"Vertically." Darmiya demonstrated by moving her trembling hand from the ground up. "Like so. In that direction."

"Damn," Admiral Heigel said softly. "This girl is brilliant. Darmiya, you've given me enough to work with for now. I'll explain to everyone while you recuperate. You look like you're ready to pass out."

"I'm all right. I can still—"

"No. You will rest now. Right, Spinner?" Pamas said, glancing at her daughter.

"Right." Spinner looked taken aback, perhaps since Pamas had readily used her call sign rather than her name. "You look like death. Honestly."

"Why, thank you." Darmiya huffed, but that breath alone seemed to take the last of her energy.

Pamas adjusted the hoverchair to lower the back and raise the footrest. Calagan came over to kiss his sister's cheek. "Rest a bit. We have use for that mind of yours later. Let us just catch up with you first."

Darmiya smiled wearily. "You always were a charmer. You'd think I'd be immune to your flattery."

Calagan smiled. "As long as it works and gets you to rest up." He turned back to the main desk area, and Pamas began pushing the hoverchair over to the far end of the ECC tent. At this end, cots were lined up for the staff to rest on when given the opportunity during a crisis. Pushing a few cots aside, Pamas aligned the hoverchair with the wall and pulled a privacy screen around it. "Are you comfortable in the chair like this, or should I lift you onto one of the cots?"

"The cots are horrible. The chair's fine." Darmiya pressed another sensor, making it extend fully into a flat surface. "But perhaps a pillow?"

"Absolutely." Pamas took one of the pillows from the closest cot and tucked it under Darmiya's head. "That good enough?"

"Perfect. It's really ridiculous how quickly my energy ran out. I'm normally so alert that I drive everyone else crazy. Perhaps that's why Calagan looked so worried. And Spinner, too. They are used to me being more…perky."

"Of course they worry about you. They love you." It was obvious that everyone Pamas had come across in Darmiya's company adored her. And Pamas was no exception. She had known Darmiya for only a few days, yet when she had feared Darmiya was dying, Pamas had panicked in a way far more personal than how she would feel about a new acquaintance. It hurt Pamas's head when she compared how she had walked around the cubes of *Pathfinder* for the duration of the journey to Gemocon, still traumatized, yet very numb and with no desire to interact. She could have looked up Pherry on the ship, but fear had kept her from doing so. What if he had accepted her then, only to reject her once he got together with Spinner and followed her lead?

What had happened to that Pamas when she stepped off cube eleven and met Darmiya at the gate? Did she change from numb and apathetic to infatuated in a second, or did all these emotions simply start from there and race to magnetar speed in a few days?

Darmiya turned on her side, facing Pamas. "You look like you're trying to solve a mystery."

"Shh. Just rest, Dar. I'm going to sit here with you while you do just that." Pamas patted Darmiya's shoulder.

"Actually," a voice said from behind them, "I've been drafted to keep the lovely Darmiya company." Fleet Admiral Caydoc came up next to Pamas in her hoverchair. "And before you object, I'm bringing my personal assistant, Minna, with me."

"All right with you, Dar?" Pamas looked down at the pale woman before her. She seemed half-asleep already.

"Is fine." Darmiya nodded.

"All right. I'm over by the main desk if she needs me. Or something." The latter was meant for Caydoc and Minna.

"Understood, Lieutenant." Caydoc placed her unsteady but mobile hand on Pamas's lower left arm. "It's nice to see you back in uniform, Pamas. I hope we get a chance to catch up in a more private setting, if you're interested."

"I am." Pamas surmised they both had questions. Nodding politely, she hurried back to the desk where the briefing was still going on. Part of her wanted to remain by Darmiya's side and keep her safe. The other part wanted to be in on the plans of how to proceed with the new threat. For now, Pamas had to prioritize being on the team that would bring the terrorists down.

CHAPTER TWELVE

Darmiya glanced up from her computer tablet, not quite sure what had stirred her from her calculations. As soon as she saw the blond head at the other end of the ECC, she knew. President Tylio and her entire entourage strode between equipment and desks toward the center of the ECC. Soldiers stood at attention, but Tylio kept waving dismissively, and Darmiya could read the words "as you were" even from her corner. After resting for two full hours, she had eaten some food, and Calagan had even taken the time to fetch some of his miracle soup. She couldn't even begin to count the all-nighters they had pulled with her brother's soup as sustenance.

Darmiya quickly found that she couldn't focus if she remained at the central desk in the ECC. Instead she took her tablet and what maps she required, and arranged a table for herself in the far east corner. It was a blessing not to have to use the hoverchair anymore. As long as she didn't have to walk any long distances, she managed all right.

Pamas kept an eye on her, she could tell. So did Spinner, but rarely at the same time. As far as Darmiya could tell, mother and daughter remained entirely professional and seemed to have put their unresolved issues on hold, an ability they appeared to have in common. Darmiya had often wondered which one of her parents Spinner favored when it came to her physical appearance. While Spinner's hair consisted of black, unruly curls, Pamas's was smoothly brushed into a tight, black bun. Their eye color was the same, golden brown, though Pamas's were hooded and with more lines around them. Pamas's skin was paler than Spinner's, and whereas Spinner had a wider nose, Pamas possessed a finely chiseled, elegant one. Both women were tall, wiry, and lanky.

Shaking her head at how easily Pamas's mere presence could make her lose track of her task at hand, Darmiya punched in the new coordinates and double-checked them against her previous findings. The more she tried to figure out how and why the bodies of the wounded and dead had ended up in such a contradictory position, the more frustrated she became. If she intended to come up with something Dael and her soldiers, together with the law-enforcement agents, would find useful in their hunt for the terrorists, she needed a miracle right about now.

She rubbed her cheeks and was about to chuck her tablet across the ECC when she spotted it. At first she thought it was some strange illusion that her tired brain had created. She flipped the tablet upside down and then back again, a technique she had often used when she was an art student on Gemosis. When she examined the grid showing the bodies as well as the alignment of the black-matter shells, she began to tremble. Quickly she tapped in a few commands that superimposed the pattern on one of the maps. No matter how she adjusted the size, the result was the same.

Darmiya felt across the desk for her mug of soup. It had gone cold, but she sipped it greedily. She was onto something, but the theory forming in the back of her mind didn't make sense to her yet. She needed a fresh pair of eyes.

Glancing up, Darmiya waited until she caught Admiral Heigel's eyes and discreetly waved her to her corner. Nodding briskly, Heigel strode over to her.

"Got something for me, Doctor Do Voy?"

"Please. Call me Darmiya. And yes. I need your take on this. Look at it yourself first, and then, if you don't see what I see, I can ask my questions." Darmiya pushed her tablet across the desk to the admiral.

"Then call me Korrian. Enough titles in here to drive me crazy anyway. Now, let's see." She studied Darmiya's data, graphic tables, and maps. At first, she merely looked puzzled, but then Korrian began flipping between the different maps with increasing speed. She went back and forth, examining everything twice before she slowly looked up over the edge of the tablet at Darmiya.

"They're not exaggerating. You truly possess a one-of-a-kind mind, Darmiya." Korrian shook her head. "I'm not sure I would have noticed this—and if I had, it would have taken me days, perhaps weeks. We need to put this up on the big screen again."

"Already? I mean, you're certain?" Darmiya wasn't sure where her indecisiveness came from, or her lack of self-confidence. It wasn't like her.

"Absolutely. We need the others' input, and when better than now, when we have the president here?"

"Oh, dear. Well, of course. Let the others brainstorm and poke holes in my theory." She welcomed any thoughts her colleagues might have.

"Listen up," Korrian said as they approached the central desk. "Darmiya has discovered something utterly brilliant, and entirely new. I need each of you to look at this from your particular point of view, your area of expertise. I'll put it up on the big screen and forward it to your tablets. Before we start, though, the privacy drapes, please."

Pamas pressed the sensor for the drapes and then rounded the table to join Darmiya. Pulling up two chairs, she motioned for Darmiya to sit. "I can tell your stamina will improve with more sitting and less standing around."

"Thank you." Darmiya sat and stretched her legs out in front of her.

"Now let's see if I can even understand one percent of what you've uncovered." Pamas took one of the tablets on the table and pulled up Darmiya's data. "Oh, Creator."

"I know it looks like a mishmash of numbers, but—"

"Shh. I'm going to try. Patience, Dar."

Darmiya had to smile. Patience really wasn't her strong suit, but she liked for Pamas to call her Dar. Nobody had ever shortened her name or invented any sort of nickname for her before. Perhaps Pamas wasn't aware that she was doing just that, but the name gave her a nice feeling just the same.

President Tylio tapped her lower lip with her index finger before she spoke. "Did you implement all of Caya's findings from when she did her readings? I think she missed only two of the wounded, who were in surgery at the time."

"Yes, sir." Darmiya nodded seriously. "Every single one she sent me before she returned to her room."

"Good." Tylio pressed a few sensors on her tablet and tilted her head. "I realize that you've indicated their heads and feet, but why are some lines blue and some yellow?"

"Yellow means wounded, sir, and blue means diseased." Darmiya watched Tylio press her lips together.

"These patterns can't be accurate, can they?" Adina browsed through several pages, back and forth on her tablet. "The epicenter of the explosion at cube eleven was just inside the doors. We have verified that. Look at how the rescue workers and guards have indicated the position of the wounded and dead. They should be thrown in a uniform pattern outward from the center, disregarding unmovable objects." Glancing up at Darmiya, she frowned. "Can there be a mistake?"

"No mistake on the data, Commander," Darmiya said calmly. "However, I'm not saying my analysis is the only one that's correct. Hence Admiral Heigel's bringing it to the central desk." She let her gaze travel around the inner circle. Before *Pathfinder* came into orbit and began landing its ferries and cubes, Darmiya had been in awe of being part of the advance team. Now, when she realized that more than two million souls depended on her, on everyone within this privacy drape, to keep them safe and solve the terrorist issue once and for all, she found her position immensely humbling.

"I realize not everyone here is a scientist, or an engineer, but Adina, considering that these are verifiable facts, what deductions would you make looking at the grid pattern superimposed on the maps?" Korrian pulled it up in even better resolution on the big screen.

"Wait. The maps. Let me access them." Adina swiftly rearranged the documents and added a few new algorithms that Darmiya was dying to read. She was aware of the exact moment Adina spotted what Darmiya and Korrian already had. "Fuck. I'm sorry, sir." Sending an apologetic glance at Tylio, Adina turned back to Korrian. "They're like—like damn arrows!"

"They are, aren't they?" Korrian took a large stylus and began drawing along the grid on the big screen. "Let's follow their path." She drew a straight line from each victim's feet to their head, one by one, extending them across what would soon be christened the capital of Gemocon and over toward the mountains. The lines seemed random at first, but the more Korrian filled in, the clearer it became that they all converged on the slopes of a very tall mountain in the center of the mountain range.

"How—how can that be?" Pamas gripped Darmiya's hand. "What's out there that can do this?"

"Nothing indigenous," Darmiya said darkly. "As I only know what I've read about black garnet, not having studied it in person for obvious reasons, it took me a while to formulate a hypothesis. Should I go first, or you, Admiral Heigel?" Darmiya's cheeks warmed. Perhaps even having the audacity to ask made her sound presumptuous?

"Oh, you go first. I have a feeling we're not that far apart." Korrian waved for Darmiya to continue.

"Thank you, sir." Standing up on somewhat stronger legs, Darmiya took another stylus and extended it so she could reach the large screen. "As you can tell by the way the admiral has drawn lines from each body, something in the mountains shifted the wounded and dead during the exact moment of the blast. Once they were on the ground, whatever pulled at them couldn't make them budge anymore. I spent an hour binge-reading about black garnet, and from what I could deduce, removing the shell from the black-garnet fibers would hypothetically create a magnetism of such force it could literally move objects. Or people."

"Then why didn't it—if that's what happened?" President Tylio asked.

"This is merely an educated guess, but I think the mountains saved our people caught in all this from slamming into bulkheads, walls, buildings, other people. Either by sort of standing in the way or because of the potential metal ores that run through them."

"How?" Tylio followed the lines with a nail.

"I think they're trying to return to join the original source." Darmiya felt Pamas squeezing her hand. Without thinking, she returned the touch. "Somewhere in the mountains, perhaps in a cave or stored out of view in other ways, someone keeps genuine black garnet."

Everyone seemed to stop breathing for several moments.

"Creator of all things," President Tylio pinched the bridge of her nose. "Admiral?" She turned to Korrian.

"Regretfully, Madam President, Darmiya's and my conclusion are the same in every essential aspect." Korrian's complexion was bordering on gray, making Darmiya realize that the woman wasn't young anymore. This was her life's work, what she had eaten and breathed for the last forty-five years, at least. To find out that evil of this magnitude had followed them all to the new, supposedly calm and peaceful world, must be such a blow to everything Korrian and her wife, Meija, stood for. The same went for the rest of them, whether they had given their all to science, the military, medicine, or politics.

People had put them all at grave risk, and now Darmiya waited for the question that would devastate them even more.

"How could they have had time? How can they have moved such a volatile substance off *Pathfinder* and transported it into the mountain right under our noses? Do invisible changers exist?" Tylio spoke with such hatred that Darmiya was startled, yet she knew she had to answer.

"The black garnet didn't come with *Pathfinder*." She held up an unsteady hand as everyone snapped their heads toward her. "I know this about black garnet: no matter how careful you are, you can transport it only very slowly and carefully. The closest cube is more than 150 kilometers away from that mountainside. It would take the person or persons at least forty hours, probably more, considering they'd have to be on foot and traversing rough terrain with risks of avalanches and so on. Add the time it takes to split the shells from the core—not to mention the equipment it takes to perform such a thing. I don't think they'd dare perform this process anywhere near any settlements. The risk of being detected is too great, and it would be hard to explain why you'd suddenly need a completely anaerobic laboratory." Darmiya saw that they understood now. Dael was pale, apart from the bright-red hue on her cheekbones. Spinner's dark eyes were black, as were Pamas's, who hadn't let go of Darmiya's hand.

"Already then." Dael sounded devastated. "Already when we all risked our lives to find a home for our people."

"Yes." Darmiya was furious, and for once she let it show. "While the rest of the advance team worked around the clock to provide for those joining us, imposters, stowaways, or whatever we should call these traitors were building weapons of mass destruction in the mountains. I think we can surmise that today's two explosions were merely a dress rehearsal meant to instill terror."

Chapter Thirteen

Once the discussions erupted around the central desk area, Pamas didn't leave Darmiya's side. She spotted the president taking Korrian and Dael aside, speaking rapidly but not loudly enough for anyone else to hear. Two generals were at each other's throats, and Pamas looked on in fascination to see if they would actually come to blows.

Meija Solimar had joined Adina and was obviously filling her in. When she was done, Meija strode over to Darmiya and Pamas, taking Darmiya's right hand between hers. That was when Pamas realized she was still holding Darmiya's left hand.

"Please, Darmiya, sit down again," Meija said, shaking her head. "You look exhausted. All that work after you were poisoned earlier today. This is not good for you."

"I'm all right, Madam Solimar."

"Meija. Believe it or not, I hate formality as much as my admiral of a wife does." She cupped Darmiya's cheek. "You need something to eat. In fact, we all do. Why don't we send for something from the canteen? I heard their menu includes some wonderful additions from the *Pathfinder* chefs."

"I can take care of it, Meija," Pamas said and reluctantly let go of Darmiya's hand.

"No. You stay here with our genius. Once everyone calms down, they're going to need her. I don't think I'm speaking out of turn when I think you're the best person for the job of Darmiya's protector. I spoke to Helden Caydoc yesterday, and she told me of your amazing career cut short through no fault of your own. If anyone can anticipate and spot hostility or anything untoward against Darmiya, it's you."

Pamas was sure she was hallucinating. She had heard many stories about Meija and Korrian while aboard *Pathfinder*, as the two women had become legends for their role in creating the ship. It was surreal for Meija to say she had talked to Helden Caydoc about her.

"If anyone wants to so much as talk to Darmiya, they'll have to go through me first," Pamas said darkly. She had no idea why she was so protective of the young woman, but she was. "Yes, we need her and her expertise, but if she's not up to it, they can wait."

"Good. That's what I want to hear. I'm going over now to let everyone know that we need sustenance before they start tearing out each other's jugulars with their teeth." Meija smiled wryly and walked over to her wife. Pamas realized Korrian and Dael had objected to her suggestion at first, only to surrender when Meija's hands ended up on her hips and her chin jutted out.

"Wait." President Tylio nodded slowly. "Actually, a small break would be practical. We need Caya and Briar here. It will save time. I'll go over to the hospital to see if Caya can manage it. She was tired but doing much better last time we talked." Tylio rubbed the back of her head just under her chignon. She wore her trademark ten-row beads, which accentuated her light-blue caftan and trousers. "Let's open up the privacy drapes. That way the esteemed generals over there will have to shut up in order not to talk about classified material in front of junior officers."

Korrian snorted. "True enough." She pressed the sensor on the desk. "Drape's going up, people. We're not in a secure mode anymore."

"Aye, sir." Pamas let her eyes scan every face around the central desk. It was clear that the generals hadn't heard what Korrian had just said. "Generals, *sirs*, you are discussing classified material in an open setting." She found it remarkably easy to resume the stark voice she found worked so well with male subordinates and even peers twenty years ago. The generals looked up and blanched when they saw the drape was raised. At least they shut up, Pamas thought.

Turning to Darmiya, she crouched next to the chair. "Want me to get the hoverchair, Dar?" Stealthily she placed her fingertips against Darmiya's wrist. To her relief, her pulse was strong and steady.

"Thanks, Pam, but I'm all right. I just need a good night's sleep, and then I'll be back to my annoyingly perky self." Darmiya did look all right, but also a little awkward after the rushed words.

"You couldn't be annoying if you tried," Pamas murmured. "Want an example of annoying, take a look at the general, the taller of them. He's using Calagan's tablet without permission."

"What?" Darmiya sat up straight. "Where's my brother?"

"I think he went to assist Meija with the food." Pamas looked up at Darmiya. "Want me to grab Calagan's tablet and give it to you?"

"No, thank you. I'll deal with him. I've had to assert myself many times since I joined the advance team. Perhaps it's the perky part of me that makes people think I'm such an airhead?" Darmiya shrugged and stood. Her steps were steady as she rounded the table, walking past the president, who was speaking via her communicator.

Pamas watched Tylio, keeping an eye on Darmiya as she strode up to the tall general.

"General Mindero it is, I believe?" Darmiya said softly, but Pamas could easily hear the steel behind her benign tone.

"Yes, dear?" the general answered, and Pamas wanted to groan aloud at his attempt to sound fatherly. Why did some men need to establish some sort of pecking order as soon as a woman was present, especially if she was young?

"I believe that's my brother's personal tablet, sir. It contains his private correspondence and work assignments. If you try to enter anything into it without the proper identification algorithm, you might inadvertently set off an alarm that will have the military police and other law enforcement here instantly. We had to establish such routines once we began working here. Not that we don't trust each other—we do—but information is easily compromised even when the individual has the best of intentions."

"I'm sure it's fine. I have very high security clearance, dear."

"I'm sure you do, but that won't help matters So, I need that tablet. Now. *Sir.*"

General Mindero looked around as if to ascertain how many had heard a young woman lecturing him. When his eyes met Tylio's and the president merely raised her left eyebrow in a very clear challenge, he bowed and handed over the tablet. "I thought it was mine."

"I see." It was obvious to Pamas that Darmiya didn't believe him but wouldn't pursue the fact that Calagan had placed a bright-orange supportive and absorbent shell around his tablet. Hardly military issue.

Returning to Pamas and her chair, Darmiya sat down with a sigh of relief. "Did you see how he looked at me? I think I seriously aggravated that man."

"He doesn't matter. If things develop like I think they will, he won't be part of the next phase."

Darmiya turned sideways in the chair and pulled her legs up against her chest. "As we can't talk about it until the drape is down again, I'll just say I look forward to being enlightened." She tilted her head and smiled, not the wry smile from earlier, but a broad, blinding smile that made Pamas's stomach clench.

"Hmm, all right." Pamas couldn't remember when she had last experienced a physical response toward another person. She plucked at the seam of her jacket, feeling foolish for sensing her heart ache.

"Oh, no. Did I embarrass you, Pam?" Darmiya covered her mouth. "I'm sorry. Sometimes I don't know when to shut up." She blinked hard.

Distraught and feeling completely inept at handling someone else's pain, Pamas took Darmiya's left hand again. "No. You could never embarrass me. I'm the one who should apologize for...for everything, really." She wasn't quite sure what she meant, but she carried so much guilt for so many things, it tended to spill over and color everything else in her life. It was a dark, horrible feeling that loomed over her every day. Sometimes, if it was a busy day, she could keep her thoughts away. On slow days, when she had far too much time to think, she could drive herself mad when mulling everything over, time and time again.

"I'm not sure I understand." Darmiya kept her hand in Pamas's, which was a good sign. "I just know that I tend to babble even more than usual when I get self-conscious or nervous."

Pamas would never have thought she'd find such a trait charming, but she did with Darmiya. "You're fine, whether you chat away or if you're in a silent mood. Truly."

"Thank you." Darmiya's eyes looked seriously into Pamas's. "Truly." Now she smiled because she'd repeated Pamas's word.

The ones fetching food and carrying out assignments began to return. Last to arrive was the president, accompanied by Caya and Briar Lindemay. Caya was doing much better. Her translucent complexion had regained some color, and she no longer looked like the slightest gust of wind would blow her away. Her sister seemed to be sturdier, even if she was on the petite side as well. She did look a bit tired, however.

"Welcome to the ECC, Caya, Briar," Korrian said. "I trust you're feeling better, Caya?"

"I'm fine, thanks, Korrian. If I can snag some food, I'll be back to normal." Caya turned to her sister. "And you too, Briar. Honestly. You've worked nonstop since the explosions. You need nourishment like the rest of us, you know?"

"Creator. My sister is lecturing me. My *younger* sister, at that. Don't worry. I'll get some for you and Thea as well." Crinkling her nose at Caya, Briar walked over to the table holding the food boxes.

Pamas joined her. "Hello again, Ms. Lindemay," she said quietly as she grabbed two boxes for her and Darmiya. "Glad to see you're okay."

"Oh, hello, um, Lieutenant Seclan." Briar looked up at Pamas after glancing at her rank insignia. "You've regained your rank. How great. And don't worry. I've tuned out everybody's thoughts today, and that includes yours." Briar looked exhausted, and Pamas mulled over her words.

"That's what takes a lot of strength out of you, doesn't it?" she asked discreetly. "Not the part of being on your feet saving lives all day, but tuning everybody out, not to mention having to reassure people about it—about the fact that you're not invading their privacy."

Blinking rapidly, Briar seemed at a loss for words for a few moments. "That's…that's exactly right," she said in a gush. "How can you possibly know?"

"I'm no changer, that's for sure, but it dawned on me that both you and your sister must have to reassure people on a continuous basis—especially if they're new acquaintances."

"Not many people understand this fact, yet still you are as new to us as most others are." Briar tilted her head. "Even without reading you, or listening into your mind, I can tell that you're carrying around a lot of experiences that will need an outlet sooner rather than later. Caya and I read you deeply enough when we first met you to help Dael ascertain if she could put you back on active duty, but I think we could be of assistance to you on a personal level if you want."

Her heart rate reaching record levels, Pamas merely wanted to decline and put distance between herself and Briar, but one glance in Darmiya's direction made her change her mind. She wasn't sure why the sight of Darmiya's soft smile right then made any difference, but clearly it did. "Later," Pamas said quietly. "Once we have things under control regarding this whole mess."

"Fair enough." Briar nodded and then looked down at her food boxes. "Better go eat before my sister decides to embarrass me even further."

Pamas returned to Darmiya with their food, and they ate in silence. As they were finishing, Spinner joined them, balancing three mugs of tea. "I put four sweeteners in yours, Darmiya." She turned to Pamas, hesitating. "You still take yours with two sweeteners and *tion* spices?" Spinner sucked her lower lip in between her teeth.

"I sure do, when available." Pamas had to steel herself to not do something foolish. Torn between hugging her daughter fiercely or running away from the entire situation, she only said, "Thank you."

"No problem." Spinner didn't stay but returned to Dael's side when everybody resumed their seats and the privacy drape went down.

Pamas sipped her tea, glad to feel the hot beverage scald the tip of her tongue. She couldn't even begin to count the times she had craved physical pain, or at least discomfort, for distraction. Normally, she tried to focus on anything but her years in captivity, but this time, she merely needed not to read too much into the fact that her daughter had taken a very small, but so very important step toward her.

"Spinner will need a lot of time," Darmiya said. "Please, don't give up on her." She placed a hand on Pamas's thigh, squeezing lightly.

"Never. I've come too far, literally and figuratively, to give up on my children. They may not want me in their lives the way I dream of, but that won't deter me." Pamas knew she sounded gruff, but the idea of losing what was just within her reach scared her. Perhaps it was this notion that made her continue without filtering her comments. "Same goes for you. I hope you will still want to be my…my friend. I mean, despite everything."

Darmiya colored faintly, which made her even prettier. Her dark eyes glittered as they reflected the screens around them. "Absolutely." She patted Pamas's leg, but then it was as if she realized exactly which of Pamas's body parts she was touching, and she quickly turned forward in her chair. "Looks like we're about to start again."

Pamas had to smile. Darmiya was probably unaware of how easily Pamas could read her body language and facial expressions. Perhaps it came from being held by changers who had so many tricks up their sleeves that trying to decipher their expressions was all she could do?

Dael stood, raising her hands to silence the murmuring voices around the central desk. "All right. Listen up, people. We need everyone to stay silent and try to cleanse their minds of anything that has nothing to do with the task at hand. Caya and Briar will initiate a session, and the less their minds are clogged with personal matters, the better. The only reason they have to do it in here is that we cannot let any of the documents come into view of junior officers with lesser clearance."

"Oh, Creator of all things…" One of the generals rolled his eyes and huffed. "More witchcraft, Admiral? I just don't buy into—"

"General Kallos. If you aren't prepared to sit through this session with an open mind, we can't use you." A tall, older man entered the draped-off area. Pamas realized immediately who he was. Fleet Admiral Orien Vayand. He outranked every military individual on Gemocon.

General Kallos looked shocked. "Sir. Surely you don't put any stock in these amusement park tricks?"

"I have seen firsthand what these young women can accomplish. They have risked their lives on multiple occasions and deserve our respect and support. If you cannot see yourself giving that to them, I will replace you. It's not a punishment. We just can't have negative energy present." Vayand opened the drape again and motioned for General Kallos to vacate his seat.

"How about you, General Mindero? You ready to set aside your doubts, sir?" Darmiya asked the man who had so blatantly examined her brother's tablet.

"I'm all right," Mindero answered, his eyes narrow as he regarded Darmiya and Pamas.

"Something I need to know about?" Vayand asked as he took a seat next to Darmiya. "Good to see you up and about again, Doctor Do Voy."

Darmiya blinked. "Oh. I mean, thank you, sir." She glanced quickly at Pamas, who merely raised the eyebrow above her good eye. Clearly Darmiya hadn't expected Vayand to recognize her.

Dael sat down next to Spinner. "Looks like we're ready to start."

Pamas looked at the two sisters, fascinated by the warm compassion they radiated. Gripping each other's hands, they closed their eyes. Slowly they leaned toward each other until their foreheads touched. Briar hummed lightly, but Caya quickly began squirming in her chair. Briar opened her eyes, obviously concerned.

"Something's wrong, sis." Briar freed her hands and placed them against Caya's cheeks. "Is it the concussion?"

"No. That's not it at all. I'm feeling, I don't know, blocked somehow." Caya stood. "Thea? I need something from our quarters."

Pamas saw the president wince slightly, probably because Caya mentioned them living together so casually.

Tylio nodded at the wiry commander. "I'll send Commander KahSandra for it."

KahSandra walked up to Caya, who murmured her instructions in her ear. "Aye, sir." After saluting, KahSandra strode out of the draped area.

"I'm not being deliberately mysterious," Caya said where she stood. Her long, blond hair lay around her like a sorceress's cloak, and the lilac-colored dress accentuated her translucent turquoise eyes. "Something is blocking me, and if I can't get through that, it will hinder Briar's readings as well. I've asked Commander KahSandra to fetch a…a tool of sorts. Or perhaps calling it a tool is blasphemous in a sense." Her cheeks reddening, she smiled self-consciously, suddenly looking much more like the very young woman she was.

"What kind of tool?" Calagan asked, looking intrigued.

"Three changers who sacrificed their lives to save mine and that of many others gave it to me. They told me it had been their mother's—and that it now belonged to me, as it responded to me."

"Responded to you?" Admiral Vayand leaned forward on his elbows. "It's a personalized tool?"

Caya smiled again and nodded. "That is about as accurately as I can describe it. An amplifier of sorts. I'm hoping it will help my sister and me cut through whatever is blocking us."

It took only ten minutes for Commander KahSandra to return with a square metal box. She placed it on the desk in front of Caya, who waited until everyone was sitting down again before opening it.

"Only Thea and Briar have seen me use this. I have practiced every day since the day I received it, which was just before cube eighteen was destroyed." Caya pulled aside a silky golden fabric. Carefully, she pulled out an orb that looked like it was made from rough, crackled stone, about twenty-five centimeters in diameter.

Gripping it firmly between her hands, Caya raised the orb above her head and closed her eyes. Pamas was so fascinated by Caya's expression, serene and content, that she jumped when the first silvery flash shot out from the orb and lit up the ceiling of the central desk area. Darmiya gripped Pamas's hand as another flash singed the air. The orb began to tremble and then spin, faster and faster. Flashes kept sparkling around it until they appeared to engulf the orb completely. Caya tossed her head back, and the orb now hovered a few centimeters above her palms

Briar placed her hands on her sister's shoulders, and this act seemed to raise the orb a few more centimeters. Caya was breathing faster and trembled where she stood between her sister's hands. Briar, in turn, looked serene and was humming again, barely audible above the orb's hissing sound.

After what seemed like an eternity, the orb began to slow, and the two sisters opened their eyes. Pamas gasped, and she wasn't the only one. Normally a translucent turquoise, Caya's eyes seemed transparent, like water, and possessed an amazing light from within. Briar, whose eyes were green, now looked at them through pupils surrounded by golden-yellow irises.

"Caya?" Thea whispered, raising a hand to touch the young changer but stopping herself halfway.

"I have seen what will come if we do not act," Caya said, her voice deep with conviction and emotion. "If we do nothing, our mission, the Exodus operation, will fail."

CHAPTER FOURTEEN

From where Darmiya stood to the side of the whirlwind of activity that had erupted an hour ago, she gazed around her. The central desk was now separated into four groups, virtually consisting of the same members established during the meeting several days ago, all of them tasked with vastly different assignments.

"Darmiya? What do you think?" Adina nudged her gently.

"What? Oh. I'm so sorry. All the noise in here made me tune out for a bit." Darmiya shook her head. "Please, ask me again."

"No problem. It sure is loud in here. If we could only raise the drape…"

Everything being discussed among the four groups was highly classified. Only the people in the center of the ECC, whom Caya and Briar had vetted, were privy to it.

"Should we travel by foot or use hovercars? They don't do as well in rough terrain, but the hovercraft might expedite our journey into the mountains." Adina ran her fingers through her short, dark hair.

"We've tried all the types of vehicles that we brought on the advance ships. You're right. The hovercars do very poorly. Perhaps they can be calibrated, but it'll take too long. Caya stated clearly that we can't delay anything. Reinventing technology isn't worth it. The cars, even in the best of circumstances, wouldn't take us there fast enough to make up for the time we lost." Darmiya tugged at her braid. "But we can build more hoverskids fairly quickly."

"I was just going to suggest that, even if I'm not an engineer or a scientist," Pamas said.

Darmiya was so glad she was in the same group as Pamas, Spinner, and Adina. Caya and Briar were rotating from group to group, adding their thoughts and ideas, and answering questions. Later they would join Darmiya's group, which would be exciting despite the circumstances. Darmiya guessed that the relationship between Adina and Briar had something to do with it.

Spinner had been poring over the maps for the last half hour. Now she looked up and nudged Darmiya. "Isn't this the field where we picked the green and purple berries that had the same basic ingredients as antibiotics? It was during our first month here."

Darmiya moved closer to Spinner and followed her finger. "Wait. Yes. I think so. Does a twin brook run through it northeast to southwest?"

"Um…let me see…" Spinner leaned across the horizontal screen and scanned the map.

"Here," Pamas said and pointed a few centimeters to the west. "Can that one be it?"

"Yes!" Spinner looked up and met her mother's eyes. Darmiya held her breath, but Spinner merely nodded approvingly, which in turn made Pamas smile. "It's a pretty sight. A natural double brook that flows through the field of flowers like it was manmade. I could barely tear Darmiya from it, as she insisted on first taking samples and then bathing her feet."

Pamas shifted her gaze to Darmiya. "I can picture that," she said huskily, her eye a golden shimmer rather than its normal amber hue.

"So, what if we spend the night there?" Spinner said, returning to the subject. "It's located about two-thirds of the distance to the area we need to reach."

"Good plan." Adina entered the information into the tablet that was connected to the other groups. This way, they didn't have to repeat any information or take unnecessarily long to figure something out that one of the other groups had already solved.

President Tylio and Fleet Admiral Vayand came over to their desk, the president reading her tablet. "I'm glad someone found a good place for the teams to catch some sleep. I was getting worried. After all, you have more experience with the local surroundings."

"You'd think establishing a good place to camp out would be simple, sir." Spinner shrugged. "This meadow isn't on a straight trajectory to our goal. We'll have to veer off course for an hour, but it reduces our risk of being detected, should the terrorists be doing runs at the same time. I'd hate for them to surprise us from any direction."

"We also need to think about mine detection," Adina said. "If I was hiding black garnet in a cave, I'd place mines or otherwise booby-trap along the paths leading there. I'm sending an order to Lieutenant Dodgmer to calibrate some detection devices for every individual in the expedition. They will be worn as bracelets, one on the wrist, another one around the ankle. I can have him outfit them with stealth signals for us to keep track of our team members."

"Good idea." Spinner nodded. "Did you get Darmiya's idea about the hoverskids?"

"I did," the president said. "But I have no idea what they are."

Darmiya explained briefly. "They're quite safe and very easy to maneuver, sir."

"I've used one, and considering I haven't driven anything for a long time, I only needed a minute to get the hang of it, sir," Pamas said. "Why don't I take one inside for Adina to examine? It really is made from very few parts."

"Do so." Tylio looked pleased. "You're doing really well, all four teams. I'll be back in one hour for another report."

"Yes, sir." Adina saluted, and they watched the woman who carried the entire responsibility for the success of the Exodus operation on her shoulders make her way to the last table. The members in that group nearly fell off their chairs as they rose to attention, but Darmiya saw how quickly Tylio put them at ease. No doubt, she had to do that a lot.

Time passed quickly, and eventually Darmiya's legs couldn't carry her anymore. She vaguely remembered having something to eat that Pamas had pushed into her hand. Probably some type of sandwich and some herbal tea.

"I'm sorry, but I need to go lie down," Darmiya said, feeling embarrassed at how she slurred her words. "I don't know about you, but I'm about to fall asleep right here." She patted the desk.

"It's past midnight. We should all get some sleep and gather again tomorrow morning. We can have a working breakfast and start here at 0700." Adina looked around the table. "Sound all right?"

It was a relief to see how grateful most of the others in the group seemed. Darmiya stood and then gripped the desktop, holding on while the room spun around her.

"Hey, sis, what's up?" Calagan was at her side, wrapping his arm around her. "You need someone to take you home. I wish I could do it, but I have to design a safe containment for the black garnet. Then again, I suppose I could—"

Pamas was suddenly at Darmiya's side with the hoverchair. "No need. I'll take Darmiya home."

"Oh, no. Not that thing again," Darmiya groaned. "I've had enough of feeling like a weak flower hybrid."

"It's not for you. It's for me," Pamas said.

"Wait...what?" Darmiya looked at Pamas, who had no obvious injuries that suggested she would need a hoverchair. "I'm supposed to drive you in this?"

The corners of Pamas's mouth twitched. "Of course not. I'm driving you home. This way I don't have to carry you. I'm getting too old to do that anyway."

Gaping now, Darmiya then snorted and shook her head. "Is this an attempt at humor, Pamas?" She laughed again, knowing full well her giggles bordered on hysteria from sheer fatigue. "Very well, Lieutenant." Darmiya sat down in the hoverchair. "Onward."

"It might help if I knew where you live, Dar," Pamas said, and turned the hoverchair toward the exit.

"Actually," a gentle voice said, interrupting them, "I haven't had a vision per se, but I have a strong feeling that Darmiya shouldn't stay by herself tonight." Caya stood next to them, in the process of braiding her long, blond hair. "Any chance Darmiya can stay at your habitat, Pamas?"

Clearing her throat, Pamas answered in a low tone. "I'm in a one-person tent."

"Oh. That isn't ideal either."

"Why can't I go back to my own place? I have a door that actually locks," Darmiya said. "If you think it's necessary, Pamas can stay with me there."

"It's better than the tent, but I still have a strange feeling about it."

Dael joined the small group. "I have an idea. Ani and I have just added on to our log cabin. It's located at the outskirts of the capital, but you can ride in the hovercar with us. We're leaving in five minutes."

Darmiya saw Pamas wince. Turning to look for Spinner, Darmiya couldn't see her anywhere. "Thank you, Dael. That's very nice of you."

"Not at all. After all, you are family, as you're one of our closest friends, and the lieutenant is family by blood. I think this is a good opportunity for several reasons. All settled then?"

Darmiya blinked. Who was she to argue with their commanding officer? She hoped Pamas and Spinner wouldn't feel too cornered. "Yes. Thank you, Dael."

"Excellent." Turning to Pamas, Dael smiled politely. "Take Darmiya to the hovercar. Ours is the blue one. We'll join you in a few minutes."

"Aye, sir." Pamas saluted.

"We're off the clock as of now, Pamas. No need for titles or salutes then. After all, we are family, since I'm married to your daughter."

"Which makes Dael your daughter-in-law," Darmiya said merrily, now so tired she was starting to feel drunk. "That's pretty awesome."

Pamas and Dael stood as if struck by a bolt of plasma-storm lightning. Then Dael smiled rigidly and glared at Darmiya. Pamas, in turn, gave Darmiya a slightly exasperated look, which Darmiya found truly funny. Darmiya snorted, and Pamas pushed the hoverchair between the desks that the night shift manned now.

"Did you have to do your best to make the situation between Spinner's wife and me even more awkward?" Pamas said, sighing loudly.

"That wasn't awkward," Darmiya insisted. "It was sweet. One big happy family."

"And what the hell did they put in your last mug of tea? You sound positively drunk."

Darmiya hummed. "No. Not drunk. Just very tired. I get silly when I'm this exhausted. It's like my science brain shuts down and my party brain gears up. I think I could dance! Well, if my stupid legs would carry me. I'm awfully wobbly."

"Hmm. I wonder why," Pamas said. "Oh, wait. Could it be because you were poisoned and almost died?"

Darmiya realized that Pamas might have a point. "True. Thank you for offering to stay with me. You really didn't have to. I mean, I appreciate it, but you're not responsible for me, or anything." She knew she wasn't expressing herself well, but her head was now one big mess of jumbled thoughts.

"Am I making you uneasy, Dar? Should I just let you go on home with Dael and Spinner by yourself? I'm quite comfortable in my tent." Pamas sounded entirely neutral, but Darmiya could still detect a faint trace of uncertainty.

"No. I don't want you to stay alone in your tent. I want you with me—us." Her cheeks warming now, Darmiya was glad they had reached Dael's hovercar. She stepped off the hoverchair and saw the driver assist Pamas as they stowed it in the back of the vehicle. Sliding into the double seat in the far back of the hovercar,

Darmiya pulled her legs up and curled up on her side. The seat adjusted to her position automatically, and she closed her eyes.

She felt rather than heard Pamas take the seat next to her. Darmiya sighed, for some reason experiencing a lot of relief. Tilting her head, she let it fall onto Pamas's shoulder, not sure why that didn't make her feel awkward, only that some persistent voice in her head insisted that it ought to. She promptly ignored it as Pamas cupped her cheek and held her in place. Darmiya settled and simply watched their world go by as the hovercar left the ECC area.

After Dael and Spinner entered the seat in front of Darmiya and Pamas, the hovercar moved without haste through the night. The headlights cast beams through the dense darkness as the driver skillfully avoided people still out on the gravel roads. Some were still partying despite the two explosions. Darmiya knew that Dael, Admiral Vayand, and the president had debated enforcing martial law, but decided against it as they feared there would be more trouble if they tried to restrict people only a few days after their arrival in Gemocon.

As they reached the outskirts of the area that would soon be christened the capital of Gemocon, they didn't see any more streetlights and very few structures. Looking up through the transparent ceiling of the hovercar, Darmiya focused on the alien constellations it had taken her so long to get used to. Not that she had seen many stars on Gemosis. The planet she was born and raised on was infamous for the amount of pollution its inhabitants released into the atmosphere. One of Darmiya's goals in life had been to solve those issues once and for all. Shuddering, she pressed closer to Pamas.

"Cold?" Pamas murmured against the top of Darmiya's head.

"No. Just bad memories."

"I see." Pamas didn't say anymore but kept her arm around Darmiya's shoulders for the duration of the drive.

As the hovercar pulled up and lowered to ground level, automatic lights came on to the left, displaying an old-fashioned log cabin. However, the term "cabin" didn't do it justice. Darmiya couldn't make out everything in the limited light, but she could see it was a two-story residential structure with a traditional porch. It had been so long ago that she was out here to see what progress her friends had made on their house. Work had taken every waking hour, and the few moments Darmiya had to herself she spent sleeping. Now she wished she'd simply made more time for Dael and Spinner. It wasn't because they hadn't asked her. She was the one who withdrew. The confession caused tears to come to her eyes. No, she couldn't fall apart now. She couldn't allow herself to crumble when everyone else was holding up just fine. Besides, as usual, they needed her calculations and estimations when it came to the new assignment.

"We're here," Spinner said over her shoulder. "Can you manage that dead weight, Lieutenant?"

"Absolutely." Pamas moved from her seat. "Come here. It isn't far. I can carry you."

"No, no. I'm far too heavy." Darmiya pushed against Pamas. "As you say, it's not far. I can walk." She stood and forced her legs to move steadily as she left the car. The night air out here was cold, and Darmiya shivered. "See? I'm fine."

Pamas didn't look convinced and stayed close as they made their way to the front door.

Pamas stood in the living room area of Dael and Spinner's cabin. Here, her daughter was making a perfect life with the woman she loved more than anything or anyone. It was as it should be, and sadly enough, that made Pamas feel even more like an outsider. She was a guest who would stay one night and then leave, perhaps never to return—unless Spinner relented.

"We'd just completed the left part of the second floor before Ani went on her extended mission and *Pathfinder* hit high orbit. We plan to use it as our master-bedroom suite and have Helden come live with us and use the downstairs bedroom." Dael came up behind them and shook her head sadly. "If we can persuade her. She's staying in a medical facility geared toward the elderly and claims she's very comfortable there and that she enjoys the company. She has a valid point, I suppose. Out here it'll take a while before we have proper neighbors."

"The Helden I remember wasn't very much into socializing," Pamas said. "Guess a lot can change when you're in intergalactic space for an extended time."

"True. Now, here. Let me show you. Ani is still outside sending the car back to the capital before she does her rounds."

"Her rounds?" Pamas looked out the closest window.

"Her habit ever since we moved out here." Dael unbuttoned her uniform jacket and hung it in a closet located just inside the front door. "She makes sure the lot is undisturbed and that all the windows are locked and undamaged. We have a state-of-the-art alarm system, of course, and guards on duty around the clock."

"Did you have that type of security in place from day one here, or...?" Pamas watched Darmiya make her way to a chair over by the dining area and realized that there was no question that couldn't wait until later. "I'm sorry. I need to help Darmiya upstairs, if that's where you want us."

"Yes. I think that's best," Dael said and smiled tenderly at the sight of the wilting young woman. "She's been through a lot today. We all have, but she came close...too close." Clearing her throat, Dael placed a gentle hand on Pamas's lower right arm. "No matter what, I'm glad you're here. Ani will sort things out for herself—so just be patient and take care of our girl over there in the meantime."

"Yes, sir," Pamas answered quietly and walked over to Darmiya. "Hey. What do you say we find you your bed before you fall over—again?" She made sure her voice was gently teasing, as she had some catching up to do with social niceties.

"Clever idea, Pamas. You have a ton of them." Darmiya groaned and stood again. Gazing up the stairs, she groaned a second time. "Way up there?"

"Yes, but don't worry. This time I insist." Lifting Darmiya with one arm around her back and the other under her bent knees, Pamas was momentarily taken back to earlier in the day, when she had climbed down the twisted staircase with Darmiya slung over her shoulders. She forced herself to focus on the fact that Darmiya had made such a fantastic recovery and was all right. And here with her. "There we go." Pamas made her way up the stairs with her precious burden, careful not to stumble because of her own fatigue.

The master-bedroom suite was stunning, but Pamas was only interested in the bed and the en suite bathroom. She placed Darmiya on the big double bed. "Can you manage, or do I need to help you, Dar?" she asked quietly.

"I'm sure I can manage. Oh, damn, perhaps not." Darmiya was stuck in her blouse, giggling without much force behind her mirth. "Just tug, please."

With joined efforts, they managed to undress Darmiya down to her underwear. She looked so adorable where she sat on the side of the bed dressed in only a chemise and briefs. An insistent voice claimed that Darmiya was also the sexiest woman Pamas had ever seen. Telling it to shut up, Pamas knew sharing a bed with this woman would be a strange test of her true feelings when it came to Darmiya Do Voy.

She tucked Darmiya in and stood watching her fall asleep. Darmiya's dark curls spread across the pillow. She lay on her back with both her hands at the level of her face on either side of the pillow. Her chest moved in slow, even breaths, and her legs stirred restlessly, showing that Darmiya was already dreaming. Pamas certainly didn't want Darmiya to suffer any nightmares about today's events, but she couldn't do anything to prevent that possibility. At least she would be there if Darmiya woke up afraid or in pain.

Entering the bathroom, Pamas nearly wept at the sight of the large aqua shower. The best thing about being planetside was the abundance of water. She removed her clothes and grinned as she saw the recycler over next to the double sink. Pushing her underwear and uniform through the unit, she watched them materialize new and fresh at the exit slot. After she took off her eyepatch, she stepped into the shower, ran it hot and hard, and closed her eye at the onslaught of water. For the first time, ever since she escaped, she thought she might make an appointment with an ophthalmologist after they completed their mission. It was probably high time to lose the eyepatch—and shed some of the old Pamas as well.

CHAPTER FIFTEEN

Darmiya shifted, trying to wrap the bedding closer around her. The covers seemed to be stuck, but she was reluctant to wake up any more than she already had. It was always so hard for her to fall back asleep if she did. Grabbing the covers, she gave them a good tug. A muted *ooph* sound from behind made her instantly wide awake.

"What the...?" Darmiya sat up, ordering the lights on twenty percent. Nothing happened.

"This is a traditionalist house, Dar," a husky voice muttered. "You have to tap the sensor above you next to the light fixture."

Wait. Husky voice, yes, but still familiar. "Pamas?" Darmiya's heart accelerated and thundered against her ribs.

"The very same. Why are you awake? You in pain?" Clearly Pamas had pressed said sensor, as soft light filled the pitch-black room. Next to Darmiya, Pamas sat up, her hand covering her left eye—or rather, where her left eye should have been.

"No. I'm just cold," Darmiya said absentmindedly. She was focused on Pamas's face, framed by her shiny, dark hair. It reached just beneath her shoulders, and whoever had hacked it off was obviously not a trained stylist. Still, the choppy style suited the weathered woman next to her.

"I may have hogged the covers," Pamas said, and was now beginning to squirm and look awkward. This was definitely an expression Darmiya hadn't seen on Pamas's face before. Normally Pamas cultivated an indifferent look, or one of slight annoyance or disdain.

"That's all right. I suppose neither of us is used to sharing a bed, no matter how big." Darmiya pushed her own large curls from her face. "And you never have to hide your injury from me, unless it makes you uncomfortable. I'd be lying if I said it doesn't bother me. It does, but not in the way you may think, or fear. Your injury bothers me because they hurt you. They had no right. They took you and hurt you. I'm so very sorry."

Pamas still held her hand over her missing eye, resting her elbow on the knee of her bent leg. "They did. And others wounded you. They destroyed your world and your home." Pamas cleared her throat. "And then you lost people on *Espies Major*. You haven't gone through life unscathed."

"True. But I have all my body parts and organs intact. I don't want you to feel you have to hide any part of yourself from me. If you'd rather do so anyway, know that it is only because you feel it necessary." Tugging the covers up over her shoulders, Darmiya lay down again. She turned to face Pamas, who, and it wasn't hard to see, was mulling over Darmiya's words.

"I have repelled several people, and even if I tell myself I don't care since I don't know them, it's not true. It does matter to me. Honestly, I'm pretty much over the fact that I lost one of my eyes. Luckily my vision in my right eye is perfect. Sometimes my depth perception leaves something to be desired, but it could have been worse. They could have damaged both my eyes."

They could have killed you, Darmiya thought, but stopped her morbid thoughts before Pamas caught onto them. Pointing out the obvious wouldn't help Pamas. "You've seen me in several vulnerable situations, and we've known each other only a few days, not counting the ones you isolated yourself."

"I have." Nodding slowly, Pamas lowered her left hand from her face.

Darmiya hadn't known what to expect and thus had envisioned the worst. Now when the soft light fell upon Pamas's face, Darmiya sighed in relief. No creepy, monster-like, blood-filled hole met her cautious gaze. Instead, it merely looked like Pamas was asleep on her left side. Yes, there was scarring. The eyelid had sunken in a fraction of what it most likely had been before the injury. "I'm sorry they hurt you, Pamas." Shuffling over to Pamas's side of the bed and taking her left hand, she kissed the weathered skin on Pamas's knuckles.

Pamas trembled, and for a terrifying moment, Darmiya thought she would either leave the room or fly into a fit of rage. Surely a person who had been subjected to kidnapping and torture carried a lot of resentment and anger? But instead, Pamas covered both her eyes with her unsteady right hand. Darmiya was about to object when she realized that Pamas acted because of an entirely different reason. Tears appeared from behind Pamas's hand and ran down her cheeks.

"Oh, no..." Certainty that she had somehow managed to wound this amazing woman sliced at Darmiya's already aching heart. "I'm sorry, Pamas. I really am."

"No. Not you. Not your fault." Inhaling deeply through her nose, Pamas lowered her hand after wiping at her tears. "I tend to respond like this whenever I experience a new first."

Darmiya carefully scooted closer to Pamas and wrapped an arm around her waist. As Pamas wore only a white tank top and matching briefs, nothing kept Darmiya from feeling how her ribs jutted out. This was puzzling, as Darmiya had witnessed Pamas eating normal amounts on several occasions. Perhaps something had been done to her while in captivity to disturb her metabolism?

Gently, Darmiya stroked Pamas's back in soothing circles. She was at a loss as to whether Pamas found this gesture reassuring, but she hoped so.

"So, what first was this?" Darmiya really was interested. It was an honor to be part of a person's firsts, especially when it came to Pamas. Darmiya had never felt this protective. Yes, she had always looked out for her brother, and he totally reciprocated, but to want to care for someone with such a personal, strong conviction—this was new.

"Compassion. Void of dismay or artificial interest. Genuine caring. And to be able to show myself, and not just my damned eye, but to be me and not feel so damn guilty, if only right here, right now...so rare." Slumping back onto her pillow, Pamas pulled Darmiya with her.

Pamas reached up and pressed the sensor of the light fixture, turning it off. "There's only so much I can take at a time," she said, but Darmiya could hear a faint smile in her voice.

Darmiya wasn't sure when she might get another chance to hold Pamas like this. She gently wrapped her arms more firmly around her. "Just let me hold you for a little while. You might actually grow to like it. I just wish..."

"What?" Pamas whispered.

"Nothing. Just silly." Her cheeks burning, Darmiya hid her face against Pamas's neck. "You know. Typical for me."

"I know nothing of the sort," Pamas said firmly. She shifted her arms and wound them around Darmiya's neck. "I have no idea what happened to make people more or less brainwash you into thinking you're some silly airhead. Nothing could be further from the truth. I find all aspects of your personality fascinating and charming."

Darmiya laughed, a short pitiful bark. "Then you're clearly one of my firsts too."

Suddenly rolling them, making Darmiya end up on her back, Pamas was now half on top of her. Darmiya lost her breath. "Oh."

"Oh, indeed." Pamas's voice sounded strained. "You have no idea how you affect me, do you? How could you? You're very young—far too young."

"For what? For whom?" Darmiya wasn't angry, merely stunned. "F-for you?"

"Oh, definitely far too young for me," Pamas said, "and I'm not just thinking about years, weeks, and days. I've lived a whole life in a way that ages a person beyond belief. To even consider taking you on that journey…would be utterly selfish."

"Then…why are you trembling so hard against me?" Darmiya wasn't sure where her courage to contradict Pamas came from. She only knew she had to argue any points the other woman made that would put distance between them before they even had the slightest chance to grow close.

"Despite my attempts to act with valor, I'm just human. I'm here. You're here. You. And I'm not made of stone."

"So, you find me attractive?" Darmiya shifted and made sure Pamas felt every part of her undeniable curves against her. Was this playing dirty? Perhaps. Then again, they could die from a black-garnet explosion any day, so who cared if she had to resort to this strategy?

"Oh, sweet Creator, I do." Groaning now, Pamas lowered herself firmly onto Darmiya and captured her lips in a kiss that seared through all Darmiya's defenses.

Whether Pamas intended for Darmiya to respond the way she did, or experience such a revelation, was unclear. As Darmiya wrapped her arms more firmly around Pamas and kissed her back, one kiss after another, deep and passionate, all she could think about was how much she loved Pamas Seclan.

CHAPTER SIXTEEN

D ar, this isn't…I'm sorry." Pamas tried to stop the caresses, but feeling the soft curves under her own wiry body was so alluring, she had to bite the tip of her tongue until she nearly bled to get a grip on herself.

"Don't apologize. Please, don't. If you don't want to do this, that's all right. Of course it is. Just don't say you're sorry." The hurt tone in Darmiya's voice made Pamas wince. She was too out of practice, both when it came to physical love and the tender heart of young people. She just knew that she hated hurting this woman and would rather lose her other eye than do so.

"I'm not sorry. Well, that's not entirely true. I'm sorry for my appalling sense of timing, but not for kissing you. How could I be? You're amazing, and so wonderful to hold, I'd have to be dead not to respond to you." Pamas wasn't sure her frank words expressed how she felt. She cupped Darmiya's face in the dark and pressed her lips to her forehead.

"I wish you weren't the noble kind." Darmiya sighed. "Or that I was sexy and experienced enough to make you forget about timing and such things."

"Creator, don't say things like that!" Groaning, Pamas hid her face against Darmiya's neck. "I'm really trying to do the right thing and not—not just take what I want. I'm not like that. Or at least I didn't used to be." Her throat ached, and she wanted to drown in this woman, forget about everything that had happened to her the last twenty years. She could simply kiss Darmiya again, taste her, and explore the emotions simmering under her skin once she was near this vibrant young woman.

"But who says restraining ourselves is the right thing? What if the right thing is to let go and give ourselves over to what we really want? It's hardly a secret that I'm attracted to you." Darmiya pushed her fingers into Pamas's hair. "And I may be a science nerd who's happiest at my computer or conducting tests, but I've seen how you look at me at times. I chalked it up to wishful thinking, but…clearly there's more to it than that."

"I had no idea I'm that transparent." Pamas wasn't sure she liked that part of what Darmiya just said, but it still didn't quite matter to her when Darmiya was running her blunt nails along her scalp, making her shiver. "Damn. I want you so much, it hurts. I…I don't know…I just don't know how to handle this." Pamas was aware she had opened a door to her inner self that had been firmly closed and locked ever since she was taken. She needed to close it again, or she might end up hurting both Darmiya and herself.

"Why not let everything happen, you know, little by little… and besides, considering what our current mission is, what we're forced to fight against, who knows if we'll be around later? I'm not saying we should do this because we might die tomorrow. That's not what I mean. But, that said, we shouldn't waste time." Darmiya's voice trembled.

"I agree. We shouldn't." Pamas's mind whirled with fantasies about Darmiya's curvy body, her full lips, and the cascading dark curls. "You know…I think being close like this, just holding you, doesn't feel like wasting our time at all. Not to me. Remember. I've been out of commission, so to speak, for so long. Holding you, and oh, Creator, kissing you, is a miracle I never thought I'd live to experience."

Darmiya lay still beneath Pamas. Then she rolled them onto their sides. "You're right." She sounded calmer, even happier in an odd sort of way. "And if you still want me later, after we've dealt with this impending disaster, we could really, you know, take our time."

If she would want her? Pamas nearly snorted in disbelief. She couldn't imagine being able to resist this woman ever again. "I hope you won't change your mind," Pamas said lightly and pulled Darmiya onto her shoulder.

"No. Never!" Darmiya moved as if to sit up, but Pamas pulled her down with gentle hands.

"I wasn't being serious, Dar." She kissed the top of the curly head, inhaling the sweet scent that was all Darmiya. "You're the most loyal, honest person I've ever met."

Darmiya relaxed and snuck an arm around Pamas's waist. "I try to be, but I'm not perfect. Don't put me on some pedestal as 'young, unspoiled, and innocent.'"

"I promise I won't." It was almost impossible to not do so, though. In Pamas's eyes, Darmiya was all of that. Most of all, Pamas was afraid of hurting Darmiya, as she realized the risk of doing that was great. With her past, where she had done things she wasn't proud of in order to survive, she was light-years away from the fresh-faced woman in her arms. Still, and perhaps that was a testament to her own selfishness, she couldn't stay away from Darmiya. Maybe she did have a chance to find some sort of happiness, even if it couldn't last.

Darmiya moved up and caressed Pamas's cheek with the back of her bent fingers. "May I kiss you good night. Again?" Her voice contained a shy smile.

"You don't need to ask, but yes. Please."

Darmiya's lips pressed gently against Pamas's and nibbled their way from one corner of her mouth to the other. Running her tongue along Pamas's lower lip, she clearly asked to be granted access. Pamas knew they were playing with fire but parted her lips and invited Darmiya's inquisitive tongue in to play with hers. Moaning without meaning to, Pamas tilted her head to allow Darmiya to find a better angle. Only when Pamas's hands attempted to find Darmiya's breasts almost automatically did Pamas slow down the kisses and gently pull back.

"Mmm..." Darmiya merely snuggled closer and pulled the covers up around them. "In the nick of time, Pamas."

"Excuse me?" Pamas blinked into the darkness.

"If you hadn't stopped me right there, I might have renegotiated our whole agreement and insisted on having my way with you." She pressed her lips against Pamas's neck. Pamas could feel Darmiya smile again and knew she was half teasing.

"Next time, I may not have the strength of character to stop anything you do." Pamas rolled one of Darmiya's curls around her fingers.

"Oh, good."

Pamas hid her face in Darmiya's hair, hoping they would get another chance to know each other—and not just physically. Everything was happening at warp speed, and they were up against some resourceful, innovative people who clearly didn't fear death. Pamas wasn't afraid of it when it came to herself. When it threatened her children and Darmiya, though, it was an entirely different matter. When she was a prisoner, the thought of her children had kept her strong and on point. Now, when she knew that her children—and the woman in her arms—were in danger, she experienced fear like she'd never known it before.

"Sleep now, Dar," Pamas murmured and inhaled Darmiya's fresh, intoxicating scent. She knew she wouldn't sleep. Right now, they were safe, and Pamas refused to waste time and sleep away what might be their last moments together.

CHAPTER SEVENTEEN

A dense fog made it impossible to see where the line of soldiers began or ended. Darmiya pulled the fastening of her jacket closed all the way up to her neck. The backpack she wore weighed almost twenty kilos. She wasn't complaining. Thanks to some modifications of several hoverskids, they would be transporting their scientific equipment on some hovercarts rather than on their backs. Darmiya was also well aware that the soldiers carried at least twice her load.

"Creator of all things, it's cold," a bright voice said next to Darmiya.

Turning her head, Darmiya saw that Caya and Briar had arrived, dressed similarly to her and wearing their own backpacks. The president had long thought it possible to keep the sisters safe aboard cube one, but according to Adina and Korrian, Caya had been the one explaining why they needed to go on this mission. Korrian had chuckled when she relayed how Tylio had contemplated coming along as well but eventually saw reason.

"It'll get better once the suns are fully up," Darmiya now reassured Caya.

"I hope so. I hate the cold. If I could, I'd live on a beach in a tropical climate." Shuddering, Caya rubbed her arms through the sleeves. "How about you? Where on Gemosis did you grow up?"

Grateful for some distraction, Darmiya said, "In the southern hemisphere, in Delosis, the capital. Luckily, my brother Calagan and I were on an assignment up north when the earthquakes began. Delosis was destroyed within the first hour."

"I'm so sorry. I shouldn't have asked. Trust me to bring up the hard memories." Caya looked mortified.

"It's all right. It really is. I've talked about this with Calagan, Spinner, and Dael many times. Only way to work through it. Seeing so many Gemosians all around me in the camps also helps." Darmiya meant it. She found it easier to breathe now when she saw her countrymen and women—not to mention lots of children—milling around the temporary habitats.

"You're very strong. It's something I can sense without reading you." Caya smiled faintly. "And very, very intelligent."

Darmiya tilted her head and scanned the petite woman before her. "Thank you. We were all chosen for this mission for our respective strong suits."

"So true." Caya nodded somberly. "This is going to be difficult. And dangerous."

"Yes." Darmiya already knew this. Having gone over the maps, memorizing every single one of them in case they lost their use of technology, she knew exactly how the terrain alone could make things difficult. Once they were within scanning distance of the location of the black garnet, things could either go very wrong or be resolved. Those were the two outcomes. Success or failure. Shuddering, Darmiya tugged at the shoulder straps of her backpack and adjusted it.

A loud whistle got everyone's attention. Darmiya unfolded her personal hoverskid and held the stick against her hip. Around her, soldiers and the few civilians that were deploying did the same.

"Attention! Dael called out via a loudspeaker. We are going to run one last test of everyone's augmented communicators. Once we do that, we will move out."

Darmiya heard a series of beeps and metallic noises from the team, and her communicator went off in a familiar diagnostic pattern. So far so good. She grabbed the stick and mounted the hoverskid. Next to her, Briar joined Caya, each on her own hoverskid.

"There you are," Pamas said as she appeared on Darmiya's left. "All set, I see."

"Sure am." Darmiya tried to maintain the casual tone she'd strived to use around Pamas ever since she'd woken up in her arms. Pamas had either decided to take her cue from Darmiya, or she was equally nervous and taken aback by their attraction. In Darmiya's case, her emotions went way beyond attraction. She loved this woman with all her heart and had no idea how it had all happened so fast. Perhaps her short infatuation with Spinner when they were aboard *Espies Major* together had been the precursor of these overwhelmingly strong feelings.

Pamas—along with Adina, Korrian, and Lieutenant Dodgmer—was one of the officers in charge of their part of the convoy. Four more security officers belonged to their group, and Darmiya made sure she knew their names. You never knew when calling a person's name might save their life—or yours.

Another loud tone sounded, and Dael's voice came over their communicators.

"I'm looking at this team of forty military personnel and civilians, and I feel reassured that you will carry out your assignments with valor. As you know, I'll lead the security team at the front. Commander Weniell will command the security officers taking up the rear. The two teams between us each have five security officers as well as other military experts. I know I've briefed everyone on this already, but the scientists are the key members of this mission. Without their knowledge and expertise, we won't stand a chance of dealing with the terrorists or their black garnet." A brief silence. "We're moving out now. The president asked me to convey how much faith she has in you. Walk, or should I say ride, in heavenly splendor."

Pamas glanced around her as the forty souls mounted their hoverskids. They had all been outfitted with energy sources that wouldn't need charging until they reached the destination where they would make camp for the night. Adina was a brilliant engineer, and the way she had worked with her team to spruce up the hoverskids was impressive. When Darmiya maneuvered her hoverskid to ride next to Pamas, she could feel how much more smoothly it moved

"I hope the fog doesn't ease up until we're out of sight of the capital." Pamas glanced behind her. "I don't like the idea of having traitors in our midst, but the less people figure out where we've gone, the better."

"The true terrorists might suspect that we're onto them and warn the ones potentially guarding the black garnet," Darmiya said, riding closer to Pamas so she didn't have to raise her voice. "I mean, it's only logical that a missing group of scientists and soldiers would be out on a mission to catch them."

"Possibly. But they won't know which exact direction we're going to get there." Gripping the stick harder, Pamas clenched her jaw. "Unless they have, what did Caya call them, super changers, among them that can somehow see it."

Darmiya pondered that possibility. "At least we know we have super changers with us, and they're on our side. On the right side." She looked over at Caya and Briar, who rode their hoverskids, with Adina close by. "If something sinister awaited us, Caya would sense it."

"Unless an even more powerful changer blocks her." Pamas shook her head. "I'm sorry, Dar. I'm being the pessimist here when we need to focus on succeeding."

"Well, I'm usually the born optimist, so that should balance things out." Darmiya hoped her recent bout with depression hadn't hampered her ability to look at things from the bright side. Oddly enough, since meeting Pamas, the part that never thought she'd ever feel any better or be herself had lost its grip on her. Even if she wasn't quite her former bubbly, spontaneous self, not yet, she could tell she wasn't the apathic hermit she had been in danger of becoming either.

"We complement each other, you mean? Sounds good." Pamas smiled.

"I think we do." Darmiya knew she blushed but tried to act nonchalant.

The convoy of hoverskid riders made its way toward the valley leading to the mountains. The easy route followed the river in the valley toward their goal, but Darmiya, Dael, and Spinner had mapped out another, less-apparent one. It would take them around a few of the mountains and also add a few hours to their journey.

The deities seemed to have fulfilled Pamas's wish. Just after they took off into the less-traveled area leading to the mountains, the fog lifted and showed scenery that was so beautiful, Darmiya gasped—as always. "Aren't the colors more brilliant here on Gemocon than anywhere else in the entire universe?" she asked, smiling broadly. "I mean, look at the small yellow flowers over there on that hillside. They're so little, we shouldn't be able to spot them at all, merely see them as one big yellow blur, but they're so intense, we can see every single, individual petal. Can you imagine anything like that back on Oconodos? We certainly didn't have anything like that on Gemosis. We hardly had any wildflowers left, due to the environmental problems." She stopped talking when Pamas looked at her strangely. "I'm sorry. I'm babbling. Again."

"No. Don't stop. Do you have any idea how amazing it is to be here next to you, listening to your exuberance over a flower, when all I saw for a very long time was humid, mosquito-infested jungles and damp, dark bunkers? I could easily listen to you all day."

Warmth erupted in Darmiya's chest, and she had to deliberately focus on riding her hoverskid so she wouldn't fall off and make a fool of herself. But Pamas liked listening to her. How was that even possible? Pamas, who had lived through such hard and dark times, who seemed entirely serious and aloof—what did she see in Darmiya, who so often was told she needed to act her age and be serious to a degree that suited her profession and level of genius?

"Dar?" Pamas sounded concerned, which made Darmiya snap out of her self-doubt.

"Sorry. I just don't get that a lot. Normally, people tell me I'm a bit...much. Except Calagan, Spinner, and Dael. Even Helden puts up with my chatter most of the time." Shrugging, Darmiya forced herself to smile but cringed at how she sounded. Pitiful.

Pamas frowned and steered her hoverskid closer to Darmiya. "Trust me. Those who complain don't deserve you. How they can be so callous to a warmhearted person such as you, it...it makes me furious. You're nothing short of amazing. If anyone tells you differently, or makes your feel anything less than that, they're wrong."

Darmiya was stunned. Nobody, not even Calagan, had spoken to her, about her, like that. "All right," she managed to say. "I'll, um, I'll keep that in mind." Tears burned behind her eyelids, but she refused to let them flow. She was on a mission that might mean life or death for the people they were there to save. She refused to come across as shallow enough to care more about what people thought of her than what safeguards her expertise could bring. "Thank you." She whispered the last words but knew Pamas heard her since she reached out and very briefly squeezed her arm.

The scenery shifted when they reached the first tall mountain. They planned to go through a pass that Darmiya had explored with her brother on one of their first missions after setting down on the planet. It would be a challenge to get through it since it was partly a tunnel that an underground river existing more than a hundred thousand years ago had made.

As they reached the pass, Dael rode up to Darmiya's group, stopping next to Pamas. "Here's where we need Darmiya and Calagan to be our guides, as they're the ones who've been this way before."

"We were obviously not on hoverskids then," Darmiya said, "but the tunnel is tall enough that we will get through if we're careful and stick to the center of it. I suggest, though, that our tallest guys keep their heads down."

"I'll relay that fact to them," Dael said. "Lieutenant Seclan, bring Darmiya and Calagan up front. You and Spinner will be responsible for these civilians when you lead the way."

"Aye, sir." Pamas nodded briskly and motioned for Darmiya and Calagan to follow her. Riding past the first group of the team, Darmiya focused on the opening of the tunnel. "Don't forget to switch on your head- and footlights. We have no way of knowing if the tunnel is intact." Spinner and Pamas nodded, and they all pressed the sensor on their arm consoles, making the lamps on their helmets and their boots light up the narrow passage before them.

The tunnel was as damp and cold as last time. Darmiya had taken samples from the walls, and Calagan had found some fungi he had hoped would have some medicinal benefits. Now they weren't going to bother with any such discoveries but simply get the team through the tunnel safely. Darmiya remembered a spot about halfway through where the ceiling seemed to cave in. Reaching it, Darmiya saw it had indeed done just that. A large block lay halfway on the ground and partly up against the side of the tunnel. Stopping her hoverskid, she jumped off and hurried over to it.

"Damn," she muttered when she saw how big it was. They couldn't possibly budge it without equipment. "Calagan, do we have anything to move it with?"

"No." Calagan frowned. He ran a handheld light over the boulder, cursing under his breath. "Wait. Look here, sis. It's pretty porous, don't you think?"

Darmiya probed the surface of their obstacle and had to agree. They couldn't hack it up by hand, but they could find other means. "Pamas? Can you pass the word back that we need a drill?" She didn't carry one in her special compartment for minor tools. Heavier implements were stored on the hovercarts.

Pamas called out the order, and soon a small but powerful drill was passed forward. "Are you carrying any of the blast powder, Calagan?" Darmiya asked as she eyed the boulder to figure out where she should drill the holes. "I had room for only two bottles."

"I have four. How many do you need? Three?" Calagan pulled off his backpack and helped Darmiya remove hers.

"Yes." Darmiya had found the best spot to start drilling and put on some protective glasses. "Everyone who doesn't have the proper gear on, step back," she said and started the drill. Everyone but Calagan and Pamas stepped away. Glancing up, Darmiya made sure Pamas's eye was covered. It was an automatic reaction on her part, but she filed it away for future reference.

The boulder was very porous. After drilling two holes, Darmiya determined she wouldn't need a third one after all. Pouring in two small bottles of blast powder, one in each hole, she stepped back and motioned for Calagan and Pamas to join her.

"Usually, this doesn't send anything flying, but as the rock is full of cavities and almost spongy, I don't want to risk the powder reacting in ways I can't predict."

A fizzing sound came from the rock, and it began to reverberate.

"Is it supposed to do that?" Pamas asked, tugging at Darmiya to pull her farther back. "That doesn't look right."

"It's not common, no." Darmiya looked in fascination at the rock that appeared to take on a life of its own. "Calagan? Does this seem familiar to you?"

"Not really," her brother said, appearing as captivated as Darmiya felt.

The rock seemed to jump, and a small part of it whipped past them and hit the wall to their right.

"Everybody down!" Pamas yelled and yanked Darmiya onto the ground. "Get down!"

The large boulder was now breaking into smaller pieces, but something inside it, perhaps the fact that it was porous like a sponge and filled with cavities, gave the blast powder too much space to do its job. One after another, small and large chunks of the rock tore past them and struck the walls. Darmiya prayed to the Creator that the projectiles wouldn't hit anyone. The explosion seemed to go on forever, but in reality, it took less than thirty secs for the boulder to turn into minor rubble. Once the large rock was demolished, the rocks stopped showering them.

"Damage report!" Dael called out from her place farther back.

Spinner quickly checked on the ones in the group plus Pamas, Darmiya, and Calagan. "Forward team all well."

One by one the groups called in with good news. Nobody was hurt, and the equipment was unharmed. Darmiya was so relieved she could laugh and cry at the same time, but she harnessed her emotions and sent the drill back to the hovercart where it belonged.

"We can easily pass now. The tunnel widens about twenty meters after this, and then we can move faster." Darmiya mounted her hoverskid and watched Pamas do the same. Spinner followed just behind them as they continued through the tunnel. They had cleared their first hurdle, but Darmiya knew this was nothing compared to what they faced farther into the mountains. Glancing at Pamas, she wondered if being clairvoyant was contagious, as she could easily read the same thoughts on Pamas's face.

"We'll be all right," Darmiya murmured, and smiled gently toward Pamas. "One thing at a time, right?"

Pamas returned the smile, but it was clear it was mostly for Darmiya's benefit. "Damned right, Dar."

CHAPTER EIGHTEEN

Pamas's back ached after riding the hoverskid an entire day. After the tunnel incident, their journey had been uneventful. Every hour they had taken a break, as nobody but Darmiya and Calagan was used to traveling very long on this type of vehicle.

Now they had stopped to make camp, which would allow them six hours to rest and review the last of the plan again. Pamas pulled out the portable habitat from her backpack and placed it on the ground under a protruding cliff that would provide shelter should the weather change unexpectedly. Pressing a sensor by the fastening device, she took a step back and watched the dome inflate to a hemisphere shape. Another tap on the sensor made the habitat open.

"Seems you found the best spot," a voice said behind her. Pamas pivoted and saw her daughter standing there, holding her habitat, still uninflated. "Looks like there's room for more under there." Spinner looked matter-of-fact.

Attempting not to sound too eager, Pamas nodded. "Plenty. Right there will keep you under the cliff as well. I don't think it's going to rain, but...just in case."

"I'm sure the habitats are designed to withstand worse weather than a drizzle, but I get your point." Spinner rolled her shoulders and looked uneasy. "We need to set up one more dome for Commander Vantressa and the Lindemay sisters. Darmiya is sharing with you and her brother with Lieutenant Dodgmer."

"Aye, sir," Pamas answered calmly and pulled one more box from the hovercart. Soon they had put up a semicircle of domes under the protruding cliff. It amazed Pamas how well they worked together, with hardly any verbal communication. Spinner stomped around the dome and fastened it into the hard ground with automatic anchors. Chiding herself, she had to make herself handle them with a bit more care.

"Good meeting?" Pamas asked as Darmiya walked up, looking exhausted.

"Yes. We're on schedule, and the original plan is in place unless something unforeseen comes up." Darmiya rubbed the back of her neck under the high bun. "Creator, what I wouldn't give to crawl straight into bed."

"It's all set up, Dar. All you have to do is slip into your sleeping bag." Smiling at the way Darmiya's eyes grew huge in her pale face, Pamas ran a quick finger along her jawline. But she caught herself before she committed another faux pas and simply pointed in the direction of their dome. "We're sharing, but I have to take care of a few more things before I go to bed."

"I'd offer to help if I wasn't so tired that I've forgotten my name." Rising on her toes, Darmiya kissed Pamas's cheek. "Don't push yourself too hard. I don't mean to sound rude, but you're not in the same shape as these rough, tough soldiers." She raised an eyebrow, clearly meaning what she said.

"Hey, I hear you. And trust me, I can feel it." Pamas smiled wryly. "I'll come to bed soon." Only when her words left her lips did Pamas realize what they sounded like. "Hmm. Well. You know."

Smiling wearily, Darmiya chuckled and waved to the others before ducking into her tent.

Spinner appeared next to Pamas so fast, it was obvious she had been standing close enough to overhear. "What the hell was that about?"

"What are you referring to, sir?" she responded, assuming a bland expression that had served her well during interrogations in the hands of the malevolent changers.

"You know what I mean, *Mother*," Spinner growled, her eyes radiating fury. "Are you using Darmiya as some sort of substitute for the daughter who grew up resenting you for leaving her behind?"

"What?" Pamas was stunned and unable to disguise the hurt Spinner's words caused.

"Don't you think I saw the little caresses and reassuring words? Yes, Darmiya has lost everyone but her brother in the Gemosian disaster, but she doesn't need another mother."

Angry now, and offended, Pamas straightened her back and pushed back her shoulders. "You are perfectly right, Aniwyn. I have no maternal feelings when it comes to Darmiya Do Voy. I still hold out hope for you and me, though. And Pherry. You two were my reasons for living and, later, for getting a ticket to board *Pathfinder*."

"What do you mean, reasons for living?" Hands on her hips, Spinner regarded her with suspicion oozing from every pore. "Are you saying you were suicidal?" At least Spinner had the good taste to look a little embarrassed at her blunt words.

"I was. After I escaped and reached the goal I had planned for, I deflated completely for so many years. Not until I heard how far the Exodus project had come was I able to put together a new plan, something to make me want to go on living. You and Pherry. Your names became my mantras." Pamas looked around them, and oddly enough, everyone else seemed to have gone into their domes. It didn't take a genius such as Darmiya to figure they were giving Pamas and Spinner some much-needed space. "And then we arrive here and all hell breaks loose when everyone is set on starting to plan their future. I don't know about you, but I feel lost." Pamas shrugged.

Rubbing her forehead, Spinner then pushed her fingers through her wild, curly hair. "I know we haven't had a chance to talk or even fully acknowledge, well, anything. I've kept my distance. Not so much because I resent you, not anymore, but I can't just flip a switch and turn my emotions around. They may not be factually accurate anymore, but they are mine, and they're still valid to me." Sighing, Spinner turned and sat down on some boxes on the hovercart. "And I haven't even had time to talk to Pherry. He's going to kill me for it when we get back."

"Do you mean you haven't spoken to him after he disembarked his cube?"

"Of course, I've *talked* to him!" Looking annoyed as she crossed her legs, Spinner narrowed her eyes into cautious slits again. "Just not in person. We've chatted via video-link. We did that when I was still on my assignment. I didn't know about you then."

"Maybe this isn't an appropriate time to discuss this issue, Aniwyn," Pamas said, knowing full well her fatigue showed in her voice. "So much is at stake and—"

"And that's exactly why we can't postpone it forever." Spinner sounded like she was forcing herself to remain calm. "If that black garnet goes off, we might not make it through tomorrow."

Darmiya's heart-shaped face flickered across Pamas's mind. "Don't you think I know that?" she asked quietly. "The irony of traveling across interstellar space to finally be with my children again, hoping against all odds they might want their mother in their lives even if it's been twenty years since—since…" Pamas's voice betrayed her, and she stopped trying to explain. Perhaps it would be hopeless to try after all?

"No!" The harsh tone had disappeared from Spinner's voice, and she stood next to Pamas. "Of course it's not too late. It can't be. I mean, no matter what, we're related. You're our mother. We thought you were dead. We attended your funeral." Spinner's voice became low and husky. She stared off into the darkness outside their well-guarded perimeter. "It was horrible. Pherry was barely a teenager. I was eighteen. That's when I took custody of him and kept him away from our father. He was never very nice, but after you left…"

"I didn't leave, Aniwyn." Pamas wrapped her arms around her waist. She felt as if she needed to hold her intestines together or she might bleed out right then and there.

"I know. I'm sorry. You were taken." Spinner looked up at the sky as if asking the Creator for strength. "Fuck. You were taken and held captive for most of those years, and we had no idea. The investigators told father that everything pointed to your leaving voluntarily since they found all the measures you had taken to escape him and start a new life. Nobody indicated to us, to Pherry and me, that you planned to take us with you. Father, in fact, insisted you had left the three of us. What were we supposed to think?"

"You were children. You had no way of knowing. I realize that. I truly do." Pamas wanted to embrace the tormented woman before her, but too much time had passed. Spinner had lived with her version of what had happened for too long.

"I hated you for abandoning us." Spinner's jaw was set so hard, the arteries on her neck pulsated visibly.

"Spinner? Pamas?" Darmiya's soft voice broke the tension, and Pamas took a step backward, stumbled, and took another one, steadying herself against the bedrock behind her. She slowly turned her head toward Darmiya and saw her standing outside the dome they were going to share. Briar stood by Darmiya's side with an arm around her shoulders.

"We're fine. Everything's fine. We were just, um, talking." Pamas held up her hands, palms forward, as if that would help keep the volatile feelings at bay. Nobody had believed enough in her love for her children to look for her? Was that what Spinner meant? Had everyone assumed she'd left her abusive husband and abandoned her children to fend for themselves? How could she go on knowing that everyone had thought such a lie?

"Pamas," Briar said, approaching her carefully as if Pamas was as unstable as the black garnet they were searching for. "I never read anyone without their express permission, but the emotions flowing between you and Spinner, and also involving Darmiya, are so strong they are actually keeping me from falling asleep."

She stepped closer and held the shivering Darmiya against her. "The changers who abducted you have hurt you so badly, Pamas. You suffered not knowing what happened to your children, as well as the physical and mental pain the changers caused while trying to get you to talk, to give them military intel. And you," Briar said, turning to Spinner, "you lost a mother and were told she had walked out on you and your brother. Then they said she was dead even if they found no body. They held a funeral, and you were supposed to mourn a mother who didn't seem to want you. Now that you know none of that was true, you need each other to get through this. To start over." Smiling gently, Briar held Pamas's gaze. "After we've dealt with this black-garnet situation and have returned to the capital, our offer still stands. We will work with you to help you make it easier, if you want to." Briar motioned at Caya and herself. Turning to Spinner, she smiled gently. "And if your brother wants to join us, that'd be very good for all of you."

"Perhaps by then you can explain why I keep waiting for the ax to fall." Spinner shrugged. "All right. Let's agree to keep this relationship professional and civil until we resolve this situation and get back. If we don't focus on the task at hand, people will be killed."

"Very true." The reprieve relieved Pamas. "Time to tuck you in," she said to Darmiya, who could barely keep her eyes open. "Sorry for keeping you awake." Pamas saw Spinner's eyebrows do a new detour up her forehead, but it was far too late to go into any further explanations—and no matter their history, there were things a mother didn't explain to her children, after all.

After she guided Darmiya into the dome and back into her sleeping bag, the young woman held on to Pamas's hand until she fell back asleep, murmuring something unintelligible.

"Shh. Go back to sleep, Dar. I'm right here." Without letting go of Darmiya's hand, Pamas managed to crawl into her own sleeping bag. Her thoughts strayed to her daughter and the images of her children Pamas had kept in her heart during her entire abduction. A lot had changed and Spinner wasn't the same—but neither was Pamas.

CHAPTER NINETEEN

The morning arrived with the same mist as the day before, only it was much colder this far up in the mountains. When Darmiya woke up, Pamas was already gone. For a moment, she was afraid something was wrong but reeled herself in when she checked her chronometer. It was still very early.

Running a cleansing wand over her body while she was still alone in the dome, she then rolled up her sleeping bag and deflated her pillow. The built-in mattress in the floor of the dome would automatically deflate when they engaged the repacking feature.

Peeking out of the dome, Darmiya spotted Pamas sitting by a smokeless fire in the center of the four domes under the cliff overhang. She was stirring something in a large pot and pouring a dark-brown powder into a large thermo-can.

"Can that be coffee?" Darmiya asked hopefully as she sat down on the boulder next to Pamas. She refused to let their surroundings intimidate her and gave Pamas a soft kiss on her cheek. "Thank you for being so sweet to me when I was so tired last night."

"You're welcome. And yes, it's coffee. From the Limanida sector on Oconodos. Quite strong, actually." Pamas turned her head toward Darmiya and smiled gently. "Feel rested?"

"Yes. I never thought I'd sleep so well while out here. I woke up a few times, but when I did, I...um...well, you were there." Sucking her lower lip in between her teeth, Darmiya met Pamas's eyes through her curls. "Having you near made me feel safe."

Her eyes softening, Pamas placed a hand on Darmiya's knee. "That makes me very happy to hear. I want to be that person for you."

"What person is that?" A bit confused, Darmiya trembled as she waited for Pamas to reply.

Stirring the pot again, Pamas seemed to hesitate. "I want you to be happy, safe, and content. If I can provide at least some of those conditions for you, it will be amazing."

Darmiya could hardly believe her ears. It sounded very much like a declaration of…of…She didn't dare to even think about the word that was so big, so overwhelming. It was obvious to her that she was in love with Pamas. More than that, she loved this woman with all her fluttering heart, and Pamas's words made her dare to believe that Pamas might one day feel something similar. Pamas was damaged in ways she could barely fathom. She had yet to share details with Darmiya, and she had a feeling it would be a while until she did—if ever. For Pamas to show this soft side, when she normally was quite remote and aloof, was promising but by no means a declaration of love.

"You mean so much to me," Darmiya said, wanting Pamas to know that, at least. "And you make me feel many wonderful things." And some frightening, mind-blowing, and confusing things as well.

"Dar," Pamas said and moved her hand to run a thumb along Darmiya's lower lip. "You're the most courageous woman I know. Can you be patient and—"

"Good morning. Am I interrupting?" Caya walked past them and sat down next to Darmiya. "Oh, that smells great. What's in the pot?" She winked at Darmiya, which made her think that Caya knew very well that she'd interrupted.

"Oatmeal." Pamas pulled out bowls. "This will keep you well fed until we reach our destination." Her tone had returned to stoic and professional. "Want me to pour you a cup of coffee, Caya?"

"Yes, please." Caya rubbed her hands.

As they started in on their breakfast, Dael and Spinner joined them, shortly followed by Korrian, Briar, and Adina. The conversation became somber and work-oriented, and Darmiya listened intently, only adding to it when they touched on her area of expertise. Calagan was the last to appear, deeply involved in a conversation with Lieutenant Dodgmer. He clearly noticed how closely Darmiya sat to Pamas, but she refused to respond to his obvious unspoken question. She wanted to be close to Pamas, and if Pamas didn't move away from her, she wasn't going to do so either. Darmiya didn't want to suddenly indulge in fatalism, but who knew what would happen later?

"All right, listen up. I want to stress a few important matters when we approach our goal." Korrian's strong voice silenced everyone. "Be cautious with your weapons. We have no way of knowing how the individuals we are after are storing their black garnet or black-garnet shells. If their technology is incompatible with ours, we might create a large crater where these mountains are standing and obviously kill both them and ourselves in the process. If you need to use a weapon, I suggest knives or batons, possibly weapons that fire darts, like crossbows." She glanced around the ring of people who were all holding mugs of coffee. "We need to keep any chemical at a safe distance, and by that, I mean at least five hundred meters."

"What about our hoverskids?" Caya asked.

"I don't foresee them as a problem, as they run on small reactors. Needless to say, if we find what we're looking for in a cave system, we're not going to hoverskid in there."

Darmiya thought fast. "Once we reach this potential cave system, who will be part of the mission team that goes in first?" She was fairly sure she knew but wanted to find out for sure.

"Good question, Darmiya," Dael said. "We need the team to be small and as inconspicuous as possible. I have talked this over with Admiral Heigel, and we have agreed that you and Caya will do a quick, first scan. Spinner will go in with you to keep you safe, and she will have four security officers on standby just inside the opening. If you run into any individuals, with or without the changer gene, they will assist and apprehend them and bring them out to us. It's important that we pull this mission off in stealth mode." Dael sipped her coffee. "I wish we could have used assault craft and taken them out that way, but even if it had been technically possible to employ any sort of shuttle or freighter, we would have not learned anything about this threat that way."

"Yes, sir." Darmiya nodded. She had guessed she'd be part of it, since garnet compounds were one of her areas of expertise. Next to her, Pamas had gone rigid, and Darmiya knew she resented not being chosen to go in. Darmiya wondered if Dael had picked Spinner because she trusted her more or because she was younger. Perhaps Dael simply needed someone with familiar capabilities. Pamas was still an untried resource to some degree. But she had saved Darmiya and several others already.

"Sir," Pamas said now, "permission to join the team going in." Her hand next to Darmiya's thigh was clenched in a tight fist.

Dael tilted her head as she seemed to size Pamas up for the thousandth time but then nodded slowly. "You can't go in with Darmiya, Spinner, and Caya, but you can be part of the security crew just behind them." Her expression softening, she smiled faintly. "I am not insensitive to the fact that one person going in is your daughter and the other your…friend. I cannot allow personal relationships to play a part in the mission, but you have proved yourself able to provide excellent protection."

Pamas exhaled slowly, as if she'd been holding her breath. Darmiya scooted closer as inconspicuously as possible. When the rest started another discussion as they finished their coffee, Darmiya took Pamas's hand. "I'm glad you're going in with us."

"As am I." Turning her hand under Darmiya's, Pamas squeezed it gently. "We'll get through this, Dar. I promise. And once we're back at the capital, we're going to…talk." She gazed into Darmiya's eyes for what seemed like minutes. "If you want to."

"I do." Her sudden fear that one single black-garnet molecule could so easily snuff out this hope of something new and wonderful broke her heart.

Around them, everyone rose and began deflating the domes and packing their gear. Darmiya ran a quick hand along Pamas's tight ponytail as she got up and followed suit. Now she should focus only on the task at hand. She was part of the main team and held a lot of responsibility, and she couldn't fail her fellow Gemoconians. Caya was going in as the expert on changers and their abilities. She would be the one who could sense danger and give them a chance to act accordingly. Spinner, the best friend Darmiya had ever had, would have their backs as they examined the place that the black-garnet shells indicated. And Pamas would be Spinner's backup in case they ran into serious trouble. It was a sound plan, albeit a rather desperate one. They had to fix this problem, or their new world would never be the safe haven they had dreamed of for decades.

Darmiya packed the last of her things on one of the hovercarts and then mounted her hoverskid. As they took off, following Briar's and Caya's directions so as not to tip off the terrorists, Darmiya told herself they would be successful. They had to be. And no matter what, when they returned to the capital, she would tell Pamas how much she loved her.

CHAPTER TWENTY

The cave, according to the careful scans Korrian had done from a safe distance, was part of a vast system that reached at least two kilometers into the mountain. Pamas stood next to the older admiral and glanced furtively at her tablet, where Korrian entered notes to pass on to the team going in.

Dael came up behind them, together with Spinner. "I have altered some of the tactical approach. When I saw the myriad of tunnels leading to countless caves, I decided we need more boots on the ground in there. Admiral, I need you out here to relay information between us and the ECC. Once we go in, they'll know we're there sooner or later."

"Understood." Korrian nodded briskly. "Here's the latest data. The first cave is large but empty, as far as I can tell. My scans show no traps or people."

"Neither do mine. Briar is wary of trying to read any potential minds in there, since that would give away our presence," Caya said, "but I can scan for individuals very shallowly, and as far as I can tell, none are in the first cave. I do sense a presence of someone, or something, farther in. I'm not sure, but I'm seeing... green? I know it sounds completely weird, but that's what I see. Also, a feeling that I'm being blocked. I mean, not me personally, but something is blocking my ability to some degree."

Pamas studied the petite young woman, this changer who had intimidated so many aboard *Pathfinder* but won the heart of the president. She could only imagine how the president loathed to have Caya and so many of the ones she had befriended on a personal level here, in danger.

"I say we push forward, Admiral," Korrian said to Dael. "The longer we wait—"

"The greater the risk of being discovered becomes." Dael looked at the team that was ready to leave. "Go in heavenly splendor. Once you are inside, we'll all move into position and will be on standby to give you whatever backup you may need. Remember that the communicators don't work in there. I know firsthand how normal it is for us to rely on them on a daily basis. So much that it's part of our lives to just slap the damn thing to reach the one we need to talk to. Be prepared to communicate verbally, person to person, and that's how you form lines of communications back to us." She smiled wanly. "I know, I know. I'm not saying anything you don't already know. Who would have thought I could become such a mother hen?"

Even Pamas had to smile at that exaggeration. Dael Caydoc was a formidable leader, a hero among their people, and nobody could ever accuse her of hovering or not following protocol. Pamas couldn't have dreamed of a better partner for her daughter. She prayed she would get the chance to know both Spinner and Dael really well one day.

"All right. Saddle up, so to speak, people," Spinner said, taking command as the highest-ranking officer going in. "I go in first, with a security officer, to clear the first cave. We will signal the rest of you once we've done that. All right?"

"Yes, sir," the security officers said in unison, gripping their batons and knives.

As they hurried along the bedrock that gave them protection from being visually detected, Pamas made sure Darmiya and Caya were right next to her the entire time. She wouldn't lose any of the three she was there to protect.

❖

The cave opening was narrow, approximately two meters wide and low enough for the tallest of the men to have to bend their necks as they stepped inside. Darmiya stood next to Pamas just behind some shrubs, keeping a steady grip on the straps of her backpack. She carried a lot of the vital, fragile instruments, some of which she meant to put up in the outer cave and some farther inside.

One of the security officers reappeared and made the all-clear sign. Spinner stepped in front of Darmiya and Caya, taking the lead as they approached the cave entrance. Darmiya cast a glance upward and immediately wished she hadn't, as the tall, looming mountain seemed to move toward her as clouds passed in the opposite direction. It was nice outside now, sunny and with a lovely, sweet-scented breeze. The idea of stepping into damp caves didn't appeal to her. She looked at Spinner, who walked with long, certain strides, carrying a crossbow loaded with carbon-fiber arrows. Normally, the military-grade crossbows used high-tech projectiles, but in this case, those were out of the question.

They passed the opening and entered the cave. The only signs of anyone being there before them were a few lanterns and some empty crates by the left wall. The bottom of the cave consisted of bedrock partly covered with dirt. Darmiya nodded at Caya and Spinner and pulled off her backpack. "This will take me a few minutes, but I'll be ready to continue once I have my first readings."

"Then I'll do some readings of my own." Completely disregarding the dirt on the floor, Caya sat down, crossed her legs, and clasped her hands. With her eyes closed, she began rocking slightly back and forth.

Darmiya's fingers flew across the small boxes as she took out her pre-calibrated measuring devices. Most of these, she had built herself, and even if they weren't originally intended for this purpose, she hadn't had to change very much to make them scan for black-garnet nuclei as well as the shells. She placed the instruments against the right wall, where she unfolded a small shelf for them. Quickly checking the diagnostics that automatically occurred prior to the scanning, she saw the most important instrument was working as it should. Turning her head back over her shoulder, she saw Spinner stand just behind her. "It's scanning."

Caya stood and came over. "I'm starting to think something is really strange about this substance, the black garnet. I can see scattered images of people in long robes, either black, blue, or gray, and even naked bodies, for some reason, but I get no context. The same with the sounds. Rumbling, noisy, and with chanting... or something similar to chanting."

"Perhaps you will get better readings when we go in farther," Spinner said, sounding hesitant. "Though, if your strange results are due to the black garnet, it might get worse."

"We won't know until we try." Caya shrugged, but the dark shadows beneath her eyes emphasized her paleness, making her look close to transparent.

Darmiya heard a faint tone from her major instrument and tapped the screen. "I read a lot of black-garnet shells. From the data, I would assume they keep them in canisters. We would be getting sick if it weren't stored securely, so that makes sense." She pulled up another screen and tried to decipher the numbers. "Damn, this doesn't add up. I get a reading of black garnet, but it's barely showing up. I realize it must be contained meticulously, but still. If they have the same amount of black garnet as they have shells, the readings should be through the roof."

"Any of those instruments portable?" Spinner asked.

"Yes. This one. I can wear it attached to my harness." Strapping the smaller scanner onto her chest, Darmiya stood. "Ready."

"Good. We've been lucky that they haven't detected us yet. Perhaps their powers are compromised in the same way yours are, Caya."

"Would be logical," Caya said, closing the fastening of her coverall. "The same mutated genes supposedly affects all of us."

"I don't compare you to them, Caya," Spinner said seriously. "I hope you know that."

"I know. Truly. But perhaps you should."

"What?" Darmiya was appalled. "You're a hero, Caya, they are...they're..."

"I only mean compare us in the sense that we may be more alike physically than we are different." Caya swallowed hard. "I will submit myself for extensive testing when we get back. It's vital."

"Sweet Creator," Darmiya muttered as they began walking toward the inner part of the cave. "That will go down brilliantly with the president."

"Not her decision," Caya said darkly. "I love her, but I make my own decisions."

Darmiya was about to reply but thought better of it, as they needed to stay focused. Still, there was no way the president would allow anyone to experiment on Caya. She could think of a few people, including herself, that would strongly object. There were other ways to do things than perform experiments on humanoids.

The inner part of the cave was damper, to such a degree that moisture ran off the walls. The opening into the next area went through a thicker wall in the bedrock, and it was only a meter wide and even lower than the previous entry. Spinner led the way, holding her crossbow at chest level. Darmiya made sure she was next, keeping her eyes on the readings and praying that the small amount of electricity in her instrument wouldn't cause any problems as they walked farther into the tunnel. Behind them, one security guard, who took up the rear, would also guard the next entrance until they moved on.

"I hear chanting, a weird kind of buzzing almost." Caya tapped Darmiya on the shoulder. "Tell Spinner to be careful."

"I heard," Spinner muttered before Darmiya had time to open her mouth. "I'm feeling some strange vibrations. Can that have anything to do with the buzzing, Caya?"

"No idea, but it sounds plausible." Caya came up and hooked her arm with Darmiya's. "I don't mean to invade your personal space, but I need to touch someone normal to clear my head. That buzzing is getting to me."

Darmiya, who until now rarely thought of how young Caya was, patted her arm. "We are stronger in numbers, or so my brother always says. Then again, he is a mathematician, among other things. I bet he's quite upset that he wasn't chosen to go inside. I wager you a serving of ice cream with berries that he's in a sprinter's start position at the cave entry."

Caya giggled quietly, and it warmed Darmiya that she had managed to distract the young changer. She was perhaps in a unique position to know what it was like to carry such a huge responsibility at such a young age. Back on Gemosis, Darmiya and Calagan were the golden children in the world of science and soon also the go-to people when unusual solutions were required.

"Heads up." Spinner murmured. "Next entrance in ten meters."

Darmiya glanced at her instrument. "Readings are stable," she said quietly.

"Good. Stay back a few secs." Spinner sent a mirror attached to an extendable rod through the opening, angling back and forth. "Lots of instruments but void of people. Let's move in. Stay behind me. Keep very quiet."

Darmiya and Caya joined Spinner just inside the opening. Looking around the green-tinted cave, Darmiya felt her mouth fall open. Throughout the tall cave, row after row of tall, square canisters gave off a green glow. Screens attached to all of them showed different readings.

"What is that?" Caya whispered.

"These canisters must hold the black-garnet shells. That's far more than what permeated the air after the explosions." Darmiya moved slowly along the wall toward the closest canister. It did buzz some. Perhaps that was what Caya had sensed? As soon as she was close enough to read the data on the screen, Darmiya knew she had been correct but also so very—and horrifyingly—wrong. She flipped open the side of her instrument and started receiving more readings, this time a lot easier to make sense of, no matter how gut-wrenching.

"What about this?" Spinner showed a row of five canisters. "They're glowing red instead of green. They can't contain black garnet, can they?"

Darmiya hurried among the canisters over to Spinner. Caya still stood by the entrance, her arms folded around her and her head lowered.

"None of these canisters hold any pure black garnet," Darmiya said, wiping at an errant tear. "Let me check these red ones." She ran her scanner along the red-tinted, tall, metal-and-glass objects. "Creator of all things sacred. Save us from these sins. Save us from this evil." Her voice broke.

"What the hell?" Spinner blanched as she regarded Darmiya. "What's wrong?"

Darmiya swallowed back against the tears and forced herself to remain focused. "These five canisters hold five humans. Three men and two women."

Spinner looked at the screen, and Darmiya pointed out the readings showing heart rate, respiration, blood pressure, and metabolism. "Fuck. So, these five are humanoid? Not changers?"

"I can't be sure, but—"

"No," Caya said dazedly from the opening they had come in through. "Not changers. I would sense if they were changers. We must save them. They can't be in there by their own volition."

"Wait a minute," Spinner said, holding up a hand. "If these are humanoid, what are the others? All the green ones?"

Darmiya gazed around the cave. All the green reflecting on the wet walls gave it an eerie ambiance. Knowing what was in the rest of the canisters made the place a nightmare.

"Clones," Darmiya said quietly. She scanned the closest one, wanting to prove her point to Spinner. It took only a few moments, and then Caya covered her ears and screamed. "Stop! It'll explode!

Stop!" She began running toward them, but Darmiya had already slammed her instrument shut. Despite this, a rumble began shaking their feet, and the closest canisters tumbled and fell, pieces of glass shards flying around them. Pieces of the bedrock started falling from the cave ceiling.

"Caya, get out of here!" Spinner yelled and tugged at Darmiya, but something nudged Darmiya from behind, sending her flying.

In her mind, Darmiya yelled for Caya and Spinner, but then she hit the floor among the broken glass and canisters. After that everything went black.

❖

As soon as the tremors in the bedrock reached them, Pamas began running. Next to her, after a quick inhale containing Spinner's name, Dael did the same. Thinking only of her daughter and Darmiya, Pamas ran so fast, she was sure she would fall and plunge headlong onto the uneven ground.

As they got almost into the first cave, a cloud of dust shot toward them. One of the security officers who had been in the first cave awaiting Spinner's go-ahead stumbled out, coughing as he donned his mask. "Masks on, sirs," he managed between coughing fits. "The entire inner cave gave in."

Shoving her mask into place, Pamas pressed herself past the soldier and entered the smoke- and dust-filled cave. Two other guards were pushing at rocks over by the far end, but she could see them since they wore headlights. "Report," she barked.

"I think we can enter the larger tunnel here, no problem, but farther in, I don't know, sir." The men cleared the entrance to the tunnel. "We should go in first, perhaps, sir?"

"Negative. I'm going in. Admiral Dael and the rest are right behind me. They'll give you what orders you need." Not about to wait any longer, Pamas started walking in the dusty tunnel, letting her light sway to minimize the risk of banging her head. As an after-thought she donned her lightweight helmet, lowering the visor. The tunnel was occasionally very narrow, but she had no problems approaching the inner opening. Hoping she could reach Spinner, Darmiya, and Caya within minutes, she lengthened her strides.

Pamas reached the slight bend of the tunnel that the scans had showed meant she was almost at the opening. *Hold on. Just hold on.* Pamas turned the corner and saw nothing but a solid wall of debris consisting of rocks and stones of all sizes. She was blocked. There was no way in.

CHAPTER TWENTY-ONE

L ieutenant, look at this," Calagan appeared at Pamas's side and pushed an instrument into her hands. Staring with dry, aching eyes at the screen, Pamas saw the devastation and knew that Darmiya, Caya, or Spinner had at most a minimal chance to be alive. Not only was half of the cave system pulverized, but large pieces of rocks had fallen, and judging by the new scans, they had crushed everyone inside. Sobbing inwardly, she couldn't fathom that she had come to Gemocon only to lose her daughter…to find she could still fall in love and then have that love wrenched from her, taking her heart and soul with it.

Tearing at the rubble with bare hands, she felt her nails break painfully, but she didn't care. She had to find them, had to know for sure. Her lungs screamed for air in the dusty tunnel, her mask already plugged with the stuff and each raspy breath grating like sand against the frail tissues.

"Ani! No, no, no…" At first Pamas thought the pained voice was her own but realized in her frenzy that it came from Dael, who pushed herself in next to Pamas. "Please." Finally she seemed to register Pamas's presence and yanked the instrument from Pamas's hands. "Was Ani in there? Was she?"

"Yes." Pamas moaned. "Yes! And Darmiya, and Caya. I felt the rumble. I was on my way. I was planning to get them out, but I was too late. I'm so sorry…" Pamas dragged a large rock over to the side and pushed her hand through the hole she had made, trying to feel for anyone or anything.

Dael wiped angrily at her face and stood. "I refuse to give up on them until we find them. Keep digging. I'll get some machinery up here." She turned and disappeared down the tunnel in the dust. Pamas vaguely heard her bark orders outside.

Somewhere, Pamas registered that her left lower leg hurt. She took a second to glance at the tear in her uniform trousers, where blood trickled down into her boot. Not caring about such a minor wound, Pamas kept digging, pulling, tearing, every now and then calling for the three women.

Just as Dael returned to the tunnel, bringing reinforcements, Pamas thought she heard something.

"Shut up, everyone," she called out, then pressed her head and shoulders farther into the hole she'd managed to create. "Hello? Please talk to me. We're trying to get to you. Hello?"

"Pamas?" a husky voice said and coughed violently afterward.

"Yes, it's Pamas. Who is this? Are you hurt?"

"Caya...it's Caya. I'm hurt some. Not sure how bad. I can see the light where you've dug through. Ow." Caya coughed again. "I don't know about Spinner and Darmiya. Everything went black and...and I woke up and...oh, damn, that hurts!" Her voice rose to a screech. "Please dig faster. It hurts."

"Is that Caya? Is that my sister?" Briar was now next to Pamas, wrapping an arm around her as she called into the narrow hole. "Honey? It's me. Hang in there. We're going to dig you out."

"Briar. Oh, thank the Creator." Caya began to cry. "I'm so sorry. I really am. I should've waited, but we had to get in to save the humanoids...to get the...ah!" She screamed again. "It...hurts...and it's so dark..." Her voice faded.

"She's about to pass out. We need to get her out fast." Briar began helping Pamas move the rocks. "How the hell can they be so heavy?" she gasped as she tossed one of them aside onto the growing pile.

"Their density is different from Oconodian bedrock." Pamas wasn't sure where she'd picked up on that geological fact, but it gave her something else to think about right now.

"Ah. I see." Briar kept at it, ripping at the rocks, shoving them aside with the same frenzy as Pamas did. Then she stopped, holding her breath. Covering her face with both of her dirty hands, she hummed intelligibly, rocking back and forth. Pamas had no idea what Briar was doing, and honestly, she didn't care, as she was entirely focused on yanking the rocks aside and widening the opening.

"Spinner...I...I sense her." Briar crawled out of the way and sat down with her back against the bedrock next to the rubble. "She's not conscious, but she's not dead."

"What?" Dael yanked Briar's sleeve. "Can you sense Spinner? She's alive?" Desperation tinged her voice that tears had already thickened.

"Yes."

"What about Darmiya?" Dael asked, making Pamas flinch so hard she hit her head against the edge of the opening.

"I don't know. I hear a lot of voices in there. They're hard to separate. I hear profound fear. Most of them are unconscious, but it's almost as if they're dreaming...or...what the...I hear chanting. And..."

Pamas stopped what she was doing and turned to Briar. "What?"

"Monotonous voices that seem to chant. I don't get it." Briar pressed the heels of her palms against her temples. "And it hurts. How can it hurt?"

Remembering something she had tried a long time to forget, Pamas moaned inwardly. Not this. This couldn't be happening here. The implications of what Briar sensed had to have other explanations. She put up a hand, raising her voice. "Stop your readings immediately," Pamas said, raising her voice. "Unconscious, but also conscious, changers are in there. They sometimes use chants to revive wounded or fallen this way. Don't get pulled in. They might recognize you as one of them, and I mean as a changer in general. I've seen them pull some crazy shit, such as taking over other changers' minds. It's easy enough for them unless you have a technique to keep them out."

"Damn," Briar said and stood. "Are you sure? I wanted to search for Darmiya, for signs of her."

"We just have to dig faster and get to her and Spinner." Pamas was half relieved that her daughter was at least alive, but her entire being felt frozen as soon as she thought of Darmiya. *So, just dig, don't think.* The rocks became more and more slippery, and then she realized her palms were bleeding. When a cold hand suddenly gripped hers, Pamas winced but closed her fingers around Caya's.

"Thank the Creator you're here," the young woman sobbed. "As far as I can tell, Darmiya and Spinner are to the left of me. They shouldn't be too far away. I tried to read their minds, you know, to let my mind follow Briar to enhance her reading, but all I got was their voices, their demands, all permeated by their chanting. I'm so sorry. I'm failing them…"

"No. Listen to me, Caya," Pamas said quickly as she kept digging, pushing, shoving to get to their loved ones. "You can't use your gifts right now. Trust me on this. There are forces around you…you have no idea what they're capable of. Just hold back on your readings."

"But I can—"

"No. I'm dead serious. Close your mind to anyone or anything around you. You may think you're reaching Spinner or Darmiya, but it might be a false reading. It might be a sinister attempt to gain control of your mind."

"Damn." Caya didn't speak much after that.

"Can't we use what Darmiya poured into that big rock in the tunnel yesterday?" Dael asked from behind.

"I can't see how it would be advisable to add yet another chemical compound to the mix in here. The environment is volatile as it is." Korrian spoke curtly, and Pamas was relieved that at least one scientist had joined them. "I sent Calagan to take some readings outside. We can use his talents better out there for a few moments. He'll be able to tell us if he finds any bio-signatures farther in the mountain."

Furious and so exhausted now that she had trouble breathing, Pamas gathered what was left of her strength and pushed at a large rock to the right. Surprisingly enough, it fell away from her and to the side. Now the opening was a lot bigger than before. Without asking for permission, she crawled into the cave, letting her headlight shine around the opening. To her left, Caya lay very still. A deep, long laceration on her forehead was the most obvious injury, but Pamas also saw what looked like a deep gash on the side of her neck.

"Caya? Can you hear me?"

"Mmm. Get me out of here." Caya murmured the words through almost unmoving lips. "Right after you told me to shut my powers down, I felt them attempt to pry open my mind. I'm holding them off, but it's hard. My capacity is diminished."

"Send a bodyboard through," Pamas called out through the narrow path she had just dug. "Caya is conscious and bleeding from at least two wounds." Waiting impatiently, Pamas held Caya's hand as she waited for the board. When it was pushed through, she tugged it toward her and gently slid the petite woman onto it, mindful of her spine and neck. After yanking on the cord attached to the bodyboard, she watched it begin to disappear through the hole. She helped guide it, and when she heard Briar call out, "Sweetie," Pamas knew Caya was safe. Now her own search would begin.

Darmiya forced her eyes open, frowning, as this didn't help her vision. What was going on? Had she lost her sight? A tiny flame of panic licked the inside of her chest, making it hard to breathe. Feeling her head with her left hand as the right one seemed stuck somehow, she looked for the headlight, but all she could feel was mussed, dirty hair.

"Hello?" She had to try a few times before her voice carried. "Spinner? Caya?" The last thing she remembered was the bedrock wall lit up by a multitude of green lamps as one canister after another crashed to the floor. Darmiya had found the purpose of this cave and explained to Spinner, who stood guard, holding her crossbow firmly. Then…Darmiya frowned. She truly didn't remember anything after that.

Something ran into her mouth, and the salty iron taste made her realize it was blood. Feeling along her forehead, she found a deep gash just above her left temple. Though she whimpered at the pain, she let it be since it didn't seem that an artery was bleeding. Carefully, she moved her legs one at a time, making reasonably sure she hadn't fractured any bones. Rolling onto her side, she felt around her, trying not to hurt herself on sharp debris or injure another unconscious individual.

"Hello? Please. Anyone there? Caya? Spinner? Please…" Darmiya sobbed, trying to keep her panic at bay, which was nearly impossible. The utter darkness was enough to scare her into complete apathy, not to mention being alone in a cave, perhaps with several dead people…or worse, with newborn clones going through animation. The thought that Caya and Spinner might be dead singed her soul. If she went down that path in her mind, she would have a panic attack.

Slowly, Darmiya crawled until she reached one of the cave walls. Here she sat down for a moment, closing her eyes against the dust. After she regained her equilibrium, she began to crawl along the wall. How long had she been unconscious? If it had been hours, the rescue teams would have been there to perform a search-and-rescue mission. Now, all she could do was follow the wall, feel as far as she could reach for Caya and Spinner. Darmiya tried to disregard the sharp debris cutting her knees and palms, and as she forged ahead, she was sure she was losing her mind, as she could hear chanting.

❖

Pamas saw more lights enter through the hole she had made. Flashlights lit up more of the cave, and her stomach turned at the sight of several bodies. Now, she could move around faster, examine the people lying on the floor as if a giant had tossed them around aimlessly.

Closest to her, a naked female body lay at an unnatural angle. She was clearly deceased. Her face was bluish white in the flickering light, and oddly, the woman had no hair. Suddenly the entire cave lit up, and a quick glance to her right showed the soldiers had put up a spotlight. Getting to her feet, since she also spotted a lot of broken glass, Pamas frantically moved from person to person, all of them naked, all of them dead. Some had obvious injuries, yet others seemed unscathed. Broken canisters were strewn around as if they'd fallen from the ceiling. Then she reached a person she immediately identified by her short, wild curls. "Aniwyn! Oh, Creator, Spinner. Oh, no." Forgetting about the glass, Pamas fell to her knees, pressing her fingertips against Spinner's carotid. At first, for a terrifying, life-altering moment, she felt nothing. Realizing her fingers trembled so much, it was impossible for her to check for a pulse that way, she bent over Spinner and pressed her ear to her chest. And there it was. A rapid, slightly weak heartbeat. But she was alive. She had a chance if they could get her out quickly enough.

"Pamas! Is that her. Is it Ani? Pamas!" Dael's voice penetrated the buzzing noise in Pamas's ears, and she looked up to see the pale woman stepping over bodies to get to her wife. "Is she alive?"

"Yes. But barely. She needs a mask and to be evacuated quickly. After that, we should find Darmiya and then get the hell out. I recommend you give the order that nobody stays behind in here."

"All right." Turning around, Dael signaled her crew with a series of fast hand gestures, which sent them into a flurry of activity. Two came skipping over the unmoving people on the ground with a bodyboard, clamped a neck collar around Spinner's neck, and readied her for transfer.

"You going too, ma'am?" one of the medics ask, indicating Pamas's bruised and bloodied knees peeking through her trousers.

"Not yet, Ensign. Carry on," Pamas said and began moving again, aching to find someone with long, black curls. She barely registered that Dael went with Spinner back through the hole while she continued her search.

"Hey, Pamas," Briar called out from the opening. "You have about ten more minutes. I'm being very careful not to open my mind, but something is stirring in here, and we should be gone before whatever it is shows itself."

Shuddering, Pamas only raised her hand to show she'd understood. When she came farther up along the cave wall, she saw an indentation where no glass or debris had reached. She glanced inside, saw it was empty, and was about to leave when a weak voice whispered, "Pamas?"

Swiveling so rapidly that she nearly fell, Pamas looked around her. She couldn't detect anyone resembling Darmiya, no matter how she tried. "Dar? Talk to me. Where are you?"

"Here. Down here." A small hand waved at the level of Pamas's boots.

Cursing, Pamas once again threw herself down on her knees. More glass pierced her skin, but she couldn't care less. She reached into a recess below the opening in the wall and stared right into Darmiya's glimmering eyes. "Oh, Dar. Come here. Are you hurt?"

"Yes. I…my vision is almost gone in my right eye." Darmiya spoke so matter-of-factly, she frightened Pamas.

"Don't worry. I'll get us out of here. We need to evacuate ASAP."

"Can you hear the humming?" Darmiya asked drowsily. "Like a lot of insects."

Reaching into the tiny opening, Pamas found Darmiya's hands. They felt so small in hers that it broke her heart. "I'm going to pull gently now, all right? We need to leave."

"Sure. Pull me along." The slurred words troubled her, but at least Darmiya followed obediently when Pamas got her out of the hole. She didn't wait. Feeling as if history had repeated itself within just a few days, she pulled Darmiya up over her shoulders in a rescue grip. Stumbling over now-stirring bodies, Pamas refused to bother with them. She aimed for the light over by the hole. Halfway over the expanse of broken glass, green substance, and something else, something sticky and, judging from the state of her boots, corrosive, an arm appeared in front of them and tried to grab Pamas's leg. She kicked herself free and called out to the security officers. "We have one alive over here."

She glanced down at the fumbling woman, who stared unseeingly toward Pamas, obviously guided by her voice. Unlike the ones Pamas had seen so far, this woman had long, flowing hair. Passing the approaching guards, she said, "Consider her an enemy combatant until proven otherwise. Grab her, and then get the hell out of here. Once outside, make sure you gag her and secure her limbs. If she's a changer, we have no way of knowing what her powers are."

"Where will she end up?" one of the ensigns asked as the two men dragged the woman between them. "The brig?"

"No. I'll get back to you with information where to take her." Pamas took a firmer hold of Darmiya and made her way to the opening by the far wall. It was getting harder to move as more of the bodies were stirring, and she heard the men behind her who were dragging the changers swear.

"Fuck. They're waking up. All of them. I thought they were all dead! And what the hell's that humming? It's like there's insects in here."

"Keep walking, Ensign. If you step on someone, so be it. Your priority is to get out of here. If you have to let go of the woman to save yourself, then do so. Just keep moving." Pamas barked the orders while she steeled herself against the nausea rising every time she stepped on someone. Arms waved like pale, newly sprouted plants, as if the people on the floor were feeling for her and the others in unison. Like one mind.

"Hurry, Pamas!" Calagan called from the hole. He was inside the cave, pushing away the forest of arms that seemed to be between her and freedom. Flashbacks of other damp places, like the bunker cells she'd spent so many years in, darted back and forth in her mind, but she murmured the names of her children over and over, adding Darmiya to the litany to keep her eye on the man who now used the back of his rifle to drive back the bodies rising like one, now on their knees, reaching, clawing…and humming.

"What the fuck?" One of the ensigns was close to losing it. She could hear it in his voice. "Sir?"

"Keep walking, Ensign. Step on them or kick them aside. That's an order!" Gasping for air after her command, Pamas staggered the last steps before her legs began to give way

Calagan threw himself forward, catching both Pamas and Darmiya. "Come on! I have her. You go first, and I'll push her through. No time for a bodyboard."

Thinking fast, Pamas went into the hole feetfirst, calling to those on the outside, "Pull my feet when I give the order!"

Calagan struggled to help Darmiya headfirst into the hole, but Pamas grabbed her wrists, inwardly apologizing for hurting the woman she loved as she was about to seriously bruise her. "Pull now!"

Strong hands tugged her back at a steady pace. Darmiya slid forward, moaning in pain.

"Sorry, Dar. Just a little bit longer," Pamas said. "Calagan. Are you there?"

"Helping the others. Soon."

"For the love of the Creator, don't get yourself killed. Darmiya will never forgive me." Growling, Pamas felt herself being pulled free, and she landed in waiting arms.

"Good job, there, Lieutenant," Korrian said, and helped Darmiya out of the hole, together with Adina. "You look a bit worse for wear, kid. Why don't you hop onto the gurney over there, and we'll take you too—"

"No. Not yet." Briar came running. "Caya managed to talk to me before she passed out again. She said to seal the cave. I know I didn't misunderstand. She was frantic, and for her to say something like that, it has to be bad." She was pale, but her jaw was set. "Until we know what we're dealing with in there, what and who they are, we have to seal the cave."

"But they'll...it's inhumane." Korrian stared at them in disbelief. "They'll starve. They..." She closed her eyes briefly. "I know, I know. I trust both you and Caya with my life. And it is up to me to keep everyone else on this planet safe," she added. Turning to the two security officers who had just helped Calagan out, she said, "Stand guard while we gather enough explosives to do the job."

CHAPTER TWENTY-TWO

Pamas watched the freighter touch down on a small field between the mountain they had sealed and the one north of it. She had refused to let any medics approach her, telling them they could bandage her hands and knees when they were on their way back to the capital with the three women who nearly gave their lives—and who were not in the clear yet. Sitting on a small crate between Spinner and Darmiya, she held their hands, not caring how it stung her own wounded ones, looking back and forth between them.

Dael came and went while they waited for the freighter. Spinner had not woken up from her unconscious state yet, but her color was looking better, which Pamas thought was due to the fresh mountain air. They had sent all Darmiya's data to the capital, and the engineers were calibrating the freighter so that anything potentially permeating the environment around the mountain with the sealed cave system wouldn't affect it.

Dael had conferred with Korrian, and an engineering team was deploying to put up a warning signal system around the mountain. Briar doubted it would sustain a serious attack by potential terrorists, but it was better than doing nothing.

As the freighter's hatches opened and medical staff and engineers milled out, Pamas reluctantly let go of Spinner's hand and knew Dael would be at her wife's side, as one of her captains was relieving her.

Darmiya opened her eyes as they carried her gurney onto the freighter. "What...I mean, where are...we going?" she asked huskily.

Ecstatic that Darmiya was conscious, Pamas kissed her forehead. "Back to the capital. We're going home."

"I'm glad." Darmiya squeezed Pamas's hand, only to wince. "I'm so sorry! You're injured. Did I make it worse?"

"No." Pamas lied tenderly. "Just a scratch, really. How is your eye? It looks better." It did. It wasn't as red as before.

"I can see." Darmiya smiled tremulously. "It's a bit blurry, but I can see."

"Thank the Creator. One of us having an eyepatch is enough."

"No joking matter." Darmiya frowned. "Wait...it's important. Is Dael here? Has she talked to Spinner or Caya? Does she know yet?" Words ran from her lips like water, slightly slurred but with great urgency.

"No. You're the only one conscious right now." Pamas looked over at Dael, who sat with Spinner's hand in hers, looking pale and solemn. "Let me get her." She reluctantly let go of Darmiya and walked over to Dael.

"Sir. I'm sorry to disturb you right now, but Darmiya has important information. She's adamant. Want me to sit by Spinner?" Pamas regarded her daughter with a twitch of pain in her chest. Why wasn't she waking up?

"No. I don't want to leave Ani for a moment. Have someone move Darmiya's gurney up here," Dael said, her voice throaty. Pamas knew instinctively that Dael was fighting tears and emotional collapse.

"Yes, sir." Pamas nodded briskly and motioned for a medic to help her move Darmiya's gurney.

Dael turned to Darmiya. "How are you doing, sweetheart?" she asked, her tone entirely different now, soft and tender. "You look better, I think."

"I am." Darmiya took Pamas's hand again, holding it gently. "We found at least ninety to a hundred canisters holding what I now am certain are clones."

Pamas had hoped, prayed, even, that this wouldn't be the case. Thinking of the rumored experiments conducted in the jungles, sometimes in the bunkers below ground, she wondered if the changers had perfected the technique.

Glancing at Dael, Pamas could tell the admiral was shocked.

"How can you be certain?" Dael asked matter-of-factly.

"Because we found the canisters holding the five original humanoids." Darmiya closed her eyes briefly. "I scanned them. I had to."

"This isn't the first time I've heard of this atrocity," Pamas said, brushing an errant lock from Darmiya's forehead. "There were rumors when I was captured. I never quite believed them, as a lot of rumors about our captors were always flying around, and though a lot of it was true, some was exaggerated. But when Caya started talking about humming, chanting, that sort of thing, I recognized that as part of the clone rumors. But I don't understand why they'd need clones in the first place. The changers, if it indeed is changers behind this, are powerful enough as they are."

Dale motioned for an ensign to approach them. "Send a message to the ECC that we need another meeting. Schedule it for an hour after we touch down."

"Aye, sir." Saluting, the ensign hurried to the nearest communication console.

"Thank you, Darmiya, for bringing us this news, as dire as it is." Dael patted Darmiya's shoulder, which made Darmiya start crying again.

"I'm so sorry. I may be responsible for the chain event that led to the explosion because I performed those last scans." Darmiya sobbed. "It's my fault Spinner is unconscious and Caya hurt. I saw her bandages when you rolled me over here." She pressed her tear-stained face against the back of Pamas's bandaged hands. "I had to find out the truth for the sake of all our people, and I hoped it wouldn't cause a catastrophic event, but I also knew there was a risk."

"And we realized the risk going in," Dael said starkly. "Ani would be the first to say this. You know that, Darmiya. I don't want to hear anything about guilt. You performed your job, and you did it admirably. Thanks to you and the readings you took, we know a hell of a lot more."

Darmiya looked up, and her forlorn expression was like a knife through Pamas's heart. "Please, Dar. Listen to the admiral. Don't allow guilt to overwhelm you. I've lived like that for so many years, and not until you came into my life did that begin to change." Pamas didn't care that Dael heard what she said. "You know you are important to not only the people of Gemocon, but to me, personally. Not to mention that you're Spinner's best friend. She'll never forgive me if I let you go on feeling like this."

"Damn straight," another husky voice whispered, and then Spinner turned her head to look over at Darmiya. "You didn't kill me."

Dael's valiant attempt to keep her emotions in check failed gloriously. "Darling!" She bent over Spinner and kissed her on the lips, again and again. "Ani…oh, thank the Creator."

Darmiya's tears flowed again, but for different reasons, Pamas could tell. Then something dawned on her. "Hey. The woman I came across that the two ensigns dragged out of the cave, she was different than those pale, bald people. She had long hair and was talking. The others, the, um, clones, seemed to just moan and hum. They had poor motor skills at that."

Spinner focused on Pamas. "You rescued only one of the humanoids? We found five."

Pamas couldn't tell if Spinner was accusing her of not trying harder. "We didn't know that. We barely got that woman out after saving Darmiya. Briar kept hurrying us along as she sensed danger approaching. I…I couldn't risk Darmiya. Or any of you." Feeling awkward now, Pamas still held Spinner's gaze, which slowly softened.

Spinner extended a shaky hand toward Pamas, who took it without hesitation. "I know you had to save Darmiya." She raised a deliberate eyebrow, and the tiniest of smiles played at the corners of her mouth.

"Yes." Spinner had guessed that her mother loved her best friend. Strangely, Pamas couldn't detect any disapproval whatsoever in Spinner's expression. Instead, she looked more teasing than anything else.

"What about Caya?" Spinner asked, and tried to sit up, but Dael kept her lying down by pressing gently against her shoulders.

"Caya is sedated, and the medical professionals are fusing her wounds. I thought it best to have most of that done before Tylio boards the freighter. I don't think we can expect her to wait in the ECC. Briar is by her side and helping her through the process of being sedated. Apparently, that's hard for an oracle. It doesn't quite take, and when it does, it brings on old demons. Briar and her sister have a special connection, obviously, and doing it this way is best for Caya."

"Creator of all things. The president is still going to freak out," Spinner muttered. "And the woman? Is she conscious?"

"Not yet. She was semi-conscious when we literally stepped on her, but now she's out like a light." Pamas glanced back to where medical professionals and guards hovered around the woman. She saw the long hair was auburn and her complexion pale and freckled. "I hope she makes it. We need answers, and perhaps she wasn't there voluntarily, if changers were holding her prisoner. Can we at least investigate that possibility?" Pamas spoke cautiously to Dael.

"Of course," Dael answered softly. She clearly understood how this matter ate at Spinner.

"ETA two minutes, sir," the communication officer said.

"Time to take our seats. Is Darmiya properly strapped in?" Dael stood and placed her hand around Pamas's elbow and helped her stand. "You look a bit worse for wear, Lieutenant. Sit over here, by me." She showed Pamas to the seat next to her own, and they sat down. When Dael even helped her engage the safety harness, Pamas wondered if this was Dael's way of showing she accepted Pamas's presence. That, or merely gratitude that Spinner was safe and would soon be home.

Chapter Twenty-three

Darmiya went through annoyingly numerous examinations at the hospital she had left only two days ago. She kept telling them she was fine, but when even Spinner insisted they all needed proper checkups, which was so out of character that Darmiya thought Spinner had a concussion, she relented.

Now, after the doctors had indeed concluded she was banged up and would be sore and bruised for the next week or so, she was glad to leave the hospital. She had had to promise to return for another minor checkup in two or three days, which was far better than being admitted again.

Spinner managed to stay out of the hospital as well, but only because Briar stepped in and promised to check on her every day and that Spinner would not be alone—and she was grounded until the doctors gave their go-ahead.

Caya, on the other hand, had to stay in the hospital, as she had to undergo more surgery. She had woken up from her emergency procedure and shown signs of concussion and broken ribs that had bruised her left lung. It hadn't been perforated, but until it was clear that it wouldn't suddenly burst, they planned to monitor her. The fact that Caya didn't object the way she would have if she'd been herself made everyone who knew her worry.

Darmiya had watched in shocked fascination when President Tylio barreled through the freighter's passenger area, heading straight for Caya. Her otherwise perfect chignon was gone, and her hair flowed freely around her shoulders. Dressed in stark gray, she seemed frail and completely in command at the same time. Caya had just been let out of the sedation, and Briar had tried to inform Tylio about what had been done, but it was clear the president wasn't quite listening. She had knelt next to the gurney, cupped the bandaged face gently, and pressed her lips against what bare skin she could find.

Darmiya had turned away then, not wanting to gawk at something so intensely private. If she had ever doubted that Caya Lindemay held the president's heart, she now knew those two were meant for each other.

"Ready to go home?" Pamas nudged Darmiya's hand gently. "Dar?"

"Why do you call me that?" Darmiya asked, knowing she sounded abrupt as she turned to Pamas. They stood outside cube eleven, where crews had worked around the clock to clean up after the explosion. If you didn't know where to look, you would never know it had happened. Now Darmiya needed the truth. If she was going to have her heart broken, she had to start taking precautions. Better know now...than later. She had already invested her entire being, but she could pretend it mattered that she had known Pamas only a short time. That would make being let down easier.

Pamas looked honestly confused. "Call you what?"

"Dar. You keep calling me Dar. Nobody calls me that but you."

Pamas suddenly appeared apprehensive. "I wasn't aware I do. Well, that's not true, but I mean I don't do it consciously."

"So, it's not a nickname?" Darmiya clenched her fists but relaxed them immediately as the motion hurt her sore muscles.

"No, not per se, even if it can be interpreted as such, since your name is Darmiya."

"What does it mean, then?" So tense now that she was ready to scream, Darmiya jumped when Pamas took her hand and tugged her toward the hovercar.

"Let me take you home, and then I'll tell you what you want to know."

"Home?"

"Well, your home." Pamas colored faintly. "If it's all right that I accompany you?" Letting go of Darmiya's hand as she climbed into the hovercar, Pamas seemed to be the one who felt tense now.

What was she doing? Was she truly trying to act difficult and push Pamas away? Darmiya pinched her own leg. What an idiot she was. An immature idiot at that. Pamas had been nothing but wonderful to her, saved her life. Saved Caya and Spinner too. Of course, Darmiya had to pick that time to act like a child.

"It's more than all right," Darmiya said and heard how her voice had turned soft and warm. "And you don't owe me any explanations, Pamas. Truly."

"But I do. Not in here though. When we're at your place."

"But Calagan will be there. I mean, if you want to talk in private." Her cheeks going hot, Darmiya examined her fingers before she dared look back up at Pamas.

"Oh. I didn't think about that. Do you mind joining me at my tent? As you know, it has a great view." Pamas smiled.

"Good idea." Darmiya sat back as Pamas gave the driver new directions. They rode through the capital that would be named when everyone had healed as much as possible after the terrorist attacks. Foundations for new houses and structures were popping up everywhere, and Darmiya hoped this meant it wouldn't take long before she could live in her own house again. Or with…She stopped her thoughts immediately. No pushing her luck here. One thing at a time.

They reached the camp, where several people recognized them. Darmiya hadn't had to live with the press since she left Gemosis. Remembering being famous on her native world, she realized they were now some sort of celebrities, as rumors spread of them saving someone from something. A young boy, perhaps eleven or twelve, boasting a mop of blond hair, came up to Pamas as they stepped out of the hovercar. "Can I shake your hand, Lieutenant Seclan?" he asked, sounding precocious. "My name is Veilan."

"Sure, Veilan." Pamas extended her hand, but he looked wide-eyed at her bandages.

"I'm so sorry, sir. I didn't realize you were wounded." Veilan took a step back.

"I'm not that wounded, trust me." Pamas took the boy's hand, and he held hers so gently between both of his, which looked a little dirty, Darmiya's tears rose.

"I hear you're a hero. If any of the other kids give you problems because of your eye, just let me know. I'll deal with them." Veilan let go of Pamas's hand. "I'm two habitats behind your tent." He looked proud of the fact they were neighbors.

"Good to know. Thanks, Veilan." Pamas placed her hand at the small of Darmiya's back and guided her into the tent after pressing the sensor. "Now I believe you have a question." Pamas tilted her head and rested her hip against the small table.

Darmiya knew she had reached the end—or the beginning, and she hoped it was the latter. "I vowed to myself when we were up among the mountains, that I would tell you the truth." Darmiya stepped closer, placing her hands on Pamas's upper arms. "I've fallen in love with you, Pamas. I love you, and I hope you might one day feel the same."

As long as she lived, Darmiya would never forget the moment the light ignited in Pamas's eyes. It was more than that. Pamas's entire body seemed to relax, and her skin took on a healthier glow. Afterward, Darmiya often wondered if, in her memory, she had exaggerated what she really saw, but in her soul, she knew it was accurate.

"Dar is short for darling in the province where I was born. The fact that your name starts with it is just a wonderful happenstance, because I love you very much, Darmiya." Pamas still didn't touch her or even move.

Darmiya sensed that she had to take the first step. Perhaps Pamas had some age issue, or, on a deeper note, she was still battling her years in captivity and feared she might not be enough or good for Darmiya. This woman was a noble warrior. Darmiya had always known that.

"I want you to take me to bed, Pamas," she said, knowing full well this statement would startle Pamas into some sort of action. Probably another noble one. She wasn't wrong.

"You've just been signed out from the hospital, and I—I—" Pamas held up her bandaged hands.

Darmiya smiled broadly, so happy right now, she feared she might strain her facial muscles. "I didn't say I wanted to make love, although that's high on my agenda when your hands are healed, but take me to bed. To hold me and let me hold you. I need to be near you, and now that you've told me how you feel, I need it even more. We nearly lost each other—damn, we almost never found each other because of so many things that could have gone wrong. What if I hadn't been the greeter at your particular gate? What if you hadn't thought yourself worthy of finding your children? What if you had lived in cube eighteen?"

"So many things, yes. Don't work yourself up, Dar. We found each other because somehow fate decided to compensate us both by letting us meet." Pamas wrapped her arms around Darmiya and hugged her close. "And I'd be happy to take you to bed. When my hands are better and you feel your old self again, we'll make love. As often and as much as you want. I, being an old woman, will try to keep up."

"You're not old!" When Pamas laughed, Darmiya knew she'd walked right into a trap. It was the first time she'd ever heard this woman laugh out loud like this, and the sound sent shivers of happiness throughout Darmiya's body. "So, old woman? Bed?"

Tucking her bandaged hands in under Darmiya's shirt, Pamas ran them up and down her back. "Mmm. I can tell you're going to be delightful."

"Oh, Creator…" Darmiya lost her breath and captured Pamas's lips with hers, deepening the kiss as she needed to, so very badly.

She glided her tongue against Pamas's, tasted her, explored every part of her hot mouth. Pamas groaned and pulled her closer.

"You test my resolve, you vixen." Nibbling down along Darmiya's neck, Pamas licked along her collarbone and under her shirt. "I'm starting to think I don't need my hands."

"I like…how you think." Darmiya moaned. "And come to think of it…my hands are just fine."

"Oh…" Pamas drew a damp line with her tongue up to meet Darmiya's lips, pushing her tongue inside her mouth again. "Come with me. Come to bed. Dar…"

"Yes. I have to. I need you so much, and I can't wait. I need you against me." Darmiya tugged Pamas's shirt off as they stumbled toward the narrow bed. There, they tumbled down, ending up in a bundle of arousal and tenderness. Darmiya didn't mind being the one who undressed them. In fact, she reveled in each garment that ended up on the floor since it exposed them to each other physically…and when their skin connected, Darmiya knew she would never love someone like she loved Pamas. Pamas rubbed against her, scorching hot against Darmiya's skin, feverish and with wet cheeks. The tears didn't startle Darmiya. In fact, she saw them as a victory. In the last hour, she had heard Pamas laugh aloud and cry, which was a miracle, considering the somber, rigid woman she had greeted that first day.

"Dar, you feel amazing and I love you. I can't think of anything but you." Pamas pressed kisses against any naked skin she found. Darmiya's arousal escalated with each word and each kiss.

"I think you're going to make me come just from this. I have no defense against you." Darmiya arched, pressing her nipple firmer into Pamas's mouth.

"You don't need one." Pamas sucked at the nipple and tugged at it gently with her teeth.

Whimpering loudly, Darmiya pushed her hands in between them and cupped Pamas's sex, rubbing against her. Gasping, Pamas lost her connection with Darmiya's breast and tossed her head back, convulsing over and over. "Creator…"

Watching Pamas climax after only a brief touch was so amazing, and so beautiful, Darmiya gently kept her hand in place against Pamas's wet folds, wanting very much for her to orgasm again.

Rolling Pamas onto her back, Darmiya pressed her lips down her breastbone, making detours to taste the small, dark nipples. As she traced every faded scar while weeping for the pain behind them, Darmiya vowed she would give so much of herself and deliver all the pleasure Pamas would ever need. Sliding down the wiry, slender body, Darmiya nudged Pamas's legs apart, eager to reach the part she knew would love some of what she wanted to give.

"I was supposed to make love to you," Pamas said, moaning and laughing at the same time. "Dar?"

"Don't worry. You will." Darmiya proceeded to kiss, lick, and devour the slick folds before her, and the only time she hesitated was when she placed her fingertips at Pamas's entrance. No way was she going to push inside without explicit permission.

"I want you to take me, Dar. I just want you up here with me when you do," Pamas whispered.

As Darmiya crawled up to lie next to Pamas on the pillow, she suddenly felt fingers between her own legs.

"May I?" Pamas asked and kissed the corner of Darmiya's lips.

"Your hands?"

"I have two fingers that aren't bandaged, and I'm sure I can put them to excellent use, if you'll let me."

"Oh, yes. Please, please, please..." Darmiya hooked her leg over Pamas's hip and pushed her own fingers into her lover... Pamas...her lover...The words resounded in her mind with each thrust. Pamas didn't hesitate any longer but slid inside Darmiya, and that was all it took. She had wanted Pamas and despaired about her urge for only a few days, but it felt a lot longer. Perhaps she had waited for Pamas her whole life.

When Pamas curled her two fingers inside her, Darmiya arched her back again and quickened the pace between Pamas's legs. The orgasm hit so fast, Darmiya cried out and pressed her face against Pamas's neck. It was her turn to sob and let her tears flow freely. The relief was so overpowering, and sex had never, ever felt like this.

Pamas began convulsing against Darmiya, wrapping her free arm more firmly around her as she sobbed the name she'd given her. "Dar, Dar, Dar…"

"Here. I'm here." Darmiya carefully withdrew her hand and shoved it into Pamas's hair. "I'm here. You're here. We're together."

"Yes, we are." Pamas slowly opened her eye and gazed into Darmiya's. "I hope you realize that I won't ever be able to let you go." It clearly wasn't a question, but Darmiya still nodded.

"I know that, and I feel the same way. Now that you've told me you love me, you're stuck with me." Darmiya kissed Pamas lightly. "I know we're very different in many ways, but I still maintain we're a good fit."

Pamas tilted her head, looking tenderly at Darmiya. "You know what? We really are."

Closing her eyes, Darmiya felt an immense fatigue overtake her, but it wasn't an unpleasant feeling. "Mind if we take a nap?" she asked and yawned.

"Not at all." There was a definite smile in Pamas's voice. "I don't mind at all."

CHAPTER TWENTY-FOUR

Pamas stood next to Darmiya in the part of the hospital that held the incarceration ward. The room had a window where those outside could observe the sick or injured prisoner, but from their side, it was only a screen showing their vital signs and chart notes.

The woman in the bed was as pale as the bedding, which made her auburn hair and freckles stand out starkly. Her eyes were closed, and she wore patches on several parts of her body.

"We're still waiting for Admiral Caydoc, Spinner, Thea, and Caya," Briar said as she approached. "I'm glad to see you looking so well, Darmiya. Three days of rest can do wonders." She winked at them, which made Darmiya blush and Pamas chuckle.

"How are your hands, Lieutenant?" Briar asked, glancing down at Pamas's now-unbandaged hands.

"Just fine. The ointment, together with the wand Darmiya augmented, did wonders."

"Augmented?" Briar looked curiously at Darmiya. "Something you need to show me, then."

"Absolutely. Just tell me when you have time, and I'll give you one of the three I rebuilt." Darmiya leaned slightly against Pamas, looking so happy.

"Here they are now," Briar said and walked over to embrace her sister. Caya was still recuperating, but her scars had already faded to pink lines.

"Is this her?" President Tylio said darkly and strode up to the window. She stood there for a moment, her back rigid and her hands balled into fists. Then she slowly relaxed, and Caya walked up to her.

"She's just a very young girl," Caya said slowly. "I told you. I don't think she was in that chamber locked into that canister of her free will."

"Madam President. Sirs." A civilian physician of Gemosian descent strode up to them, shaking hands. She was short and stocky and wore her hair cropped short. Clear blue eyes regarded them matter-of-factly. "I'm Doctor Chardi Lo Gjorda, the chief physician on the incarceration wards."

"What can you tell us about this woman?" the president asked.

"Physically, quite a lot, thanks to Doctor Do Voy's data from where she was found. I'm fully briefed on the mission and have level-one security clearance, just to reassure you." Doctor Lo Gjorda took out a smaller computer tablet and scrolled through some data. "The woman, whom we refer to as Female Eight-Six, has not regained consciousness since she was brought in from the freighter almost four days ago. She suffers from serious malnutrition and was initially heavily dehydrated as well. We rectified the latter immediately, starting already on the freighter, but the malnutrition will take longer. She receives a special blend of different types of glucose, as she has an imbalance in her brain we have never seen before. I have consulted the chief neurologist, but even she has not come across these readings done by the magnetroneum camera."

"This supports my theory," Caya said. "Who would willingly inflict these injuries on themselves?"

"Considering that suicide bombers sacrifice their lives, why couldn't this woman give her well-being for some 'cause'?" The president frowned. "Any idea what was going on with her in that canister, Doctor?"

"I'm not sure about its purpose, but the forensic investigators found traces of a liquid on her skin that was infused with melted black-garnet shells. When we drew blood, we found more traces of the agent in her bloodstream. I dare to wager that it will go away with time, since each time we've drawn blood, the traces have diminished."

"I know you haven't been privy to the full circumstances around how we found her," Dael said. "We found bald, pale humanoids, all reacting as if they were controlled by one mind, or at least working on a very basic level as a hive mentality. Apart from Female Eight-Six, we discovered four more humanoids looking fully developed and not unfinished, like the bald ones, which we had no time to save before we had to seal the cave."

Doctor Lo Gjorda blinked. "Clones? Is that what you're saying?"

"Yes. That was our response as well." Dael turned to look at the woman. "Does she carry the changer gene?"

"I was certain she would, but no. She doesn't. As far as we can estimate after checking her bones and her teeth, she's around twenty-one years old, humanoid, of Oconodian descent. Her retinal scan and fingerprints don't show up in any archives or databases. Whoever she is, she wasn't a registered passenger on any of the ships. We have sent basic identity-determination data back through the buoy system to Oconodos to see if anyone there can help us find out who she is, but that might take a while, or we may not hear back at all, as you know, sir."

Dael nodded. "Briar, are you still determined to go in and try to read her?"

"Yes, sir. I think it's our one chance to at least know if her brain shows any activity. Has she had a brain scan today?"

"Not yet," Doctor Lo Gjorda said. "I wanted to hold off on that procedure until after this briefing."

"Good. The less others have handled her, the better."

"I should go in with you," Caya said.

Briar turned toward her sister. "Absolutely not. I'll take Darmiya in with me, since she can use one of her new scanners, but that's it. What I need you to do, sis, if you're up for it, is to stand out here and see if you catch anything from her past via me."

"How can I do that when you're in there and I'm out here?" Caya looked frustrated.

"That's what Darmiya's scanner is about. Right?" Briar nodded at Darmiya to take over.

"I'll put this transmitter on your temple and this other one on Briar," Darmiya said, and pulled out a small, square object from her bag. "I'll monitor you and keep the connection stable. It should be the same as when you have physical contact."

"How did you come up with that this fast?" President Tylio looked at the transmitters. "You've been on medical leave as far as I know."

"I have," Darmiya said, blushing. She glanced at Pamas as if asking for permission.

"Go ahead," Pamas said, waving her hand. She was so proud of Darmiya and was only now truly understanding the brilliance of this young woman she adored.

"Well, Pamas and I were, um, snuggling, and I was thirsty. I was *really* thirsty, but I didn't want to leave her, so I stayed and sort of suffered the thirst, thinking, what if I could have kept the connection and still been able to go fetch a bottle of water and that someone should invent a transmitter that allowed for such a connection to be sustained." Crimson now, Darmiya giggled. "So, I, um, I did."

President Tylio had to cover her mouth. Spinner and Caya both studied their boots carefully, but Dael merely looked impressed. "You never cease to amaze and surprise us, Darmiya."

"Well, let's hope it works for changers as well as sappy lovers," Spinner said, but her expression was kind.

Pamas regarded her daughter with longing. They had spoken every day, but only about trivial things. Still, she couldn't force Spinner to talk about anything she was uncomfortable with. It was miraculous enough that her daughter had contacted Pherry and persuaded him to bring his wife and children to a family reunion. As she had guessed, he took his cue from Spinner, and sooner or later, they would deal with the harder topics.

As Briar entered the room with Darmiya, Pamas stood close to the window, not about to miss anything of the exchange. A movement next to her showed Adina had joined them and was now focused on Briar.

Briar took the limp left hand of Female Eight-Six and closed her eyes. Caya gave a soft hum and did the same where she stood on Pamas's other side.

"It's actually working," Caya whispered. "Amazing." She stood silent for a moment, and then she began to speak in a dreamy, monotonous way. "Green fields. Tall grass. Soft summer wind. It's on Oconodos. Running, fast, fast. Sunshine. Happy. Very happy. Small house by the water. Children. Siblings." Caya swayed some, and the president gently took her by the shoulders.

"This all right, darling?" Tylio asked quietly, clearly not wanting to disturb the connection.

"It's fine." Caya nodded slowly. "Large city. Classroom. Teaching young people, teacher, loves children. Rides the jumpers to home. Dark in a tunnel. Damp. Cold. Alone. Running, running, running, running. Falling. Black." Caya was breathing faster now, and perspiration had broken out on her forehead.

In the room, Briar was now sitting on the side of the bed, holding the woman's hand with both of hers. Her lips were moving fast, and Darmiya looked slightly concerned but kept tapping at her tablet that monitored the transmitters.

"Wake up. Dark, damp room. Hear foreign animals. Prisoner for many days. Hungry a lot. Thirsty a lot. The one comes often. The one I fear. Comes often into the dark, damp room."

Pamas was nauseous now. Every word was a cut by a dull, rusty blade against her nerves. Clutching at the window frame, she trembled. A dark, damp room in a place with foreign animal sounds. That could only mean one place—somewhere in the Oconodian jungles.

"Scares me. Persuades me, threatens, says my siblings will die. Mother will die. Father will die. I must go. I must be one of the five. Don't understand. Don't know." Caya paused, frowning. "I say yes. I'll go. The one says I will be revered. I'll be a Nestrocalder muse."

In the room, Briar collapsed and slid onto the floor. Doctor Lo Gjorda and Adina rushed into the room, helping Darmiya get Briar to a chair. Next to Pamas, Caya tore off the transmitter and wiped at her tears. "She's an innocent."

Pamas barely heard them. She slowly sank to her knees, her hands clamped over her mouth as she swallowed back the rising bile. Whimpering into her palms, she felt hands on her shoulder.

"Pamas? What's the matter?" It wasn't Darmiya; she was still in the room. It was Spinner.

Pamas couldn't speak. She was back in the jungle, in the bunker, and she heard other prisoners scream, plead, and pray. She felt her own punishment for never giving in inflicted on her over and over. Whippings, cuts, electrodes, faked drowning—they tried it all. At times, she gave in and handed them fake information, knowing full well it would come back to haunt her.

"No, no, no," she whimpered. "Stop, please, stop. I can't take it anymore. I just want to go home. I have to go home. My children need me. I have to go home to my children. Please." She folded over and curled up in the strong arms belonging to her daughter.

"Mama?" Large tears splashed down, landing on Pamas's cheek and temple. "Mama. You're home now. You're home with us now. Mama." Spinner rocked her, her daughter who had taken over her role and kept her brother safe, and Pamas allowed herself to relax.

"Pamas? What happened?" Darmiya asked quietly, and Pamas started to breathe properly as her lover stroked her hair.

"Flashbacks," Spinner said huskily. "Something that Briar read from the woman's mind triggered this reaction in Mama."

"Oh, Creator." Briar joined them, and Pamas looked up at her.

"She was in the jungle like me. And met Nestrocalder, like me."

"I'll be damned," Tylio said from behind them, where she stood with her arm around Caya's shoulders.

Pamas began to stand and was pulled off the floor by strong hands. She looked carefully at her daughter and saw nothing but affection, perhaps tinged by remorse. "Hey, little girl."

"Hey, Mama." Spinner smiled through her tears. "Been too long since you called me that."

Pamas smiled tremulously. "I promise to do it only every now and then."

"Everyone feeling better?" Doctor Lo Gjorda asked and seemed to take all the commotion in stride. "So, I think this is proof that this woman is still in there."

"Not only that," Briar said after sipping a bottle of water. "I have a name."

The president and Dael snapped their heads up at the same time. "A name?"

"Yes. Just before I couldn't manage to keep the connection any longer as it was so emotionally draining, and downright frightening, she gave me her name. I had the strongest feeling she knew I was trying to reach her, even if she couldn't actually wake up and talk."

"Who is she?" Dael pulled out her tablet.

"Her name is Zoem Malderyn. At least now we can search other records that we brought with us." Briar looked at the still woman in the bed. "And she is an innocent. If I found out one thing beyond doubt, it is that she sacrificed herself to save her family. She must have been smuggled here, either aboard *Pathfinder* or one of the advance ships."

Dael and the president walked to a corner to talk. Pamas found a chair and sat down, her legs not quite steady yet. Darmiya came over to her and crouched next to the chair. "I saw."

Pamas didn't have to ask what. "I never thought she'd call me Mama again."

"But she did. And perhaps she needed to witness what you went through during your abduction to drop the wall around her feelings." Kissing Pamas's cheek, Darmiya smiled gently. "And perhaps you needed for her to truly understand."

"I think you're right. Is that going to be a habit of yours in the future, being right all the time?" Pamas tugged a long, curly tress that had escaped Darmiya's headband.

"I'm sure it is," Darmiya said and chuckled. "Regrets?"

"None."

"All right. We have a lot of work to do, when it comes to the aftermath of our operation in the mountains. We're going back and unseal the tunnel with enhanced equipment and see if we can perhaps save the other four, if they're still alive." Dael tapped her tablet.

"More important and infinitely worrisome, can this changer called Nestrocalder have stowed away on any of our ships?" the president asked solemnly. "As you can tell, arriving at Gemocon wasn't the end of our problems—merely an exacerbation of some new ones."

Pamas had feared all along that Nestrocalder wasn't done with her. But now she had friends and family who knew what she had been through and would help her go after this person.

Holding Darmiya closer, she vowed not to rest until she had destroyed Nestrocalder, but in the meantime, the best revenge on the malevolent changers was to be happy with the woman she loved and the children she had been given a second time.

EPILOGUE

Commander Neenja KahSandra stood outside the recently inaugurated Dodgmer City Hall, and when the double doors hissed open, she called out the command to stand at attention to the military personnel present. Saluting the two women exiting the structure surrounded by the presidential guardsmen, she couldn't keep a smile from ruining the protocol that said she needed to look stern and solemn.

President Gassinthea Mila Tylio and Caya Lindemay held each other's hands, and KahSandra didn't think she'd ever seen any two people so happy—or so beautiful—before. Both blond, though very different hues, they wore traditional crisp linen caftans over dark-red trousers and shirts. Caya had her hair loose, and the wind caught it and wrapped it around the president, who merely laughed and left the silver-blond tresses where they were. Tylio wore her hair in a low chignon, as was her habit, and her usual ten row pearls. New was the equally traditional bracelets both brides wore on their left wrists. Made from precious black onyx-marble stones, the bracelets symbolized the longevity of their union.

"At arms!" KahSandra barked, inwardly grinning at how Darmiya Do Voy jumped where she stood, just behind the brides, with Lieutenant Pamas Seclan. The young genius was a lovely girl, and a lot tougher than she looked, from what KahSandra had heard. At her command, the forty soldiers took aim with their rifles, ready to fire the traditional firework salute next.

As the brides began to walk between the two rows of soldiers that flanked their path to the adorned hovercar waiting for them, KahSandra called out, "Aim sky-high! Fire!" And this time she could swear Darmiya gripped Lieutenant Seclan's arm and ducked.

Behind the brides, the rest of the guests began to leave the Dodgmer City Hall. Caya Lindemay's sister, Briar, was gently sobbing as she mopped her cheeks with a tissue. Next to her, her fiancée, Commander Vantressa, did a good job trying to appear less affected, but her shiny eyes spoke of withheld tears.

KahSandra spotted Admiral Caydoc and her wife, Spinner, with former Fleet Admiral Helden Caydoc. They looked happy, and only a person who knew what had taken place in the northern mountains could spot traces of stress and sorrow. Having been assigned back at the ECC, KahSandra had received a full report, which had left her feeling enraged and murderous. She had to tell herself constantly that she wasn't out for revenge. Only justice. Even if it meant going against everything she was trained to do, she would make sure that those responsible for the callous use of the innocent five humanoids to create some sort of clone hive were dealt with. Nobody knew her personal story and why she couldn't settle for any less than a personal vendetta, but when she was done, the one they called Nestrocalder would be dead, and justice would be done.

Now she had to focus on making this day a time of celebration when President Tylio and Caya officially moved into their new home, which was nothing like the old Oconodian presidential palace, but a true home befitting a loving couple that had done so much for their people.

Back at the hospital incarceration ward, a nurse adjusted the parenteral infusion for her patient before she tapped the new data into her tablet. Turning around to check the numbers on the infuser, she flinched and dropped the tablet on the bed.

Zoem Malderyn had opened her eyes.

About the Author

Gun Brooke resides in the countryside in Sweden with her very patient family. A retired neonatal intensive care nurse, she now writes full-time, only rarely taking a break to create websites for herself or others and to do computer graphics. Gun writes both romances and sci-fi.

Web site: http://www.gbrooke-fiction.com
Facebook: http://www.facebook.com/gunbach
Twitter: http://twitter.com/redheadgrrl1960
Tumblr: http://gunbrooke.tumblr.com/

Books Available from Bold Strokes Books

Change in Time by Robyn Nyx. Working in the past is hell on your future. The Extractor series: Book Two (978-162639-880-1)

Love After Hours by Radclyffe. When Gina Antonelli agrees to renovate Carrie Longmire's new house, she doesn't welcome Carrie's overtures at friendship or her own unexpected attraction. A Rivers Community Novel. (978-163555-090-0)

Nantucket Rose by CF Frizzell. Maggie Jordan can't wait to convert an historic Nantucket home into a B&B, but doesn't expect to fall for mariner Ellis Chilton, who has more claim to the house than Maggie realizes. (978-163555-056-6)

Picture Perfect by Lisa Moreau. Falling in love wasn't supposed to be part of the stakes for Olive and Gabby, rival photographers in the competition of a lifetime. (978-162639-975-4)

Set the Stage by Karis Walsh. Actress Emilie Danvers takes the stage again in Ashland, Oregon, little realizing that landscaper Arden Philips is about to offer her a very personal romantic lead role. (978-163555-087-0)

Strike a Match by Fiona Riley. When their attempts at matchmaking fizzle out, firefighter Sasha and reluctant millionairess Abby find themselves turning to each other to strike a perfect match. (978-162639-999-0)

The Price of Cash by Ashley Bartlett. Cash Braddock is doing her best to keep her business afloat, stay out of jail, and avoid Detective Kallen. It's not working. (978-162639-708-8)

Under Her Wing by Ronica Black. At Angel's Wings Rescue, dogs are usually the ones saved, but when quiet Kassandra Haden meets outspoken owner Jayden Beaumont, the two stubborn women just might end up saving each other. (978-163555-077-1)

Underwater Vibes by Mickey Brent. When Hélène, a translator in Brussels, Belgium, meets Sylvie, a young Greek photographer and swim coach, unsettling feelings hijack Hélène's mind and body—even her poems. (978-163555-002-3)

A More Perfect Union by Carsen Taite. Major Zoey Granger and DC fixer Rook Daniels risk their reputations for a chance at true love while dealing with a scandal that threatens to rock the military. (978-162639-754-5)

Arrival by Gun Brooke. The spaceship *Pathfinder* reaches its passengers' new homeworld where danger lurks in the shadows while Pamas Seclan disembarks and finds unexpected love in young science genius Darmiya Do Voy. (978-162639-859-7)

Captain's Choice by VK Powell. Architect Kerstin Anthony's life is going to plan until Bennett Carlyle, the first girl she ever kissed, is assigned to her latest and most important project, a police district substation. (978-162639-997-6)

Falling Into Her by Erin Zak. Pam Phillips, widow at the age of forty, meets Kathryn Hawthorne, local Chicago celebrity, and it changes her life forever—in ways she hadn't even considered possible. (978-163555-092-4)

Hookin' Up by MJ Williamz. Will Leah get what she needs from casual hookups or will she see the love she desires right in front of her? (978-163555-051-1)

King of Thieves by Shea Godfrey. When art thief Casey Marinos meets bounty hunter Finnegan Starkweather, the crimes of the past just might set the stage for a payoff worth more than she ever dreamed possible. (978-163555-007-8)

Lucy's Chance by Jackie D. As a serial killer haunts the streets, Lucy tries to stitch up old wounds with her first love in the wake of a small town's rapid descent into chaos. (978-163555-027-6)

Right Here, Right Now by Georgia Beers. When Alicia Wright moves into the office next door to Lacey Chamberlain's accounting firm, Lacey is about to find out that sometimes the last person you want is exactly the person you need. (978-163555-154-9)

Strictly Need to Know by MB Austin. Covert operator Maji Rios will do whatever she must to complete her mission, but saving a gorgeous stranger from Russian mobsters was not in her plans. (978-163555-114-3)

Tailor-Made by Yolanda Wallace. Tailor Grace Henderson doesn't date clients, but when she meets gender-bending model Dakota Lane, she's tempted to throw all the rules out the window. (978-163555-081-8)

Time Will Tell by M. Ullrich. With the ability to time travel, Eva Caldwell will have to decide between having it all and erasing it all. (978-163555-088-7)

A Date to Die by Anne Laughlin. Someone is killing people close to Detective Kay Adler, who must look to her own troubled past for a suspect. There she finds more than one person seeking revenge against her. (978-163555-023-8)

Captured Soul by Laydin Michaels. Can Kadence Munroe save the woman she loves from a twisted killer, or will she lose her to a collector of souls? (978-162639-915-0)

Dawn's New Day by TJ Thomas. Can Dawn Oliver and Cam Cooper, two women who have loved and lost, open their hearts to love again? (978-163555-072-6)

Definite Possibility by Maggie Cummings. Sam Miller is just out for good times, but Lucy Weston makes her realize happily ever after is a definite possibility. (978-162639-909-9)

Eyes Like Those by Melissa Brayden. Isabel Chase and Taylor Andrews struggle between love and ambition from the writers' room on one of Hollywood's hottest TV shows. (978-163555-012-2)

Heart's Orders by Jaycie Morrison. Helen Tucker and Tee Owens escape hardscrabble lives to careers in the Women's Army Corps, but more than their hearts are at risk as friendship blossoms into love. (978-163555-073-3)

Hiding Out by Kay Bigelow. Treat Dandridge is unaware that her life is in danger from the murderer who is hunting the woman she's falling in love with, Mickey Heiden. (978-162639-983-9)

Omnipotence Enough by Sophia Kell Hagin. Can the tiny tool that abducted war veteran Jamie Gwynmorgan accidentally acquires help her escape an unknown enemy to reclaim her stolen life and the woman she deeply loves? (978-163555-037-5)

Summer's Cove by Aurora Rey. Emerson Lange moved to Provincetown to live in the moment, but when she meets Darcy Belo and her son Liam, her quest for summer romance becomes a family affair. (978-162639-971-6)

The Road to Wings by Julie Tizard. Lieutenant Casey Tompkins, Air Force student pilot, has to fly with the toughest instructor, Captain Kathryn "Hard Ass" Hardesty, fly a supersonic jet, and deal with a growing forbidden attraction. (978-162639-988-4)

Beauty and the Boss by Ali Vali. Ellis Renois is at the top of the fashion world, but she never expects her summer assistant Charlotte Hamner to tear her heart and her business apart like sharp scissors through cheap material. (978-162639-919-8)

Fury's Choice by Brey Willows. When gods walk amongst humans, can two women find a balance between love and faith? (978-162639-869-6)

Lessons in Desire by MJ Williamz. Can a summer love stand a four-month hiatus and still burn hot? (978-163555-019-1)

Lightning Chasers by Cass Sellars. For Sydney and Parker, being a couple was never what they had planned. Now they have to fight corruption, murder, and enemies hiding in plain sight just to hold on to each other. Lightning Series, Book Two, (978-162639-965-5)

Summer Fling by Jean Copeland. Still jaded from a breakup years earlier, Kate struggles to trust falling in love again when a summer fling with sexy young singer Jordan rocks her off her feet. (978-162639-981-5)

Take Me There by Julie Cannon. Adrienne and Sloan know it would be career suicide to mix business with pleasure, however tempting it is. But what's the harm? They're both consenting adults. Who would know? (978-162639-917-4)

The Girl Who Wasn't Dead by Samantha Boyette. A year ago, someone tried to kill Jenny Lewis. Tonight she's ready to find out who it was. (978-162639-950-1)

Unchained Memories by Dena Blake. Can a woman give herself completely when she's left a piece of herself behind? (978-162639-993-8)

Walking Through Shadows by Sheri Lewis Wohl. All Molly wanted to do was go backpacking...in her own century. (978-162639-968-6)

A Lamentation of Swans by Valerie Bronwen. Ariel Montgomery returns to Sea Oats to try to save her broken marriage but soon finds herself also fighting to save her own life and catch a murderer. (978-1-62639-828-3)

Freedom to Love by Ronica Black. What happens when the woman who spent her lifetime worrying about caring for her family, finally finds the freedom to love without borders? (978-1-63555-001-6)

House of Fate by Barbara Ann Wright. Two women must throw off the lives they've known as a guardian and an assassin and save two rival houses before their secrets tear the galaxy apart. (978-1-62639-780-4)

Planning for Love by Erin Dutton. Could true love be the one thing that wedding coordinator Faith McKenna didn't plan for? (978-1-62639-954-9)

Sidebar by Carsen Taite. Judge Camille Avery and her clerk, attorney West Fallon, agree on little except their mutual attraction, but can their relationship and their careers survive a headline-grabbing case? (978-1-62639-752-1)

Sweet Boy and Wild One by T. L. Hayes. When Rachel Cole meets soulful singer Bobby Layton at an open mic, she is immediately in thrall. What she soon discovers will rock her world in ways she never imagined. (978-1-62639-963-1)

To Be Determined by Mardi Alexander and Laurie Eichler. Charlie Dickerson escapes her life in the US to rescue Australian wildlife with Pip Atkins, but can they save each other? (978-1-62639-946-4)

True Colors by Yolanda Wallace. Blogger Robby Rawlins plans to use First Daughter Taylor Crenshaw to get ahead, but she never planned on falling in love with her in the process. (978-1-62639-927-3)

Unexpected by Jenny Frame. When Dale McGuire falls for Rebecca Harper, the mother of the son she never knew she had, will Rebecca's troubled past stop them from making the family they both truly crave? (978-1-62639-942-6)